# one for sorrow

a novel

Amanda Gilsenan

Chicory Press

Editing services by Rebecca Sweeney

Cover/interior design and formatting by Stephen Reney

Graphic design and promotional materials by Emilie Jolivet

Additional illustration by Érin Gilsenan

Chicory Press first edition 2024

ISBN 979-8-9911582-0-6 (pbk.)

*For Erin and Patrick:*
*No matter where you go,*
*what dreams you may follow,*
*I'll always be proud.*

# Chapter One

JANE HELD ON TO the passenger seat of the car so tight that her knuckles were white. Her legs dangled as she slid around the seat, the seatbelt hanging loosely around her waist. She shut her eyes as her mother sped erratically around the winding country roads.

"Mammy, please slow down!" she cried. Her mother laughed and drove faster. The car shuddered, rattling over every bump on the road, and 's empty stomach heaved. She could smell stale cigarettes and vodka off her mother's breath every time she opened her mouth to laugh. It filled the little car and nauseated her.

Her mother said she drank vodka because no one could smell it, but Jane could. It was a smell not unlike wild garlic, a scent that seeped out of every pore. Whether her mother had one drink or ten, at six years of age Jane had learned to sense the subtle differences in her mood, the changes her mother tried to conceal. Jane knew by looking at her whether it was a sad drink, a happy one, or an angry one. This was different, though. It was a mix of every emotion all rolled into one. And it terrified her.

The car turned up the narrow road towards home and Jane's mother sped up, the back wheels skidding on some gravel before she laughed again and straightened the car.

"Reach down into my bag and pull out a fag will ya, good girl?"

Jane looked down but couldn't see her mother's handbag at her feet; she turned to find it lying half open behind the driver's seat. From a brown paper bag a glass bottle with a red cap poked out. With one hand clutching her mother's seat, Jane stretched to pull at the handle of the handbag and bring it a little closer. She moved the cold glass bottle aside and spotted the red and white box of cigarettes nestled amongst abandoned coins, a red Rimmel lipstick, a compact, and some papery things her mam needed when she went to the bathroom. And there, at the very bottom, was the silver Zippo lighter Sean had bought her for her birthday.

Just as Jane pulled a cigarette from the box, the car swerved again. Hard. A loud *thud* sounded from outside and Jane was thrown back, towards the dashboard. She threw her free hand out to stop herself banging her head. Her heart raced. For a second, she thought she could hear her mother's heart beating loudly, too.

"What was that?" Jane asked. All the colour had drained from her mother's face.

"I think...it was just a sheep," she said, looking into the rear-view mirror.

"Do you need to stop, Mam?" Jane asked as she craned her neck to look back, but she was too short to see anything. "Want me to look and see if the sheep is hurt? Mam?"

"It's fine, Jane. It's fine. I'll talk to the farmer in the morning. Now drop it!" her mother shouted. The smell of her breath hit Jane again and she turned her head to look out the window.

The car didn't slow down. Her mother seemed to speed up as she turned the last bend before home. Jane's bladder felt as if it was going to burst and the now-crushed cigarette in her hand was all but forgotten. She closed her eyes again and clenched her legs together. They were only minutes from the house.

"Don't mention that sheep to anyone," her mother slurred as she pulled into the driveway. She misjudged the distance and bumped the front passenger side against the wall, knocking the wing mirror off and leaving a trail of red paint along the brick as she tried to straighten it up and drive in.

"This car has a mind of its fucking own tonight. Heap of shite." Jane's mother grabbed her handbag from the back and walked into the house. She hadn't spotted the growing wet patch on Jane's skirt. Jane knew she had to get changed before her mother spotted it or a fresh hell would await her.

She crept in behind her mother who was shakily pouring a vodka into a coffee cup, the brown paper bag discarded on the kitchen table. With her free hand she spilled the contents of her handbag onto the table, searching for her cigarettes. She didn't take her eyes off the clear liquid as it was being poured. Even though her hands shook, she didn't spill a single drop. Jane slunk by quietly and made her way towards her bedroom.

"Just getting ready for bed!" she called from her bedroom door.

"Come back! We're best friends and we need to have a chat," her mother shouted back as she slid her jacket off and fell onto the back of the wooden chair. She often sat in the same spot when she'd had too much to drink, her back to the wall and slumped at the table. Jane had become an expert at extinguishing lit cigarettes after her mother had passed out. She always called Jane her best friend, but Jane never felt like it.

"It's just you and me now," she'd say before spewing bad things about Peter. That he had abandoned them, that he thought he was too good for his home. "Just us girls forever," she'd say. Jane hated the thought of forever.

Jane was already sitting on the edge of her bed in her nightdress. Her wet clothes lay in a pile in the corner and she quickly got up and kicked them under her bed, not wanting to anger her mother any further. She decided she would wash them herself in the morning.

"Well fuck ya, then!" came a screech up the hall. "You just stay there and I'll talk to myself." Jane knew her only option was to crawl into bed. Her mother's mood had already swung.

✄

Jane had drifted off into a light sleep when the sound of voices coming from the kitchen woke her up. She recognised Sean's loud guffawing laughter followed by her mother's raspy cough. He visited on the weekends, a married man who could match her mother's drinking abilities, and they held each other in fierce competition when they propped each other up at the bar.

Her mother loved Sean and changed slightly when he was around; she became less angry and bitter but made Jane feel like an unwanted guest. She didn't mind Sean too much because having him there lifted her mother's mood slightly, but when he left to go home and get into bed beside his wife, the emotions that had dissipated upon his arrival became amplified. His parting gift to Jane was more misery.

She heard laughter. She knew it would be short lived, and began preparing herself to ask her mother for some toast. She tried to understand how a whole day had gone by without her mother giving her some food. Most times she'd be offered crisps in the pub while she sat quietly, praying that the next drink would be the last or, depending on the pub and barman, that the rule of no kids after seven would be enforced. But her mother knew the ones where she could drink her fill and not be bothered, and Jane knew it was in her best interest to stay quiet and not draw attention to herself. Because doing otherwise stirred an anger in her mother that terrified her to her core.

She was routinely forgotten while her mother and Sean sat at the bar, laughing and having drink after drink. Inhibitions lowered, they were often seen with their arms draped around each other, their knees intertwined as they shared passionate, sloppy kisses. His care and consideration for his wife dwindled with each drink and her mother revelled in it. She was no longer the other woman: she was the only woman. Jane wished her mother loved her as much as she loved Sean.

Her thoughts were interrupted by a car pulling into the driveway. She knew by the sound of the engine, the car door closed softly, and the footsteps on the gravel that it was her brother. Peter. He was a man in his own right with a car of his own, a girlfriend, and a life outside of the bungalow they called home. He was seldom there but when he was, he only had eyes for his little sister. He crept in through the back door, not wanting to see either his mother or Sean, and came straight to Jane's bedroom.

"Hey, are ya hungry?" he asked as he stuck his head in the door.

Jane leapt from her bed and wrapped her arms around his waist. She felt safe in his presence; he had stood in front of her so many times, protecting her from whatever wrath their mother was directing at her.

He had often been seen sporting the black eyes that were meant for her. She loved him more than she loved anything else in her life.

"I'm starving! But it's not mam's fault. She just forgot. Don't remind her again because she'll get mad," she pleaded.

"Where's your coat?" he asked, looking around, hoping he wouldn't have to go into the kitchen.

"I can put a jumper and my shoes on," Jane said as she pulled a woollen jumper from her drawer. Her excitement was contagious. Peter smiled as he watched Jane try to put on her jumper and her shoes at the same time. He chuckled when she put her shoes on the wrong feet.

Jane followed Peter out the back door, stepping around piles of unwashed laundry, and climbed into the small black Renault Clio. His car always felt safer, cozier, and most definitely cleaner than her mother's. There were no empty bottles or cigarettes in the footwell, no burn marks on the seat, and it smelled of the blue tree air freshener. He took pride in his car and spent hours on the weekend cleaning it until she could practically see her reflection in the black dashboard.

"Put your seatbelt on now. You're not with her," Peter said, but Jane was already reaching around to put it on.

"I always wear it! You told me why it's important and I don't want to fly out the window," Jane said matter-of-factly before falling silent. She looked down and twisted the bottom of her jumper with her fingers. Peter had already started the car and noticing Jane's silence, he turned in his seat and looked down at her.

"What is it, Janey? Something happened, I know by ya. What did she do?"

His arm resting on the headrest behind Jane made her feel closed in, and she ran over the earlier incident in her mind. Even at her young age she knew Peter would quit college to stay at home to look after her. His life would be over just as it was beginning. She was used to omitting some details of their mother's antics and she knew in her heart this would be the right thing to do.

"Mam hit the wall driving in tonight. I think she broke the car," Jane said, still looking down.

"Was she driving the car drunk again? Fuck's sake, she'll kill someone one of these days, or she'll kill the both of yas," Peter was almost shouting. But he knew Jane heard enough shouting when he wasn't there, so he cut his rant short. As he drove he talked about his girlfriend Lucy, college, his part time job and how much fun he was having with his new friends. Jane envied him slightly but was happy to see his eyes light up when he spoke.

"You know why I'm doing this Jane?" he asked. "I want to get a really good job so I can buy a house for me and you. We'll have so much fun, just the two of us."

Jane didn't know what to say. The thought of leaving her mother all alone scared her. Who would put out her burning cigarette at night? Who would wake her in the morning for work? She had heard her talking to Sean about her boss and how she was on her last legs.

She didn't notice the journey; the tree line seemed to fade away in seconds and soon they were in the town. It was brighter and didn't feel so lonely. Street lights made the pavement glow, the cat's eyes on the white lines illuminating the already bright road. There were still some people walking around, mostly leaving pubs and getting into cars. It felt wrong to Jane to see so much life at that hour of the night.

Peter brought the car to a stop outside a local chipper and the smell of salt and vinegar made Jane's stomach rumble. She was so excited to be with Peter she almost forgot she was hungry. He hopped out of the car, looking back with a wink, and went in to order.

She sat looking down at her legs not quite reaching the floor, wondering what age she'd be when she could rest her feet on the ground. She settled at the age of seven and a half, and watched through the window as Peter reached into his pocket and handed coins to the man behind the counter.

The warm, brown bag sat on Jane's lap and the heat radiating from it began to steam up the windows. She felt safe and warm; she could feel her shoulders begin to relax. She never had to worry about how she spoke to Peter, she never worried about the tone she used or that she might say the wrong thing. He never got angry at her questions.

He asked her about school and she freely talked about how she hated maths but liked stories from history and how she wished all of the mammies and babies didn't have to die of the hunger during the famine. Peter told her about an inland lighthouse in a place called Kells where all the poor people were buried, and he promised to bring her during the summer holidays.

"Will we have to bring flowers?" she asked through a mouthful of chips.

"Huh? Where?"

"To the graveyard, when we go during the summer holidays?"

But she was no longer interested in the answer, her focus now on the last few chips in the bag.

"Jesus Christ, you still have a burger to eat, slow down or you'll be sick. If you puke in my car, you can clean it!" Peter smiled at her.

He felt guilty when he was away during the week but managed to stay focused on the long-term goal: getting Jane out of that house. It wasn't a home; it wasn't warm, clean and inviting and he feared the worst was yet to come for Jane.

When Jane was putting the last bite of the burger into her mouth, Peter started the car and turned for home. She felt a familiar sickly feeling in her stomach when the car turned... it wasn't nausea or the butterflies that flutter when you're nervous or excited, it was something different. A burning sensation that she had yet to find a word for. It was almost as if her stomach was tied in knots, and it got worse when mammy had an angry drink.

The journey home was always shorter to Jane, and she almost asked Peter to stop so she could look at the stars and the waning moon, to delay the inevitable. But she stayed quiet and before she could say anything the car was slowly pulling into the driveway. The lights from Peter's car shone directly on a line of red paint along the wall.

Peter told Jane to be quiet as a mouse as he stopped the car. He hoped their mother would be in bed and unaware of their little trip; if she knew he had money for food she'd sniff it out and use it to buy whatever alcohol she could. He had just got back on his feet after having to borrow off friends last month. He picked Jane up and quietly walked towards the back door.

Jane, her belly now full, hoped she could just go to sleep. As she rested her head on Peter's shoulder and wrapped her arms around his neck, she noticed the smell of his aftershave. It was a new scent for him; he had never worn it before and it made him seem older, and different. The sickly feeling persisted and jumped into her throat when she heard the back door open and her mother scream.

"Where the fuck have you two been?"

Jane buried her face into the nape of Peter's neck and felt her body begin to tremble. His whisper to her to pretend to sleep was barely audible.

"I asked you a fucking question!" Mother shouted, stepping outside and grabbing Peter's arm.

"I'm just going in to put Jane to bed. For fuck sake, will you calm down?"

As soon as he uttered the words, he instinctively closed his eyes; she raised her hand and slapped him across the face. Jane began to whimper and her body tensed in his arms but he knew he'd need a free hand to defend himself. He put Jane down and protectively stood in front of her.

"Who the fuck do you think you are talking to me like that? I'm your mother. Are you too good for us now? Look at you, the big man in college now!"

"Jane. Go to bed," Peter said firmly, not wanting her to hear any more of the viciousness that was about to spew out of their mother's mouth. He gently pushed her with one hand. "Go. Now."

Jane didn't go to bed. She closed the kitchen door behind her and stood in the hall with her back against the wall, trembling. She listened to her mother shout at her brother and heard the slaps ring loudly as they rained down on him. The more he argued the harder they got until eventually he remained silent and took whatever anger she had.

Jane's tears tasted as salty as the chips but they weren't comforting or satisfying. The lovely treat felt like a million years ago.

She hadn't realised how badly she needed the toilet until she felt the warm liquid running down her legs. Panic tore through her and she ran to get a towel to dry the puddle and quickly change her clothes. She grabbed the pile from earlier and stuffed everything in the washing machine before tiptoeing to her bedroom.

Her mother had been so angry the last time she had slapped her bum, shouting, "Big girls don't wet their pants!" A slap with each word. Her mother was right. She wasn't a baby anymore and that's why she didn't tell Peter.

The shouting in the kitchen had stopped. Jane could hear Peter sniffling in the hallway. She had never seen him cry before. Guilt gnawed at her. If she didn't admit to being hungry, this wouldn't have happened. She stuck her head around the door and whispered his name.

Peter immediately stood up straight, took a deep breath, and followed Jane into her bedroom. There were red marks on both his cheeks and a scratch under his eyebrow. Jane lifted her hand and rubber her brother's face gently.

"I'm sorry, Peter," she said as tears fell down her cheeks. He held her small hand to his face and closed his eyes to the warmth of her touch. He loved her kindness, her willingness to see the best in everyone. And he loved how their mother had not yet beat the cynic into her. He prayed she never would.

He often watched her from his bedroom window when she sat outside talking to caterpillars, telling them that no one is ugly forever. He heard her asking where their mammies were and if they were lonely. He marvelled that the child still knew how to be kind.

"This isn't your fault, Janey. It's not mine either, it's just the way she is. But promise me if she ever lays a hand on you that you'll tell me and I'll get you out of here. We'll be out of this kip soon anyway."

But lately Peter was believing his own promises less and less though he wasn't going to give up without a fight. Jane settled down on her pillow, with Peter sitting at the end of the bed. Silent tears fell as the bad feeling in her tummy slowly disappeared. She felt herself drift into a dreamless sleep.

Peter looked at Jane sleeping and began to cry. He was taller than his mother and stronger. He could easily defend himself; she was small with a slight frame, but he would never raise his hand to a woman. He came close once and when he did, she threatened him with the only thing he came back for, the only person he loved. Jane.

# Chapter Two

The morning had long broken, but the house wasn't as quiet as it normally was after a night of heavy drinking with her mother and Sean. Jane heard her mother move around the kitchen loudly, filling buckets of water and the back door opening and closing.

Jane quietly made her way to Peter's bedroom and opened the door, grimacing when it creaked. He didn't stir from his sleep; his quiet snores sounded peaceful and she glanced around his bedroom before closing the door. It was the cleanest room in the house. Peter had a way of making even old furniture sparkle and shine and no matter how much Jane tried she couldn't get her own bedroom as clean. Some days she forgot to pick up clothes from the floor and weeks would go by before she'd remember to change her sheets. It seemed like a huge task to a six-year-old, trying to keep a whole bedroom clean.

The sun was shining low in the sky when Jane stepped out the back door. The blue sky seemed to magnify the colours of the birds swooping in and out of nests, mainly crows and magpies looking for their afternoon meal. The rain that fell during the night had softened the ground; it was easy for them to find food. There was a chill in the air still, but Jane liked it. It felt clean. There was no smoke, not even the smell of stale smoke that always seemed to linger in the kitchen. Clinging to the walls. Jane took a deep breath in and closed her eyes.

"Where are you going?" her mother asked, standing up from the side of the car and startling Jane.

"I'm going down to the stream. Look." Jane held up the bucket.

"Right. Off with ya, then," her mother replied, bending back down towards the passenger wheel. Jane watched as her mother poured liquid soap into a bucket and dipped a sponge in. She didn't squeeze it out before rubbing it on the car and Jane watched the red paint drip onto the gravel below. She had never seen her mother wash the car before. She wondered if it was because of the sheep, but heeded her mother's warning from the night before and kept quiet, instead making her way down the road towards the stream.

Jane stood on the bank of the little stream where the cows came to drink on warm days. She didn't particularly like cows. They were nosey creatures and their nosiness often led a whole herd to trample everything in their path. This made her wary. Today the field was empty and the only sounds she could hear was the gently running water and the noise of the birds making the sky and the trees their own. She stood and listened; she knew well the different bird songs and the weather patterns that followed.

She heard magpies warble and knew they were looking for moss and sticks to build their nests. She loved magpies. The hue of blue from their feathers when the sunlight hit them made them sparkle and she loved their fierce loyalty, their protection over their young. She sometimes felt envious of the fledgling with two parents to protect it, but always watched with curiosity. She could sit for hours watching them swoop and peck at wild farm cats who dared to prowl and pounce around their babies.

Some people thought of them as pests, and they were symbols of good or bad luck, depending on the numbers visiting. Their opposite meanings and symbolism of trickery and deceit had made many people dread them. The associated superstitions had already been instilled in Jane and though the magpie was her favourite bird, she still waved to a solitary one while saying, "Morning, Jack. How's your lovely lady wife?" to dispel the curse of the lone magpie bringing bad luck to the home. Jane wasn't sure if she believed it, but didn't want to take the chance of not saluting her feathered friend.

Her favourite dungarees now rested well above her ankles and the straps were becoming strained, digging into her narrow shoulders. She picked up her red bucket and looked closely at the now faded seashell print on the front. The seashell once donned a smiling face and big eyes, but the smile had been the first thing to wear off.

Jane remembered how she made sandcastles on the beach the day her mother bought her the bucket. The sun beat down and a gentle sea breeze blew as she happily worked on her sandcastle, digging and digging a moat around the base, the water soaking into the sand as soon as she had poured it in. Sean and her mother sat on the dunes, laughing and chatting, and Jane felt that from the outside looking in anyone would think that she had a Mammy and a Daddy, and her life was perfect.

She allowed herself to relax on their day out. She watched the seagulls as they dived into the water or snuck up to steal someone's sandwiches or chips. She giggled as people tried to shoo them away but the persistent seagulls got their fill.

There was no vodka on the beach, only sunshine.

The sound of her mother's raspy laugh could be heard above the lapping of the waves, and Jane felt happy. She missed Peter, but she enjoyed her own company.

As Jane sat watching the people on the beach, her mother grabbed her hand and the trio ran towards the water, laughing and squealing as the cold Irish Sea soaked their feet. She clung onto her mother as they waded out further. She wrapped her legs around her mother's waist and her arms around her neck. She could smell cigarettes but no wild garlic and allowed herself to relax as she looked into her mother's blue eyes. The eyes that were firmly transfixed on Sean.

They both laughed as Sean splashed them with water and Jane coughed as she inhaled some of the salty water.

"Ugh! Definitely not like chips," she said as she tried to spit the taste out of her mouth. Her mother pried her away from her and said,

"I'll teach you to swim."

A wave of fear gripped Jane as she realised her feet couldn't feel the hard uneven sand at the bottom. Her mother grabbed her by the waist and told her to kick her feet as hard as she could and she would make it to Sean. He was no more than an arm's breadth away.

Jane had no time to process this information before her mother let go. She frantically kicked both her legs and used her arms to propel herself forward. She smiled, realising she was making some progress towards him.

She felt amazing, until Sean put his hand on her head and pushed her underwater. She desperately tried to grab the hand clamped on her head as he pushed down further. She could hear him laughing as water began to fill her ears.

She inhaled and stopped flailing her arms.

Then he grabbed her hair and pulled her up; like a baby taking its first breath, she inhaled deeply and started to cough salty water from her lungs.

She grabbed onto her mother, coughing and sobbing salty tears that mingled with the cool water that soaked her.

Scan continued to laugh as she clung onto her mother. She never found his jokes funny, couldn't comprehend how he laughed harder when his jokes made her cry. Peter called him a narcissist, but Jane didn't know what that meant.Sean had charms and arrogance that some women found attractive, though. He knew what to say to get his way and her mother fell for it hook, line and sinker. She was never happy being the other woman, but she gladly took whatever scraps of affection and attention Sean threw her way. When she tired of the scraps thrown at her feet a day trip far away from home would be organised. They were few and far between, but it was enough to make Jane's mother feel wanted.

Jane only let go of her grip when the water was ankle-deep and her mother complained she was too heavy. She to her sandcastle, the moat still empty, and grabbed a large beach towel to wrap around herself. The sand that caked her skin felt scratchy when she moved the towel over her body, and her stomach heaved from swallowing the salt water.

Jane's mother sat down beside her, handing her a ham sandwich and a yogurt.

"This'll make your belly feel better," she said, handing them to Jane. "He loves you, ya know? He just has a funny way of showing it. You need to be able to take a joke, Jane. Not be always taking things so seriously."

19

Jane found this advice strange considering Sean's jokes had made her mother cry on numerous occasions, too. She cried herself to sleep some nights; Jane heard her through the paper-thin walls at home. Jane swore to herself she would never laugh at his cruel, mean jokes. She was kind, unlike him. She slowly ate her sandwich, hoping the belly full of water wouldn't make her throw up on the way home.

By the stream, Jane's blue Wellington boots stuck down in the mud, pulling her out of her memory, and her feet and calves strained as she lifted her feet up, trying to keep the boots on as she made her way down to the water. The gentle trickling of the water eased the memory from her mind as she waded in. She stood watching the water move over and past her feet as she stood calf-deep.

Peter had taught her that if she stood still long enough, the little minnows would think she was just part of the river and swim around and past her as if she were just another obstacle, like a branch or a rock. They swam around her feet, trying to get downstream. They blended in with the life of the stream but when Jane looked closely she could see them, like rainbows in the water. She had never seen so many and stood in admiration watching them navigate the stream.

The water was always clear here. It ran right around the back of her house, but this was the easiest access point when she was alone. She could easily climb the gate and walk down through this field. The water was shallow enough for her not to be frightened of it. Since their day at the beach, Jane hated anything more than waist-deep water. But this was different; gentle, peaceful and pre-dictable, nothing like the ocean waves, crashing and pulling. The ocean felt angry to Jane, as if it desperately had a story to tell and nobody was listening.

The stream always cleared itself and the waters never stayed muddy for long. Even after herds of cows had been drinking, the stream would wash the muddiness away and become clear again. It would wash everything out to sea. Perhaps, Jane pondered, that was why the sea was so angry... because it held all the memories and badness from every river and stream in Ireland, and it had nowhere to let it go. No one to listen to it.

She gently and carefully bent down with her bucket, trying to keep her feet still. She barely took a breath as she held her bucket underwater, allowing six or seven of the little fish to swim in. She lifted her bucket and marvelled at the colours on the fish now swimming in circles around it. She wondered if they worried about how they would get out and felt slightly guilty from taking them away from their shoal. She quickly put the bucket back into the water, letting them swim out, hoping they would be able to catch up with their friends.

Jane waded further down towards the bridge, the water now seeping into and filling her boots. She didn't mind; she only wore them to save her feet from the rocks underneath. But the full boots slowed her down. She stood underneath the bridge. The noise of the babbling water was amplified but so too was the silence. She happily stood there, watching the minnows swim past her feet faster now because the water was deeper.

This was Jane's happy place. This is where she tried to become like the stream, letting all the muddiness flow away. Her thoughts became clear here, her mind only focused on what she was doing and not what she was going home to.

As she turned to walk back towards the bank, she could hear rustling in the grass. She hoped it wasn't cows coming for a drink, because she would have to climb to the bridge instead of leaving through the field to get home.

She squinted up towards the bridge, unsure if she'd be able to make the climb without Peter. But when she heard the rustling again, followed by, "Damnit!" she knew her brother was stuck in the mud.

She waded back down towards the bank and smiled as she watched Peter try to navigate the mud without losing his boots. His pose made him look like he was attempting the splits, and Jane started to laugh as he fell flat on his face, his boots still stuck in the earth. He looked up at her with a frown, but his eyes were smiling. He loved to hear her laugh.

"I suppose there's no point worrying about keeping my clothes clean now, seeing as I'm head to toe in cow shite!" he shouted over to her.

His profanity made her laugh even harder. He slipped his feet out of his boots and, still on his knees, pulled them from the mud.

"Jesus Christ, Jane, why do you have to come this way after a day's rain? Did you not get stuck?" he asked as he tried to stand up, but Jane couldn't answer. The tears rolled down her face and her ribs hurt as she laughed at Peter, now in his socks, still trying to navigate his way down to the water.

With each step he took he grimaced as though his feet were encased in concrete, desperately trying to maintain his balance, holding a boot in each outstretched hand as if they were his balancing pole and he was walking the tightrope. With each movement forward he grunted, and Jane's laugh grew louder. His legs ached by the time he got unstuck, and he sat at the water's edge trying to wash off the mud that encased his socked feet like shoes.

Jane noticed it washing away in the water, and the gentle flow making it clear almost as quick as Peter was dirtying it.

"We're going home by the bridge," he said firmly, nodding his head towards it. He took the bucket from Jane's hands, making sure there were no minnows left behind, and poured some of the clear water over his head, wiping his face with his hands as it ran down. But it didn't wash the mud off his face, just smeared it around.

Jane stood quietly for a second as she tried to suppress a laugh; when Peter looked over to her, the whites of his eyes and his teeth shone out of his dirty face and she erupted with laughter again.

Her whole body convulsed and she lost her balance, falling backwards with a squeal. She landed firmly in the cool water of the stream. But she didn't feel scared, she felt strong knowing this was a pull she could fight against. Peter reached his hand out to pull her up, and as she put her hand in his, she pulled with all her might and Peter, unsteady on his unshod feet, fell in beside her with a splash. Jane feared a rib would break from laughing. The water surrounding Peter now became cloudy as it washed the dirt and mud off him. He lay there, letting the current wash it all away. *If only it could wash away more*, he thought as he stood up.

They both made their way up the road, their boots in their hands, a trail of water following them as their sodden clothes dripped. Jane looked back at the watery trail and remembered the tale of Hansel and Gretel and knew that once the water dried, they'd still find their way home.

"So do you still play with Rachel?" Peter asked, hoping she still had lots of friends in school.

"Naw, she plays with Sara now. And Clara, but not me," Jane replied, not taking her gaze off the bucket as she swung it in her right hand. "They said I'm too sad and it was just because I cried in school once - just the once, Peter - but they're just silly anyway, wanting to play silly games all the time."

Jane tried to make it sound as if it wasn't bothering her but it was, and Peter knew it. Jane missed Rachel, but she was more content in her own company. She didn't have to explain to anyone why she was feeling a bit sad or if her backside hurt and why. She didn't like to tell anybody about her mother; it was her and Peter's secret. A bond that tied them and kept them close.

Jane and Peter couldn't have been more different. Peter was an outgoing boy who, from a young age, had always had a crowd of different friends. Though he didn't get invited to any birthday parties at the behest of his friends' parents, his friends still loved him. He had a sense of humour, a sarcasm far older than his years that both his peers and teachers found amusing. He knew how to use his humour and his wit to his advantage, when it was and wasn't appropriate to use it. He was kind and loyal to a fault, and his loyalty alone had won him the hearts of many friends.

Jane was different. She was an introvert who genuinely did enjoy her own company. She was wise beyond her years and had an affinity for nature. She was nicknamed the "weather girl" in her class because her predictions were nearly always accurate. But she had watched and learned from nature itself; she knew what the weather would be by the way the birds sang and flew, by the cows grazing or by the flow of the fish going downstream. It was not magic. She just watched.

But lately Jane had become known as the "sad girl." She carried around the weight of an unhappy home in school. It followed her in the clothes she wore. The ones that were too small or sometimes unwashed. It followed her in the unkept hair and the holes in her shoes.

But the main thing that earned her the nickname was how upset she would be on Mondays. It was the first day after a weekend filled with drinking, arguing and shouting. It was the first day of the week where she could let her shoulders relax and release her emotions. It wasn't because she was particularly sad on Mondays, not more than other days at least. It was that, for the first time since Friday, she could be a little girl in school without having to worry. The relief overwhelmed her.

# Chapter Three

JANE WATCHED PETER AS he tried to clean the kitchen. He banged cupboard doors and loudly put away plates and cups. He was in a world far away from her; his fidgety body language screamed that he physically wanted to be where his mind was. Jane was used to that kind of body language from her mother but never from Peter. It scared her. because at times it felt as if he were the only person in the world who wanted her.

Peter liked who he was at college and missed it when he was home. The hours in his part time job didn't increase when he was off during the breaks, so he threw himself into studying and cleaning. In college, he no longer wore a label. He wasn't the alcoholic's son, or the child of a single parent. He was just Peter. During his time away he was slowly breaking free and becoming himself.

His quick wit and loyalty won him many friends and hearts, but no one knew how fractured his own heart was. His badly chewed fingernails were the only outward sign of the weight he carried on his shoulders. He enjoyed getting to know himself away from the pressure that came from the bungalow, sometimes allowing himself to forget about his mother and Jane. But those moments were followed by immense guilt and an overwhelming need to turn back home and protect his sister.

He socialised with his friend often; though he drank, he quickly learned his limits and never exceeded them, always with fearful that he would turn into his mother with just one drink too many. Among his circle of friends he became the protector of the group, often stopping fights before they began and ensuring everyone got home safely. Peter and Jane had learned from a young age to read body language. They could sense a change in tone of conversation or rising tension before anyone else. It was their gift, a superpower they didn't know they possessed but used daily, with everyone. It made them chameleons; they could both adapt to suit any group, room or situation.

Peter's empathy stretched much further than Jane, but stopped short of their mother. Unlike Jane, he'd known her before she was a drinker. He knew the love she was capable of showing, and his bitterness grew day by day, drink by drink, when she stopped showing it.

Jane wasn't angry because she knew no different. Their mother's fear of abandonment had turned to paranoia. When that joined forces with her jealousy, they became tangled, singing the same nasty tune, and Jane's father left. She blamed him, insisting he was too needy, that she had scared him off. But Peter knew different; he had seen her pick up the bottle in her own grief years earlier, a secret he didn't know how to share. When the bottle became her only friend it stopped being a secret.

The grief Peter felt couldn't be explained in the sadness of death There was no grave to visit, no anniversary to mourn. His soon-to-be stepfather was just...gone. It was in those early years that seeds of resentment were planted which in time bloomed into hatred, a black thorny rose which Peter fed and nourished.

He sat down at the kitchen table with a mug of tea, warming his hands on the cup, and he realised Jane had been watching him intently.

"Rachel told me her nanny stood on a stray sod in a field down the road and got lost. She couldn't find her way home for ages."

Peter looked at Jane with confusion While he'd grown up in the same house, Peter spent his time in the local town as much as he could, finding the countryside too lonely. He liked the hustle and bustle of the town and needed to mix and talk to people. To be as far away from home as possible. His knowledge of local folklore was almost non-existent, whereas Jane lapped it up.

"A sod of turf? What would a stray sod of turf be doing in the middle of a field? I think Rachel's nanny was on the whiskey!"

At that, the kitchen door swung open and their mother shuffled in. The smell of stale alcohol and cigarettes filled the kitchen and Peter fought the urge to run out the door.

"I don't drink whiskey," she said bitterly, flicking the switch on the kettle.

"No, Mam. Rachel said—," but Jane was interrupted by her mother.

"I couldn't give a fuck what that Rachel one says. I don't drink whiskey."

Jane's mind went into overdrive as she tried to decide between explaining their conversation or staying quiet. Some days there was no right answer; explaining her side could be misconstrued as talking back. Staying silent was an admission of guilt in her mother's eyes, and she was trying to flip between the two. Which would cause less anger?

She looked to Peter, who barely spoke to his mother when he was home, and he shrugged his shoulders, already opting for silence as he drank his tea. But he sensed Jane's fear and stood up, grabbing his coat off the back of the chair and said, "C'mon. We'll go looking for that stray sod ourselves."

Peter made his way to the door and Jane followed, glancing back at their mother who was now sitting with her head in her hands. She looked up at Jane and there was a terrible sadness in her eyes. Jane desperately wanted to give her mother a hug, but Peter began pulling at her arm to leave. She smiled a tender smile as she closed the door behind her.

Peter and Jane walked down the narrow road. Tall sprouts of grass grew in the middle and an array of potholes had been badly filled by tar and loose chippings, some quickly becoming potholes again from the weight of the tractors that drove up daily. Jane took the lead, knowing the field where Rachel's nanny got lost, and they began to chat. Peter told her how he missed his girlfriend Lucy on the weekends, and for the first time Jane felt a pang of jealousy. She'd never had to compete for Peter's attention before. She could see how distant he was becoming and she knew he was drifting away from her.

The birds flew low in the sky and dark clouds were looming on the horizon. Crows cawed loudly as they looked for shelter, and Jane could feel the wind picking up. It was just a gentle breeze blowing at the whisps of hair that stuck out around her ears. It had a chill to it, and she knew a change was on the way.

"We probably have about two hours before the rain comes. But this is the field. Maybe you were right Peter, about the whiskey. I think

Rachel's nanny was a bit silly for getting lost here," Jane chuckled as she began to climb over the metal gate.

"You haven't been wrong about the weather yet so we won't delay. Let's find this sod and go home. Hey, maybe we'll find a whole plot of turf to keep the fire going in the winter," Peter joked as he followed Jane over the gate.

He watched his little sister walking ahead of him, hands behind her back and the grass above her ankles, laughing to himself as she kicked every inch of land she stepped on. But he soon found himself doing the same, his mind clearing with each step he took. He noticed a change in texture underfoot, a softer, boggier feeling under his shoes, in the shape of a perfect circle. The grass was a different shade of green here and wasn't as long. He made a mental note to ask Jane about circles of moss as soon as they had found the sod.

They started up an incline that was unnoticeable from the gate; Peter noticed a cow standing at the top of the hill, staring down at them. Puffs of air blew from her wet nostrils as she took deep lungfuls of breaths. Soon, one by one, a herd of cows joined her at the top of the hill. They stood like a black and white army waiting for their commander to give the orders to charge. Jane stopped in her tracks and watched as the first cow took a few steps forward. As the others followed, she saw two calves at the rear of the herd and her heart began to race.

"Peter. Don't panic. But we're going to need to run in a minute," Jane said slowly, with an arm outstretched to stop Peter from taking another step forward. She looked back in the direction they'd come from but she couldn't see the gate. It was gone from her line of view, hidden under thorny brambles and hedges. There wasn't even a glint of shiny metal.

"I think we stood on a stray sod, Peter! Where's the gate gone?" Jane felt panic rise in her chest as the cows started to advance, slowly. Peter didn't realise the trouble they were in until the first cow began to run and the others followed.

"Run, Peter! I know how to get out!" Jane shouted as she took a left and began to sprint. She ran towards the little stream which separated the two fields and slid down the back into the waist-deep, cold water. Her chest tightened painfully, her breath lost to her. She was quickly followed by Peter.

"Sweet mother of *Jaysus*! This is fucking freezing!" They didn't have time to stop - the herd had made their way into the stream from one of the low-lying banks where they drank. Peter hoisted Jane up onto the bank and grabbed a handful of tree roots and climbed up, like they had done many times before but in a different place. When they reached the top they were in an adjoining field, and they both laid on their backs, breathless.

"What just happened, Jane?" Peter asked, looking around to make sure there wasn't another herd of cows in the field they just entered.

"They were just mammies protecting their babies, that's all. But it was kinda scary and fun and I think I want to go home," Jane replied while looking up at the black clouds overhead.

They made their way out of the field together and onto the road home, arriving back at the gate they had crossed. It was silver, shiny and almost new; it seemed so out of place in the landscape. Both Peter and Jane looked at each other in confusion and had the same idea. They climbed to the top of the gate and looked over. There were no bushes, hedges or thorny brambles blocking the inside of it and there was a clear view of the gate from both sides.

"Jane did you stand on a sod of turf?" Peter asked in confusion. "I don't think I did."

"No, I....I don't know what happened. Can we go home now?" Jane replied, trembling from been wet.

Their shoes squeaked and squelched as they walked up the narrow road and Jane's teeth began to rattle. She smiled up at Peter who has stiffened completely from the cold and put her arm around his waist.

When they reached the bridge, they were greeted by Stephen sitting on an old tree stump, smoking from a pipe. He smiled broadly when he saw them trudging up the road arm in arm, dripping wet.

"It's a cold day for a swim," he chuckled loudly.

"Ha, ha. Very funny. You're a bit out of your way sitting here?" Peter replied.

"Ah. I'm just watching the world go by. Many cars come up this road?" Stephen asked.

"Hardly any. Rush hour is when you drive up with your tractor," Peter replied.

"Indeed. Why did ye go swimming today?" Stephen asked.

"We got lost in the field. The gate vanished and the cows chased us, so we had to cross the stream to get into the other field," Jane explained. Stephen puffed on his pipe and nodded his head.

"Did either of ye stand in a circle of moss? Sounds as if ye did. One of ye stood in a fairy ring and there was a curse placed on ye. Ye should've taken your coats off and put them on inside out to remove the curse. Ah sure, you'll know next time."

"Fairies? A curse? Do you really expect us to fall for that?" Peter asked.

"But Peter, the tooth fairy comes. They have to live somewhere," Jane replied, looking up at her brother incredulously. Her instantly softened and patted her on the head in agreement.

"You may scoff, young man, but even the most hardened sceptic of a farmer won't mess with the fae. They can bring all sorts of misery and bad luck, but you've paid your dues. What brought you into the field anyway?"

"We were looking for a stray sod but couldn't find one. Theres no turf in the field. Do the fairies bring them?" Jane asked.

Stephen didn't laugh, but he did smile at the child's innocence and stood up, walking over to the stone bridge. He kicked an odd-looking tuft of grass that grew in the concrete between the road and the bridge.

"This is a stray sod. A stray sod of grass that looks as if it doesn't belong. It's out of place, a different colour and height to the rest. They say it's a sign of the fae and if you walk on one, you'll stumble around and get lost for hours."

Peter looked at the well-spoken, older man and wondered how he could believe in fairy tales.

"Thanks for the explanation," Peter said. "I'd best get Jane home before she catches her death." He placed his hand on Jane's lower back, guiding her up the road.

They got into the house, both shivering and dripping wet. They took their shoes off at the back door and walked in. The heat from the range hit them and they could feel their bones begin to thaw out. It was a rare occasion their mother lit a fire.

*She must be extra cold today*, Peter thought sarcastically. She was sitting at the kitchen table looking only slightly more awake than before. Her hair was tied up in a ponytail, showing the thinning of her hair and her face, now clear of the thick powder foundation she used, held a slight tan. But a black eye was visible. She cradled a cup of tea in her hands. A lit cigarette smoked in the overflowing ashtray. She looked at her nearly grown-up son and little girl both soaking wet and muddy and rolled her eyes.

"What in the name of *Jaysus* happened to you two?" she asked, smiling a forced, yellow grin.

"I'm going to grab a towel. No point asking what door you walked into last night," Peter said as he walked past her. She looked to Jane instead and raised her eyebrows.

"Well? Are you going to tell me why it looks as if you were dragged through a ditch?"

Jane smiled, happy that her mother seemed sober and taking an interest. She sat on the chair to pull off her wet trousers and without taking a breath relayed the whole story to her. She didn't pause until the last word was out and then looked up at her mother who was clearly concerned by something.

"You went looking for a sod of turf? In a field? That's hilarious!" she said, laughing a fake raspy laugh. "Did you say yous were talking to Stephen? The farmer with the orchard? Don't be going in to his orchard. Them farmers would shoot you for stealing apples and scaring sheep to death. Now go and get dressed."

Jane did as she was told. As she was passed her mother, Jane placed a hand on her bony cheek and let her small thumb run gently over the black and purple bruise under her eye. Jane loved her mother in spite of everything. She closed her tired eyes and took a deep breath, as if her Jane's gentle touch physically pained her. A lump formed in her throat and she pushed the little hand away.

Jane walked into Peter's room with a blanket wrapped around her head.

"You look like E.T.," he said, glancing up from his book.

"E.T. phone home." Jane pointed her finger towards Peter's nose and then sat at the end of his bed. She watched him read, mesmerised by his brown eyes following the words and smiled as his eyebrows occasionally furrowed when he was trying to make sense of what he was reading.

Peter was her half-brother, or so her mother had told her many times. Peter's father was dead and her father was, "a selfish bastard who fucked off."

It didn't feel like he only half-loved her, though, and she certainly didn't half-love him. Jane loved Peter with all her heart. The word which her mother threw around in moments of jealousy or anger didn't hurt or phase her anymore. With Peter, there was no half measures and Jane contented herself knowing it was just a word.

She sat quietly at the end of his bed, pulling her knees up to her chest so her feet were under the blanket. The feeling of warmth and peace settled over her and the house making her feel sleepy, beside her brother. She watched out the window as the rain began to fall. When the wind began to sing through the wooden window frame, she watched Peter pull a blanket up around his chin and she closed her eyes, drifting into a peaceful sleep.

# Chapter Four

THE TAR IN THE filled potholes melted in the summer sun. Jane poked it with a stick, hoping to draw the letter "J".

In town with her mother she had noticed the name "James" written in the concrete. She walked past it regularly, that name forever etched in the earth. Forever entering people's minds. That's what she was trying to recreate, not realising wet concrete and wet tar are two very different things. When the tar stuck to the stick she held, she gave up and stuck the tip of her white canvas shoe in it.

She moved to the grass verge, frantically rubbing the tip of her shoe in the grass. A familiar smell crept into her nostrils; it was faint, but with barely a breeze in the summer air it lingered around her. Pipe smoke. It reminded her of turf fires and cozy nights with Peter and warmed her from the inside out.

The hearty smell helped her forget about her ruined shoe and she turned her head toward the bridge. She could see a pair of shiny, black shoes peering out from behind the full, leafy bushes and smoke rising up in puffs. She began to walk towards Stephen.

The tip of her left shoe felt heavy with stones and grass stuck to it. Every few steps she stopped and rubbed it on the road, hoping to scrape off some of the dried tar, but it wasn't working. The strange sound of her footsteps attracted Stephen's attention and he leaned over to watch Jane approach. She didn't notice him smiling at the sight of her shoe collecting gravel on her journey. He chuckled and sat back, waiting for Jane to make her now usual appearance on the grass before him.

"I'm not like a rolling stone today, Stephen!" Jane said as she sat on the grass in front of him, taking off her shoe.

"Indeed. You're gathering everything on the tip of your shoe today," he replied. "That sun would split the stones." He spoke while puffing on his pipe and wiping beads of sweat off his forehead with a cloth handkerchief.

Jane picked up a twig and pushed it under the sticky tar on her shoe, hoping it would peel off. The tip of the twig broke off and stuck to it.

"Indeed," Jane replied, half mocking him but half enjoying the opportunity to use that as an agreeable answer.

"I think your shoe is for the bin," Stephen said.

"No, no, it's my only summer pair! My mam will kill me if she sees this," the panic in Jane's voice was evident.

"Vinegar will take it off. When you go home, put your shoe in the freezer. The tar won't harden in this heat. When it's hard, peel it off. You'll get the rest off by cleaning it with vinegar."

"How do you know so much?" Jane asked, looking up at him. She relaxed slightly, knowing that she wouldn't get in trouble for ruining her shoe.

"I'm old. You learn a lot as you go along," Stephen replied.

"You're here every day now?" Jane asked.

"I am. I like the company I keep when it's lunch time," he said, smiling down at her. And for the most part it was true. He did like Jane, and her inquisitive nature.

"Do you not have lunch with your wife?"

"No. She passed away. Not that long ago, actually."

"That's sad. Was she old like you?"

"She was the same age as me, yes, but she had an accident."

Jane sat quietly on the grass, picking at her shoe, and glancing up to see Stephen twisting his gold wedding ring around his finger. She loved sitting and chatting with him. He never made her feel like a child; he answered her questions and never spoke down to her. She felt more at ease with Stephen than she did at home, and she often pondered if he knew who they were because most other adults ignored her. But this was one time she didn't know how to respond or what to say. She could sense a raw sadness from him and heard a slight crack in his voice when he mentioned the accident.

"Is it true that you shoot people who steal apples from your orchard?" Jane asked, now watching birds flying in and out of the bushes.

"Thrushes," Stephen said, keeping his eyes focused on the birds. "Do you see the brown arrow-shaped flecks on their stomachs? That's how you recognise them. It's the male that's singing. The female is pecking for worms."

The song of the little bird was one Jane had heard as part of the dawn chorus, a distinctive repetitive song that she was now happy to name. During the summer months the birds often woke her at the break of dawn, the delicate, gentle sound of the smaller birds inevitably drowned out by the bigger, louder and angrier-sounding magpies that nested in the trees not far from her bedroom window. They were shrill and incessant some mornings; though they were her favourite bird to watch, the noise became too much to bear on the early mornings and she would pull the pillow over her head and curse them for trying too hard to be better and louder than the others. Sometimes she even shouted at them. "Stop showing off!"

"They like snails. They'll use a rock to throw the snails at until the shells break and they can eat them. I bet the next time you're in the field close by, you'll see a rock surrounded by snail shells and you'll know then that's where the thrushes dine."

Jane looked up at Stephen and smiled at him. She hadn't forgotten her original question but couldn't imagine this quiet man wielding a shotgun. She lay back on the warm grass and closed her eyes and listened to the sound of the water quietly flowing in the nearby stream and the song of the thrushes in the bushes. There was no such thing as silence in nature. There was always a sound to be heard, like the birds, the howling wind, the water flowing. There was never a day where she heard nothing.

The heat from the midday sun had become almost unbearable, but Stephen's spot by the bridge was perfectly shaded and even on a wet day allowed very little rain in. That's what it now was, 'Stephen's spot.' He'd made the massive tree stump his own, the grass in front now bare where his shoes rested. He was always watching and always listening to the silence.

Stephen lifted the plastic Dunnes Stores bag that sat by the side of the stump. It was an old bag with the green letters faded and cracked, the same one he brought every day. He pulled out sandwiches wrapped in a yellow Brennan's Bread wrapper and opened them up on his lap. Jane kept her eyes closed and visibly cringed as her stomach loudly rumbled when she smelled the fresh bread and ham. She didn't want to so much as glance at the sandwiches, fearing it would be taken for begging.

"Here," Stephen said, handing a sandwich down to her.

Jane opened her eyes and looked at the thick white bread inches from her face and her mouth watered. She slowly lifted her arms up and gently took it from Stephen's outstretched hand.

"Are you sure? I don't want to take your lunch and leave you hungry if you have to go back to farming."

"You know, I've spent so many years making lunch for two that it's just become habit. Eat away," Stephen replied as he took a bite of his own.

Jane took a bite of the sandwich and in all her life she had never tasted a sandwich so good. The butter was the smoothest, creamiest butter she had ever tasted, and the ham had a sweet hint of honey to it. The bread was fresh and doughy had no green or blue bits and it was nicer than the sliced pan her mother bought on Fridays.

"Oh my god," Jane mumbled through mouthfuls as she tried to savour every bite.

Stephen picked up the wrapper he had resting on his knee and put it on the grass between him and Jane. There was a neat pile of six sandwiches in the wrapper, three more than he usually brought.

"You'll be doing me a favour if you eat a couple more. I'll only have to throw them out."

Stephen didn't look at Jane as he said this - he kept his eyes ahead, watching the birds - but he grinned to himself when he heard her reaching for another and muttering, "Oh my god," with each mouthful.

When they had finished the pile of sandwiches, he neatly folded the wrapper and put it back into the plastic bag, but not before taking out two red apples. He handed one to Jane and took a bite out of the other.

"I won't shoot you for eating this," he said, smiling down at her.

Jane held the apple in both her hands, twisting it around and rubbing her thumb over it. It was shiny and perfect.

"There's no worms in it, I checked," Stephen said as he watched her.

"I'm not looking for worms. I've never had an apple before. So you do shoot people who steal from your orchard? And why would there be worms in the apples?"

Jane was now looking up at Stephen, who had just taken a bite from his apple. She watched how he ate it and listened to the crunch as he chewed. He never spoke with his mouth full, so Jane patiently waited for his reply, her gaze now back at the apple she held in her hand.

"Worms will crawl into apples that fall on the ground, so they can eat them. I won't shoot you or your brother if you want to come in and take a few apples. But seeing as that's your first, it might ruin other apples for you... because mine are the best," he replied with a chuckle.

He watched Jane as she brought the apple to her nose and smelled it before taking a bite. Her eyes lit up as the juices ran down her chin, her mouth filled with the sharp juice as she chewed. Her eyes danced in her head. When she swallowed it, she looked back at Stephen and said, "I'd risk getting shot for more of these! Thank you so much!"

Stephen stood up and straightened his back with a groan.

"I had better get back to work. The cows won't milk themselves. Leave the core, that's the hard bit in the middle, for the birds. Slan, Jane."

He picked up his plastic bag and flattened it, folding it small enough to fit in his shirt pocket. The bag folded easily, retaining the memory of being carefully folded many times before, just like the ground held the memory of his feet resting at the stump and how Jane would always hold the memory of her first apple.

As Stephen walked up the road, passing the bridge, he took one look back at the little girl who was still savouring the fruit. She wiped the juice from her chin with a swipe of her wrist. His heart felt heavy with sadness, for the loss of his wife, for the life they were supposed to have together and for the little girl who had never eaten an apple.

Jane obediently tossed the core into the ditch across the road where the thrushes nested, careful not to throw it too hard. It barely reached the grass, and she kicked it in lightly, not wanting to scare the birds off. She wondered if snails tasted as nice as apples to birds, or if maybe the apple core would attract snails for the birds to eat before they would be devoured themselves. At least they'd have a full belly before their worlds would be shattered. It was a cruel way to die, being thrown against a stone. But Jane knew nature could be as cruel as it was beautiful.

# Chapter Five

JANE WALKED THE ROAD home content and with a full belly, but she'd had enough of the summer heat and felt her exposed skin begin to get sore. She thought happily of laying down to read in her cool bedroom until her mother got home.

She didn't get as many books during the summer months because she mainly got them from school, but she had found a battered Stephen King novel under Peter's bed and she liked the idea of reading something scary instead of the short books she devoured in school. She had read *Under the Hawthorn Tree* in two days and her teacher had given her another book on the Irish famine that took her a bit longer to read because it was non-fiction.

As she rounded the corner, she saw Peter's black car in the driveway; she began to run towards the house but her shoe, laden with gravel, slowed her down.

She walked in the back door and sat down beside her brother who was cradling a cup of tea. She put her head on his shoulder and told him in great detail about the nicest ham sandwich she ever had in her life and the apple Stephen had given her.

"He said he won't shoot you. You can go and get some. I'd like to see his orchard. Can we go up? Do you know where it is?" Jane asked.

"I do," said Peter. "Do you want to go now? Like, this minute?"

"I'd like to have an apple for tomorrow, and I really want to see the worms eating the apples on the ground!" Jane pleaded, but still not removing her head from his shoulder. She felt tired and really wanted to lay down, but she didn't know when Peter would be home again to bring her, so she was seizing her opportunity.

"I suppose it's not far, we can walk. I'm saving the petrol to get in and out to work. Right. Let's go then. Do you want a drink before we go? You look thirsty. And a bit red, actually."

He got up and filled a mug with tap water and watched Jane as she gulped it down. Walking up the road, they passed the bridge and Jane showed Peter the thrushes and where she often sat with Stephen. She told Peter about all the funny expressions Stephen had.

"A rolling stone gathers no moss! Imagine a stone rolling down the road, Peter. But I think I get it. Oh God, remind me to freeze my shoe or she'll kill me."

Peter only then noticed the big black lump of tar stuck to the front of Jane's white shoe and he started to laugh.

"Fuck sake Janey, you picked up half the road on your shoe! The council will be looking for the gravel back! I'll get it off for you later, don't worry about Mam. Are they fitting okay? Do you need a new pair?"

"No. They don't hurt my toes yet. Thanks."

They walked to the end of their lane and took a left out onto a bigger, wider road that had no grass growing in the middle and wasn't riddled with badly filled potholes. They automatically walked in single file, Jane in front of Peter, staying close to the grass verge.

The sun was still high in the sky and Jane could feel her shoulders and neck burning hotly. Her desperation for an apple for the next day waned as her heart began to beat harder in her chest. They walked another mile; just before a crossroads, on the right-hand side, was a garden filled with apple trees. Jane's heart raced harder and faster and as much as she tried to speed up to get to it her legs just wouldn't move any quicker. She felt tired and wobbly.

"Are you having a speed wobble there, Jane?" Peter asked as he watched her lose her footing in between where the road met the grass, only to catch herself at the last minute. She made no reply as she tried to keep her balance.

They walked over a cattle grid - Jane taking big, careful steps across the bars - and down a long, shaded driveway. The trees hanging down over it weren't apple trees, but cherry blossoms that had lost their bloom and carpeted the driveway in a dusty pink blanket. The lack of wind and rain over the previous weeks meant that they stayed exactly as they were when they fell.

Jane suddenly felt cold, being in the shade, and goosebumps began to rise on her skin as she looked around through an emerging headache. Peter walked on ahead of her toward Stephen, who was sitting on a chair in the shade.

"Jane said that you gave her the go-ahead to come here, and apparently she couldn't wait!" Peter said, turning his head just in time to see Jane crumble to the ground. A fine dust of pink blossoms flew into the air around her as she hit the ground.

Peter ran to his sister, Stephen close behind him, and knelt down, cradling her and pulling her close. Stephen took one look at Janes red skin and said, simply, "That child has heat stroke."

He picked Jane up and carried her into the house with Peter following. Stephen was surprisingly quick on his feet and Peter had to jog to keep up with him. He brought Jane in through a dark tiled hallway and into a large sitting room with an open window and lay her on the couch.

"Stay here with her, I'm just getting something," Stephen said as he left the room.

Peter knelt beside his sister and rubbed her head, pleading with her to wake up. He didn't even notice Stephen re-enter armed with a small electric fan and a wet towel. Stephen lifted her head gently and placed the wet towel at the back of her neck and plugged in the fan, turning it on. The air that blew from it was still warm, but it was better than the dead heat that suffocated them. Even Peter felt a slight relief.

"Give her a few minutes and if there's no stir in her I'll drive ye to the hospital. She's going to be fierce burned tomorrow and will be desperate sore for a few days. Maybe even a week."

Stephen suddenly stood up and left the room again. Peter heard his shoes tapping on the tiled floor and drawers in the kitchen opening and closing and the tapping of his shoes again as he returned. He looked up and saw Stephen standing at the door holding up a butcher's knife in one hand and a strange looking, flat-leafed potted plant in the other.

"What the fuck are you about to do?" Peter asked, about to stand up.

"It's an aloe vera plant. It'll soothe her burns. Soon every house in Ireland will have one of these, or rather they should have," Stephen replied. He walked over to a side table and cut into the plant; a clear gel oozed from the fat leaves.

"What the fuck is that?" Peter asked, looking disgusted.

"In your current state, I'll make exceptions for the obscene language. It's aloe vera gel from this plant, excellent for burns, which your sister has."

Stephen rubbed the gel on Jane's forehead and her eyes started to flicker open. She was startled, and her body tensed up as she registered the unfamiliar surroundings.

"It's okay, it's okay. Lie back, you're safe," Stephen said as he rubbed more gel into her shoulders and arms. Jane looked from him to Peter. She slowed her breathing and allowed her muscles to relax.

She looked at the high ceiling and at the moulding where the ceiling met the wall and around the light in the centre of the room. She noticed the doors were a dark wooden colour with black metal circular doorknobs, not at all like the white panel doors at home, some which had holes, all yellowed from smoke.

"I smell apples. Did you shoot me? Am I in a mansion?" she asked, wearily noticing the side tables which held lamps matching the colour and design of the doorknobs.

"No. I didn't shoot you," Stephen replied, standing up to leave the room once again. "You have heat stroke and bad sunburn. I'll get you some water."

Peter sat on the couch beside Jane and rubbed her forehead, grimacing and pulling his hand away when he touched the gel. He could feel the heat radiate off her and he felt guilty for not noticing the extent of the redness when she first came in.

Stephen returned with three glasses of ice water, handing one to Peter and one to Jane. He took a sip of his own.

As Jane sat up, she felt the soreness in her neck. Though her arms and face burned, the inside of her body felt cold. She sipped at her drink; it was refreshing, but her stomach felt slightly nauseous and she put it down on the side table. She felt weak and exhausted and all ideas of reading had left her mind as she lay back down.

"Drink that water, it'll rehydrate you," Peter said, picking the glass up off the table and handing it to Jane.

"I don't want to puke on the fancy, em, old rug," she said, frowning down at the brown patterned rug that lay under the tables and part of the couch. "Can we go home? I'm okay to walk, I think."

"You'll not walk home. I'll drive ye, and I can fill a bag of apples for you to take with you because I'm sure I won't see you at the bridge this week. You need to stay out of the heat for a few days and wear sun cream. A pale girl like yourself should be minding her skin. This is forecast for a while."

He picked Jane up and carried her out to the backseat of his car, wrapping the seat belt around her and closing the door. She put her face against the cool door panel and closed her eyes, listening to the tap, tap, tap of Stephen's shoes as he walked quickly back into the house. He met Peter sitting on the couch with his head in his hands, taking a deep breath.

"It's a lot of responsibility, having a young sister. A mighty task for a young man," Stephen said as he handed him a plastic bag. "Get some apples for the girl and yourself, and don't be lazy picking them off the ground. Good lad."

Stephen got into the car where Jane was now asleep and turned on the cold air while he watched Peter jumping up to reach for apples on the middle branches. He watched him with the apples as he did exactly as Jane did earlier and held each one and examined them very carefully before gently putting them into the bag. He put the car in gear and slowly turned down the driveway, meeting Peter at the gate.

Peter opened the passenger door and got in beside Stephen. He too felt tired and drained and dreaded going home. He would have stayed much longer, until Jane was fully better, because he knew she'd be well looked after there.

"I'll have to call in sick tomorrow," Peter said, thinking aloud.

"Why's that?" Stephen asked, knowing the answer.

"I'll have to mind Jane. The mother is working, I think anyway. And if she isn't, she still won't be spending her day at home."

"Go to work. The girl will be grand. She'll sleep most of the day and I'll check in on her. You just make sure she has breakfast and I'll look after the rest."

Stephen had solved Peter's dilemma without any fuss and Peter let out a sigh of relief and whispered, "Thanks," to Stephen, who just nodded his head and kept driving.

When they pulled into the driveway, Peter quickly opened his door and went to take Jane out before Stephen could offer to help take her inside. As Peter unbuckled Jane's seatbelt, Stephen got out and gestured for Peter to come to him. Peter straightened his back and walked over to the bonnet of the Range Rover and faced Stephen on the opposite side. The two men placed their hands on the bonnet and made eye contact.

"A house doesn't make a man," said Stephen. "I'll need to know where I'm going tomorrow, if I'm to look in on her."

Peter dropped his head and looked at his chewed fingernails resting on the hot bonnet and sighed. "A mother doesn't make a man either.

Nor does a father... but what the hell does? Because I'm not sure who I'm supposed to be anymore."

"You're just yourself," Stephen said. "A young man with a good heart, finding his way. I knew your father, you know. I worked with him. You're very like him, in a lot of ways. He'd be proud of you. Now, get the girl and show me around."

Stephen grabbed the bag of apples from the footwell as Peter gently lifted Jane from the back seat. She had woken when the car doors opened, and saw Peter and Stephen talking across the bonnet. She watched as Stephen's eyes were drawn to the red paint mark running along the wall and wondered if he was going to paint over it for them. Her mother's car wasn't as nice as this one, especially now it had a broken wing mirror, a dent in the front and deep scratch along the side.

She reached up and put her hands around her brother's neck like she had done many times before, wincing slightly at the sensation in her skin. He carried her to her bedroom and laid her on her bed. The blankets felt cool at first, but quickly began to heat up under her warm body. She turned her head to one side and looked at her brother who had frown lines etched into his forehead. Jane asked him if he would stay in her room tonight.

"Mam will be so mad."

"Of course I'll stay," he said, "and I'll deal with her, so don't worry. I'll leave you to get a cool nightie on you." He got up and closed the door on his way out.

In the kitchen, Stephen was unpacking the fan and aloe vera plant. He handed Peter a piece of paper with his phone number on it and explained how to cut the plant and use the fan.

"That's my number. Ring me if you need me at any time. Day or night. Don't ever let your pride get in the way of asking for help because that little girl will be the one to suffer." Stephen patted Peter on the shoulder as he turned to the door. Just as he opened it, he turned again to Peter and asked, "What happened to the wall?"

"She hit it driving in a few months back. Took the wing mirror off when she hit the wall. Nearly sliced open the whole passenger side like a tin opener. Stephen, I'm ashamed to say, she was drunk."

Stephen nodded his head and looked out the door, towards the wall. He took a deep breath. "Children shouldn't be punished for the sins of their parents." With that, he closed the door behind him, leaving Peter in the wake of the calm Stephen seemed to carry with him everywhere he went.

# Chapter Six

THE OUTSIDE OF THE bungalow bloomed during the summer months with a little help from Stephen. With Peter being home more during the summer months, Jane was living one of the best summers to date.

Stephen had taken Jane's love of nature and nurtured it, educating her using cuts of shrubs from his own garden that he rooted and gifted to her. She was now more attuned to the weather patterns than the birds themselves, and he thought of her gifted in that area.

Stephen walked up the lane with a plastic bag in each hand. The unusually dry, warm weather running into its second month had made it difficult for farmers. The grass was dry and burned; water supplies were scarce and the little stream was the lowest Stephen had seen in years. But there was one place that the heatwave and scorching heat hadn't affected, and that was Jane's new garden.

It was luscious and green, awash with different colours. She religiously watered the garden morning and night, and took great care in not watering anything during the midday sun in case the leaves or flowers burned. He didn't have the heart to tell her that she should be saving water during a heatwave; when he arrived at the boundary wall of the house and saw Jane on her knees, pulling up what little weeds there were, he knew he was making the right decision.

She hummed to herself as she pulled a weed from around a buddleia shrub she had planted mere weeks ago and was already thriving in its perfect location, its emerging purple and pink flowers vibrant against the grey pebble-dashed wall. As she leaned in, a brown butterfly fluttered from the back of the shrub and Jane squealed and jumped up. When she spotted Stephen standing at the wall, she squealed a second time in fright and then smiled.

"You scared me!"

"You're surely not afraid of butterflies?" Stephen asked.

Jane's cheeks flushed red and she twirled the bottom of her white t-shirt in her fingers.

"I am, a little. One was in my bedroom for ages. I didn't mind him in the corner at all, until one day he was gone and then when I lay down in bed, he fluttered in my face and got all stuck in my hair. Peter thought I was getting eaten by a pack of dogs I screamed that loud. But I could hear him fluttering in my ear!"

"Well," Stephen said, looking around, sensing Jane's embarrassment, "don't tell anyone this, but I'm terrified of mice. I scream like a little girl when I see one! That's why I have so many cats around the farm. But they like to leave presents at the door and one time the black tom cat left a present on my pillow. It was a dead mouse! I threw the whole pillow out and I couldn't sleep for a week."

"Ewww! That's disgusting!" laughed Jane. "Mice don't bother me, but I prefer an alive one than a dead one on my pillow. We have mice here. I seen one crawling out from the socket in the wall up the wire of the kettle once. I thought he was so cute, I named him Ben."

Stephen visibly shuddered at the thought of a mouse roaming around the kitchen and Jane knew he wasn't lying about his fear.

"Anyway," he said. "Enough about horrible mice. I have something for your garden." Stephen reached into his shirt pocket and pulled out a small white envelope and handed it to Jane. She shook the contents and knew it was seeds; Stephen's seeds in envelopes always sounded like rice.

"What are these ones?" she asked, carefully opening the small envelope.

"Sunflower seeds. They'll grow as tall as me, maybe even taller. Plant them deep and against a wall. Once they've grown, they'll attract magpies and smaller birds to eat the seeds from the flower. I know magpies are your favourite."

Jane held one of the almond shaped seeds between her thumb and forefinger and turned it over before putting it back in the envelope.

"Thank you, Stephen! You're the best! I'm going to have the bestest garden in all of Ireland!" Jane ran off to get the small spade he had given her. Stephen smiled and turned towards the back door, picking up the two plastic bags as he did. The windows and door were open, and he could see Peter inside, cleaning down the worktops. He deliberately cleared his throat as he passed, and knocked on the open door.

"Howaya, Stephen?" Peter greeted him and immediately spotted the bags in his hands. "You don't have to keep bringing stuff for us, you know. I'm very grateful but honestly, don't leave yourself stuck."

"I'm not at all, you're getting it all wrong. You're doing me a favour by taking this, otherwise it'll go off and need to be thrown out," he said, unloading fruit and vegetables out of the first bag. At the bottom sat three portions of shepherd's pie and Peter's stomach loudly grumbled. Stephen placed them on the counter next to Peter and started to empty the second bag. The smell of mixed herb stuffing and fresh bread wafted towards Peter's nose and his mouth watered.

"God, that smells good. Stephen, you need to stop doing this, but thank you, sincerely," Peter said as he turned to boil the kettle.

"Do you have any mouse traps?" Stephen asked.

"Um, yeah, why?" Peter asked, his forehead furrowed in confusion.

"Jane has a pet, and we need to get it out of your kitchen," Stephen replied, looking around.

"Ohhhh, you mean Ben? Yeah, I thought she made that up!" Peter laughed as he took the tea bags from the box and placed them in a cup.

"Not for me. It's too hot for tea. Get me the traps, please and a little bit of chocolate if you have it."

Peter stopped making the tea and pulled out two unused mouse-traps from the back shelf under the sink. He placed them on the table and went up to his bedroom to get the bar of chocolate he had hidden away. He placed it beside the traps.

"Mice are very attracted to sweet things. We'll catch Ben quicker if chocolate is melted onto it instead of cheese," Stephen said as he used a lighter to melt a small piece of chocolate onto the traps and set them. He handed them to Peter and nodded towards the shelves under the sink.

"One in there, and one in where the dry foods are kept."

Peter placed the traps gently on the back of the shelves and turned to Stephen, who was already making his way out the door.

"Where are you going?" Peter shouted after him. "And what do I do if I catch them?" He ran out the back door and out onto the driveway, following the smell of pipe smoke, and shouted the question again. "What do I do if I catch one?"

Stephen, without turning around, raised his hand and said, "You're on your own there, I'm afraid." He motioned towards Jane, who was struggling with the heavy spade. "Help your sister dig that hole, good man."

Peter sighed and walked towards Jane, who was sweating with the spade in her hand, and he rolled his eyes.

"You're like a little wife these days, ordering me about in the garden!" he said. "Go in get some water before you pass out again. I'll dig your hole."

"Make sure you dig a few holes, but deep, please, and right next to the wall!" Jane shouted over her shoulder as she skipped inside. Peter smiled as he started digging the dry ground. Within seconds beads of sweat were running down his back, but he felt content that in that moment in time; all he had to worry about was digging a hole.

He looked around the garden at the new splashes of colour and tried to remember the last time it looked so full of life. He didn't know the names of half of the flowers and shrubs Jane spent her time tending but he enjoyed seeing her immersed in her new hobby.

As he put his foot on the spade to begin digging the third hole, the smell of the sandwiches Stephen left in the kitchen filled his nostrils and he quickly turned to see Jane laying out a blanket on the grass, unwrapping sandwiches and pouring Coke from a big bottle that Peter thought he had hidden better.

"Are you going to sit and watch me kill myself digging holes, your majesty?" Peter asked as he leaned on the spade.

"No, silly! We can have a picnic! Come on!" Jane replied, laughing.

She took a bite out of a sandwich, and Peter sat down beside her, picking up the glass of coke and drinking it in one mouthful.

"So, I see you know where my stash is?" he asked when he caught his breath.

"Yeah, but I'll never take anything without you being here."

"I know, Janey. You can help yourself any time. It's for us. Especially if there's no other food in the house." Peter took a mouthful of his sandwich and rolled his eyes as he chewed. "My God, that man makes the best food," he said. "This is the nicest stuffing I've ever eaten."

"Maybe we should ask him to show us how to make it?" Jane replied through mouthfuls. She started to pick the crusts off the bread and roll them up into balls. She got up, placing them on the wall in a row before sitting back down on the blanket, watching.

Within minutes, a lone magpie landed on the wall, pecking at the crumbs Jane had left, its blue and black feathers sparkling in the sunlight. Peter and Jane stayed silent as it hopped off the wall and onto the grass on front of them. Peter tore some bread from his sandwich and threw it on the grass, watching the magpie come closer to take it.

"Brave little fecker isn't he?" Peter said, amused by the bird coming so close. "I thought they were just black and white; I didn't realise they were blue too. Did you name him?"

"Mags," Jane replied, as if he had been a lifelong friend. She sat smiling at her brother, her focus off the bird. Peter's eyes were as sparkly as the bird's feathers, and she liked seeing him more relaxed. He smiled as he threw more bread, but the magpie didn't take it. Instead, it quickly took off into flight and flew towards the trees in the nearby field.

"There's a car coming," Jane said, picking up the last bit of sandwich. She put the bread to her lips to take a bite out of it, but butterflies had appeared in her tummy.

"How did you know that?" Peter asked as he stood up, feeling the nervous energy off Jane.

"The magpie flew off," she replied. "He heard it before us." She nodded towards the tree the bird was now safely nestled in.

The black Mercedes pulled up and Sean stepped out, dressed in tight jeans and a black t-shirt which started sticking to him as soon as he left the air-conditioned car.

"Do yas like the new motor, lads?" he asked as he ran his hand over the roof.

"She's not here. She's in work," Peter replied, ignoring the question.

"Maybe I called to see you! What are we having, a teddy bear's picnic, without the teddy bears?" Sean took a step towards the wall and looked over into the garden. "Garden looks well. Something smells nice," he said as he walked in through the little gate and up a path separating the two lawns. As he moved towards them he kicked the head off the last remaining lupins that grew on the edge of the path, sending them flying.

Jane inhaled sharply and her face furrowed with anger, but she took another step back until her back was pinned up against the pebbled-dashed wall. He walked over to her and snapped the sandwich out of her hand, taking a bite. Jane looked up at the tall man, his forehead now dripping with sweat. Her legs began to tremble.

Peter took a step closer to Jane and put his arm around her shoulder, pulling her closer towards him.

"*Jaysus*, this is good," said Sean with a full mouth.

"Sean, what the fuck do you want?" Peter demanded. "She's not here and won't be for hours. If you're just here to show off the car, it's nice. Now fuck off!"

Sean stood up straighter, puffing his chest out and straightening his shoulders. He wasn't any taller than Peter but he was broader.

"Sit back down, little boy," he said as he took a step forward.

Jane watched as her brother and mother's boyfriend stared at each other, but the silence was broken by the sound of a magpie warbling, followed by another, then another, until there were four loudly warbling in unison. One by one, they swooped towards Sean, calling to each other as they did.

Sean waved his arms, still holding the sandwich. Jane giggled as the magpie she had just fed swooped down and pecked at Sean's head, her laughter barely audible over the noise as all four birds gained momentum. Sean threw the sandwich over the wall, thinking that's what they were after, but they persisted until he ran up the path, still waving his arms, and got into his car.

The magpies, not content with pecking his head, each deposited thick white droppings as he started the engine.

"They're shitting on my fucking car!" he shouted as he turned the washer and wipers on, smearing it across his windscreen.

Jane's giggles had transformed into belly laughter and tears rolled down her face as she held onto Peter's arm and crossed her legs. Peter's smile was one that even Sean hadn't seen before, and he grimaced at them through the car window before he sped off down the lane.

"Oh my god I need to wee right now!" Jane said as she turned and ran into the house, her laughs echoing within the walls.

Peter looked up into the trees and saw the lone magpie sitting on a branch. He wondered where the others went to so quickly as he saluted Mags in thanks.

# Chapter Seven

JANE HUNCHED OVER HER bowl of cornflakes and read the back of the box. She had done so, read the back of the family-sized cereal box, every day for a month now and knew it by heart, but she felt invisible behind it as her mother fussed, looking for their good clothes. They each had one or two special outfits she insisted on keeping for special occasions. Over the past few years these special occasions had dwindled down to just Sunday Mass. Nobody invited them anywhere.

"You're supposed to starve yourself a half hour before communion," Jane's mother said as she pulled at clothes from the laundry basket. She was dressed in a   white bra and navy knickers, her thin frame practically skeletal as she bent over, looking for her good blouse.

She had always been petite, but her years of drinking and forgoing proper meals had taken its toll on her body. She looked frail, older than her years. But she prided herself on her slim frame. and thigh gap, often telling Jane that she should aim to have one too.

Her idea of protecting her skin was to slather it in baby oil and bake in the sun. She had been, once, a pretty, fresh-faced girl with straight, dark, thick hair but her now bony frame held weather-beaten, ravaged skin; her fresh face had been replaced with lines which told the tales of a thousand cigarettes and a lifetime of sorrow. Years of harsh dye had ruined her shining hair.

Jane straightened up from her bowl. "I haven't made my Holy Communion yet. Do I still need to be starving?" Her mother ignored her, too immersed in her quest for a clean blouse.

Jane didn't like Sundays. It was the day Peter worked and went directly to his digs at college and the day where every muscle in her body ached from being so tense. She never knew what the day held in store, but it always started with Mass.

Her mother had been unmarried when Jane was born and that carried a stigma; a weight carried on the shoulders of children who never asked to be born, on mothers who refused abortion or adoption but never on the father who walked away. It was the women and children who carried the sin, who had to ask for God's forgiveness. While the man carried on with his life.

Jane felt it. It dragged her down like a weight tied around her ankles. Already in her short life this had become so hard to carry that she had stopped believing the priest's sermons. He would often come into her classroom and talk about God and forgiveness, but when he spoke of sins and sinful behaviour he would look directly at Jane and condemn unmarried mothers.

She could feel the eyes of every other child boring into her very soul as the teacher looked down at the ground. She had often felt humiliated but never knew why. Jane couldn't understand why she was singled out.

What Jane didn't know was that she and Peter were members of a new generation of one-parent families. The mother and baby homes had all but closed when Jane was born; they had reached a time where it was becoming normal to be part of this new breed of family.

But it wasn't normal in the eyes of their archaic parish priest. He was visibly disgusted by the mere presence of these children and made no effort to hide it. He refused to have illegitimate children serving Mass on Sundays, or any day, befouling his place of worship and letting every young woman think it was acceptable to have premarital sex. He vocally barred Peter from becoming an altar boy. This instilled a hatred towards the Catholic church in Peter that would stay with him for life.

Jane listened to every word the priest would preach on Sundays. He talked about the son of God, Jesus, and she remembered the story of Mary Magdalene. Jane knew she was an unmarried mother too, because the priest always put her and unwed mothers in the same sentence in his prayers. She wondered why Jesus could forgive that Mary, but the priest couldn't forgive her mam? She listened to his sermons on forgiveness and wondered how a man of God could be so lacking in the very things he preached about.

She wondered if her mother was so mad all the time because she had yet to be forgiven. Or maybe she didn't feel loved. But her mother went every week, and took Jane with her, to condemn her own choices and to pray desperately for what her life was missing. The answers she couldn't find in the church she searched for at the bottom of a bottle; both routes created more guilt, self-loathing and resentment.

When Mass ended, Jane and her mother left hand-in-hand, heads down. They left the older generation to gossip in the churchyard and were always first to their car, the eyes of the older ladies following them. Jane's mother would let out a throaty sigh of relief when she closed the door, as if the old car were a suit of armour, protecting her from the looks and the sniggers.

"I have an idea, Jane; will we go and get a ninety-nine?" she asked, starting the car.

Jane loved ice cream, and for once she felt that maybe this Sunday would be different. Maybe. If her mother was in a good enough mood to treat her to an ice cream, then maybe there would be no pub today.

"Yes please, mam!" Jane was excited as they turned for the shop.

They rarely spoke during the weekends; Mother was either drunk or hungover and had a very strict rule that, "Little children should be seen and not heard," so Jane never instigated conversation. But today, her mam was chatty and they talked about the good weather and, perhaps soon, another day at the beach. Jane was enjoying this rare nice conversation but a niggly feeling of doubt remained. She couldn't shake the feeling in her tummy and urged herself not to relax too much.

As Jane stood by her mother at the cash register in the shop, she spotted a green and white striped pen in the shape of a candy cane. It was the nicest pen she had ever seen, and she picked it up and turned it over in her hands. She wasn't allowed use pen in school, not yet, but she loved it nonetheless. It was unusual.

Her mother gave her a backwards glance. "Do you want it, Jane?" Before Jane could answer, her mother took the coveted object from her hands and paid for it. Jane's heart sung. Her mother was in a good mood, the sun was shining, she had an ice cream and a new pen. She knew for definite that there would be no pub today. This was her happiest Sunday.

They got into the car; when her mother began driving towards the local town, Jane felt tears fill her eyes. She didn't want another Sunday sitting in a pub, but she dared not voice her opinion. She knew how easily things could turn. She tried to content herself with her beautiful new pen.

"I have to go into the shop to do the lotto," her mother said while opening the door of the car. But Jane knew that was a lie. She knew where they were going and for the first time in her life decided to call her mother's bluff.

"I'll wait in the car for you, mam. I'm still eating my ice cream."

Jane quite honestly thought this was the best idea she had ever had; her mother wouldn't leave her alone in the car for long on a hot day. Jane saw a look of frustration cross her mother's face, but then she smiled.

"Right. Well, I won't be long, then. Few minutes," she said, closing the door.

Jane sat back in the seat of the car, relieved. She smiled to herself, knowing her plan had worked; there would be no pub today. Perhaps this Sunday would break the habit and there would be never be another Sunday spent in the pub!

The sun was strong in the sky and Jane felt it beating down onto the car. The inside of the car felt like a sauna, and she started to sweat. She never thought to roll down the window; she took her cardigan off, feeling her feet begin to swell in her little black church shoes. She picked up her pen and turned around, facing towards the back window. She found an old, faded receipt. and wrote on the back with her new pen.

*Where is my mam? Where is she?*

Jane was delighted that it wrote so smoothly, and she couldn't wait to show her classmates her unusual new present the following morning. She wondered if anyone else had a pen shaped like a walking stick as she wrote the same sentence again.

*Where is my mam?*

She turned around in the seat back to a sitting position, and felt her stomach growl. She noticed an unopened packet of Taytos on the floor, but knew if she ate them that she'd be thirsty. She already was.

Her mouth was dry as the sweat dripped down her back. The air inside the car felt hot as she inhaled, as if were burning her throat. Her mother's minutes felt like hours as she looked at the piece of paper and wrote her question again and again and again, until the back of the receipt was filled with a serious question written in a childish hand.

She was now worried. She wasn't worried for herself, sitting in a baking hot car, her stomach rumbling... she was concerned that her mother was lost. She had heard it happen before, people forgetting where they had parked their car and her heart now beat out of her chest. She began to feel as if every breath was an effort, and her chest went up and down too quickly.

Consumed with worry, Jane opened the door of the car. The fresh air hit her with a blast, and she felt like she could breathe again, but the worry and panic remained. She needed to find her mother and show her the way back to the car.

Gripping her new pen in her hand, she closed the door and walked up the street. She remembered the way to the pub they were in last Sunday headed in that direction. She knew her mother had been gone far too long to be still doing the lotto and thought that perhaps she was thirsty too and stopped in for one drink. *Maybe it was just 7-Up today*, Jane thought.

The street was busy. There were teens gathered on the corner and an unusual amount of traffic for a Sunday. Jane crossed the road to the pub and found the owner standing in the entrance. Like a man in control of the world.

He was thin and, at the very least, six feet tall. He seemed like a giant to Jane, and she wondered if he would even hear her from all the way up there. He looked fiercely proud; she couldn't remember ever seeing a man stand so straight and tall.

She stopped before him and, using her polite voice, looked up and said, "Excuse me?"

He lifted his chin in the air, as if this small child was polluting the atmosphere by her mere presence, and turned his head away. Jane instantly knew he was far too tall to hear her. So, she turned on her outside voice.

"EXCUSE ME! HAVE YOU SEEN MY MAMMY? SHE'S WEARING A BLACK COAT AND HAS BROWN HAIR AND SHES LOST!"

He looked down at Jane and a sneery smile came across his face. He shook his head and looked away. Jane's feeling of desperation grew and grew until it consumed her. She needed to find her mother and show her where the car was. She imagined her mother wandering around the town, panicking and worrying. How would she find her? Jane turned away from the giant man and started to cry.

Jane cried very silent tears. She never howled or whined, the tears themselves the only sign she was upset. She cried loudly if she was physically hurt but never if it was emotional. Loud crying helped with physical pain but Jane didn't make a sound now because she didn't know the words to explain how her heart was hurting.

As she walked along the street, adults and other children alike walked past her. They all ignored the crying, sweaty child; for once Jane didn't want to be invisible. She needed help finding her mother and to make sure she was okay. She blended into the busy Sunday streets; children with ice creams and balloons brushed past her as she made her way back to the car.

But Jane did not go unnoticed by everyone. A white Transit van pulled up alongside the pavement and the passenger door opened.

"Are ya lost, pet?" a voice boomed out. Jane stopped in her tracks and looked towards the van. A larger-than-life lady was leaning out the passenger side and peering down at her.

Her white blouse was crisp and new, and her blonde hair was freshly permed. Many heavy gold necklaces hung from her neck and she wore gold sovereign rings on her fingers. The smell of fresh cigarette smoke drifting from the van reminded her of her mother. Jane began to sob.

"I'm...not...lost! My...mammy...is!"

Jane knew where she was, and she knew where the car was, so she wasn't the one who was lost. Her mother was lost. In Jane's little brain it all made perfect sense.

"Hop in and we'll help ya find her," the lady said. She grabbed Jane's arm and pulled her up into the big van, pulling her over her lap and into the middle seat. Jane had no time to react but she felt at ease in the big lady's presence. She didn't even notice the driver until he started to shout.

"Ya can't be just takin' *lackeen* off the street in a white fuckin' van, Marie! What if someone seen us? She needs one of her own to look after 'er! Aren't we hated enough for ye? Jesus Christ, imagine if someone seen us take a country girl off the street in broad fuckin' daylight!"

Jane trembled as the man in the white vest spat fury across her. A cigarette sat between his yellowed fingers which were also adorned in heavy gold rings.

Before Jane could make an escape, the van kept moved slowly onwards, the couple continuing their argument in words that Jane didn't understand. It sounded a little like the Irish the teacher spoke at school, but she was too frightened to try and pick out any of the words.

The van drifted by the carpark where Jane's car sat, still under the sun, and still empty. Her mother wasn't standing beside it wondering where she was, and the receipt still lay at the back window. Jane held onto her pen tightly as she wondered if she would be able to write her mother and Peter letters from wherever she was being taken. Jane's fear crippled her as she wondered if she would ever see Peter again. She cried silently as the woman rubbed her arm. Nobody had ever noticed her silent tears before, but this lady did.

"Don't let Michael scare ya, he's a grumpy fecker at the best of times. What's yer name? I'm Marie."

Jane took a minute to settle her breathing. She took a big gulp of air and told Marie her name. But she didn't dare ask where they were going. The van pulled up beside a building in the centre of town and Marie opened the passenger door.

"There's men in here that will help," she said. "I'm going in to talk to them, you stay here."

She rubbed Jane's knee gently and Jane felt at ease once again. Marie directed her gaze to Michael and, with an outstretched finger, sternly said, "And you! Don't you frighten the wee *lackeen*. I'm going to talk to the shades!"

Marie was graceful for a lady of her size and she glided in through the double doors. She had a fierceness about her that didn't scare Jane, but made her feel protected. Jane looked towards Michael who had his gaze fixed directly out the front window. His cigarette hung from his bottom lip and he sat straight, as if he were poised for battle. His shoulders were tense and his fingers gripped the steering wheel.

"Why do people not like you?" Jane asked. "People don't like me because I have no daddy."

Michael's expression softened as he looked down at the little girl.

"He dead?"

"No, he left. I don't think he liked me."

Michael raised his hand to pat Jane on the head as she looked down at her pen, but stopped himself at the last minute.

"Well, that's just bad form," he said as he returned his gaze to the windscreen. Jane could feel Michael relaxing as his shoulders dropped slightly. He smiled to himself a little, though he kept his grip on the steering wheel, and Jane felt bad that her mother was lost while she herself was safe.

Marie returned to the van and opened the door. She looked at Jane who now suddenly looked smaller than when she first spotted her on the street. Her heart ached for the girl as she thought of her own children, and the one she was carrying. She wondered if Jane's mother was really lost. She couldn't imagine leaving one of her own to fend for themselves.

"The man in there will help ya, lovie," Marie said. She gently grabbed Jane and lifted her down from the van, her petite frame now evident in her hands. In that moment, Marie wanted to bring this country girl home and feed her. Show her love and kindness.

Jane turned around to say goodbye to Michael, but his gaze was still firmly fixed out the window. She waved anyway as she and Marie walked hand-in-hand into the Garda station.

The man inside looked down at Jane and back up to Marie.

"So, your mother is lost? Are you sure this woman didn't just take you from the street?"

Marie rolled her eyes. "For the love of God, why would I do that?" she asked. "The *lackeen* was crying on the street and everyone was ignoring her. I had to help!"

"Yes, my mammy is lost," said Jane, "She forgot where the car is and Marie helped me by bringing me here. Can you help find her? I'm not lost, I know where my car is, she's the one lost."

Jane was intimidated by the man's uniform. She grabbed Marie's hand, and though her grip was firm and gentle, she understood Marie was nervous too, though she didn't know why.

"Alright. Leave the child with me. I'll find her mother," the Garda said, ushering Jane in behind the counter. Jane looked back towards Marie and wished that she could stay with her, but the Garda had closed the door. She hadn't even had time to say thank you.

The back office was filled with screens and phones and there were three other male Gardai busying themselves and bustling around the busy office. The man from the desk lifted Jane up onto an office chair and sat at one in front of her.

"Can you tell me where your car is parked? Do you know where your mother went?"

The Garda who had at first been accusing and firm now had a gentle smile on his face. The laughter lines around his eyes softened his expression even further, and his blue eyes shone as he spoke.

Jane sighed as she relayed her story again. She was asked the same questions what felt like a hundred times, and she was no closer to finding her mother.

"Do you drink tea? We don't have any fizzy drinks, but would you like some tea and biscuits?" the Garda asked as he was standing up from his chair. He didn't wait for a reply before he went over to the kettle in the corner. He came back with four different biscuits, all plain with no chocolate, and handed them to Jane.

Her tummy rumbled; she hadn't eaten since the ice cream her mother had bought her, and that now felt like a lifetime ago. She held the biscuits in her hand. She wanted to eat them, but her stomach was doing somersaults and she was afraid to put anything into her mouth.

"I'm going to go down to your car and see if your mammy is there. You stay here with these other lads. Sometimes when little boys and girls get lost, the first place a mammy comes looking is here, so we'll leave you here because she will come looking for you."

Jane realised he really believed what he was saying, but he didn't know her mother and how this wasn't the first time Jane had been left alone. She'd never been left alone in the car before, that was a first, but she didn't believe that her mother would come looking for her. If anything, Jane started to fear that her mother had forgotten about her again and was already making her way home.

"Him there, he's called John, and the fella in the corner, the lazy one, he's Thomas," he pointed at the two other Gardai in the office. They both looked up from their screens and waved at Jane. "They'll mind you until I get back."

"What's your name?" Jane called after him as he got to the door. He looked back at her and smiled, his face looking younger before.

"I'm Chris. I'll be back in a few minutes. Don't worry, Jane, and make sure Thomas doesn't eat all your biscuits!"

Jane held onto the sugary treats as tight as she could without crushing them. She spun slightly on the office chair and wondered what horrible stories had been heard behind these walls. She wondered what would happen if they didn't find her mother. The nervous energy in her little body intensified as she started to tap her pen off the arm of the chair.

"Do you want paper to draw with your pen?" Thomas asked, mainly to get her to stop tapping. "I bet you can draw lovely pictures."

He handed her a blank page he had taken from the printer. Thomas was younger than Chris, but his brown eyes looked older, with deep black circles under his eyes. Jane looked up at him and smiled.

"I can draw a rainbow but the pen is only blue, so it'll be just blue lines... so, not a rainbow. Maybe a flower? I'll draw a blue flower to match your shirt, a bluebell!"

Thomas smiled at the little girl; alone in a Garda station, she still had kindness in her heart. He watched her as her tongue sat out on her bottom lip in a look of concentration while she drew the flower, and he wondered how such an innocent child had come to be left all alone. He was beginning to hate humanity but something in Jane gave him hope.

Chris eventually returned with his cap in his hand, shaking his head. Jane didn't even ask because his sullen and somewhat angry expression told her all she needed to know. He didn't find her mother.

She looked out the tall window behind Thomas' desk and noticed the sunset. The glow lit up the grey buildings and the sky reminded her of a perfect painting. She marvelled at the colours through the bars on the windows.

She turned to Chris and said, "So, if you still haven't found my mammy, am I going to jail?" The question shocked him as he glanced over at Thomas. He knelt down to the girl's level.

"Now why would you be going to jail?" he gently asked. "No, ah, *leanabh*. Absolutely not. Now, I'm a good Garda, and I always find lost things. Some things take a little bit longer than others, but I will find them. Only bad people go to jail."

He stood up. "Have ya ever been in a squad car, Jane? We'll go for a spin around the town and see can we find your mother." Jane jumped down off the chair and handed her picture to Thomas.

"Sorry there isn't more colours in it, but maybe if you get a yellow pen you can draw the sun. Then everything won't be so blue in here."

As Jane grabbed Chris' hand and walked out the door, Thomas rubbed his tired eyes and watched them leave before looking down at his new picture.

❧❧❧❧❧ ❧❧❧❧❧

Jane felt tiny in the passenger seat of the squad car. It was clean, like Peter's, but she could barely see out the window and felt as if she was sitting on the road. She grabbed her seatbelt and looked at the radio and all the switches on and around the dashboard. The equipment fascinated her as she wondered how they managed to operate it all when driving.

"Wanna turn on the siren and lights?" Chris asked with a conspiratorial smile. But Jane pondered the offer briefly before she declined.

"What if we turn them on," she replied carefully, "and my mam was walking along and looking for the car and heard them and thought she was in trouble and ran away?"

Chris was lost for words. Seldom had he met anyone, let alone a child, who thought so strongly of others. This girl found wandering the streets, crying, was concerned for her mother's welfare instead of her own.

They drove up the now quiet streets and through the town, Jane looking at every passing person and sighing with disappointment when they approached a new street. She watched people stumble out of pubs and into takeaways or taxis as Chris drove at a snail's pace. She still held the biscuits in one hand and her pen in the other.

As they rounded the corner into the car park where their car sat in the darkness, no longer baking in the sun, Jane spotted her mother there. She was crying and Jane quickly realised she was drunk. When Chris stopped the car, she didn't rush to remove her seatbelt and get out. Instead she looked down at her biscuits and her pen before she looked up at him.

His posture had completely changed and his face had hardened. He carried a new air of authority; she knew to do as she was told when he asked her to stay in the car. She felt glad he was with her as he picked up his hat and stepped out into the evening.

Jane watched her mother crying as Chris wagged his finger in her face. He hunched his shoulders slightly as he lowered his face to hers. He was shouting.

Jane couldn't hear what he was saying but she could see her mother's repeated apologies. Jane willed Chris to stop, not to anger her mother. The tears rolled down her face as a wave of exhaustion hit her. It was dark; her mother's 'few minutes' after Mass had turned into many hours. She wanted to curl up and sleep on the huge passenger seat, but her night was only beginning.

Chris opened the driver's door and sat beside Jane as she wiped at her tears with her wrists. He took his cap off and put it on his lap.

"I'm going to take you and your mother home. She's not in a fit state to drive. Jane...does—does your mother drink a lot?" Jane looked down at her pen and her biscuits. Chris already knew the answer. He had dealt with enough addicts in his lifetime to spot one a mile away. "Jane. Does she ever hurt you?"

Jane's heart skipped a beat. Nobody had ever asked her that before. She didn't know how to explain to him that her mam's words hurt her more than slaps ever did. She couldn't convey to him that her mother made her heart break every single weekend and her feelings were almost all-consuming. That her days were spent watching birds protect their own knowing she wasn't protected.

She looked up into his worldly blue eyes and simply said, "No. Never." She wondered if he knew she was lying and if he could hear her heart thumping in her ears.

The squad car pulled into the gravel driveway. Chris lifted Jane's now sleeping mother out of the back seat and carried her into the house, with Jane leading the way. He dropped her onto the bed, turning her onto her side, and followed Jane to the kitchen.

He sat down at the kitchen table and pulled out a card, writing his home phone number on it. He looked at the tired little girl and he suddenly felt tired himself.

"I can't leave you here alone, Jane. Is there anyone I can call? Otherwise, I'll have to find somewhere for you to stay tonight."

"Can I stay with you?"

"I'm afraid not, sweetie. It'll be a stranger, but they'll be nice."

Jane was silent for a few seconds and turned and ran up to her bedroom and grabbed a piece of paper from under her bed, one Peter had given her for safekeeping. In case of an emergency, he had told her, any time he wasn't around. She ran back down to the kitchen and handed Chris the phone number and sat down beside him.

"Stephen will help."

# Chapter Eight

JANE SLID INTO HER seat, placed her books on the shelf underneath, her desk and rested her head in her right hand.

"You're on my side!" Dominic snarled as he slid his elbow across, knocking her head from her hand.

She sighed, straightened up, and kept her focus ahead of her. The desks in Jane's classroom were old fashioned, even by the standards of the '80s. They had been in that classroom since the old school was built, and still carried the graffiti from the children of her mother's generation.

The wooden desks sat two children side-by-side on a bench, and on the top was a hole which was used to hold an ink pot for fountain pens. Now rulers and Bic biros stuck out of them. Underneath was a shelf to hold their books and pencil cases. There wasn't much room to sprawl, and for those who wrote with their elbows stuck out as much as their tongues, it made for even less space for their desk-mate. Jane hated her desk-mate as much as she hated the shared desk.

"Now class," Mrs. Doyle began, "over the next few weeks we're going to be getting ready for a very special occasion...your first Holy Communion! And everybody is going to have a special little job to do. Some of you will do a reading, some of you will bring up the gifts, and all of you will do the hand movements to the Our Father, but it'll be sung. Make sure you practice with your mammies and daddies every night, and we'll be having lots of practice in the church in the next few weeks."

"Who will you practice with, coz you've no daddy?" Dominic spat at Jane. The words were barely a whisper, but Jane not only heard them she felt them. She blinked back the tears and continued listening to Mrs. Doyle, but Dominic's question lingered...who would she practice with?

"The first thing we'll be getting ready for is your First Holy Confession. That's when you confess your sins to Fr. Gilroy and he will give you some penance to do. It could be to say the Hail Mary three times, or depending on how bad your sins were, he could ask you to say the Our Father, too."

Jane began to panic. She had committed so many sins; surely she'd be there forever and would have an endless amount of penance to do. She thought about the many times she felt as if she hated her mother, she had broken one of the ten commandments and she was sure for that alone she'd have to say so many Hail Marys and Our Fathers that she'd be saying them until she turned ninety. And then she wondered how she could possibly 'honour thy father' if she didn't know who he was?

The only comfort was that it was Fr. Gilroy - the younger, new priest - rather than the older parish priest, because she knew that in his eyes she was just one big walking sin, and she dreaded the penance he'd give her. She feared she'd have to become a nun just to get through the sheer number of prayers she'd have to do. She liked the new priest;

he treated her the same as he treated all the other children, and his presence put her at ease rather than terrified her.

She rested her head in her hand again as she listened to the list of 'sins' her teacher counted off and forgot about the invisible line that Dominic had drawn on the desk until he again elbowed her arm away. But this time, their teacher noticed.

"Dominic Smith! What do you think you're doing?"

His face burned crimson, amplified by his strawberry blonde hair.

"Em, well, she was on my side, Miss."

Mrs. Doyle rolled her eyes and sighed.

"Well, Dominic, don't forget to tell Fr. Gilroy your sin, because being rude to your desk-mate is most certainly a sin. Apologise to Jane, and in future have manners and ask her nicely to move. Boys don't treat girls in such a manner."

Dominic turned to Jane and muttered a half-hearted apology that Jane ignored. She now dreaded lunchtime in the yard; lately it felt, no matter where she turned, he was always there, shooting venomous remarks at her or pulling her hair. He made her upset, mostly, but she was getting so fed up that lately she was feeling angry. Another sin, no doubt. She put her head in both hands.

As Jane ate her bread-and-butter sandwich in silence, the other boys and girls started to chatter about the First Holy Communion and the types of dresses or suits they'd have, or what they hoped for the day. She continued eating with her head down, wishing for the bell to ring so that nobody would ask her any questions.

All she hoped was that her mother would be sober and happy, or that at least Peter would be able to go. When the bell rang for outside time, there was a rush to get to the yard. As she got to the door, Dominic pushed her aside, knocking her into the doorframe. She stood back, rubbing her arm, and waited for everyone else to go ahead of her.

Stepping out into the yard, the sun was low in the sky, and she shielded her eyes from the glare with her hand. She watched as groups formed. Some played football, others played basketball, some played chase. The groups of older girls sat in corners chatting and laughing and she wondered where she would fit in.

She spotted Dominic by the basketball hoops with two other boys from their class and she decided to give him a wide berth and go to the football pitch around the other side of the school. She felt invisible as she walked past the other children, and it wasn't until she got to the junior yard that she was acknowledged; the younger children loved the big girl who always stopped to help tie a shoelace.

Some said hi and others waved, but they carried on with their games and Jane felt a bit sad that she wasn't needed today so she kept on walking towards the pitch. At the very back of the football pitch was an unkempt patch of land which housed many different types of wildlife from wild rabbits to hedgehogs; if she was lucky, she might see some ladybirds and smaller birds nesting in the hedges. She was very rarely bothered down here and was generally left alone. Then she heard his voice.

"My mam said you're a bastard," Dominic said. "That's someone who has no daddy." His two companions, usually happy to follow his lead in everything, looked shocked at the swear word. Each took a step away from him, knowing he had stepped too far. But he kept going. "My mam also said that your mam is a slapper."

Jane turned to face him, her face glowing red and her eyes, though filled with tears, burning with fire. For the first time in her life she felt real anger surge through her veins as she grabbed Dominic by the hood of his coat and swung him, watching him fall face first into a bunch of nettles.

"You don't talk about my mammy like that!" she shouted after him, but her anger quickly dissipated when she heard Dominic howl in pain. He quickly jumped up but already Jane could see his face and hands erupting in angry red welts. She quickly pulled two dalken leaves and rushed to hand them to him, but he pushed her hand away and ran towards the yard.

Jane took a deep breath and followed a few steps behind, ready to accept her punishment. She walked with her head down and her heart racing.

As they set foot onto the yard, one of the teachers on yard duty immediately ran to Dominic when she saw his face, ushering him inside. He was now in floods of tears as the stinging worsened.

"What in the name of God happened to you?" the teacher asked as she ushered him towards the door.

Dominic took a look back at Jane and replied, "I tripped over a piece of wood hidden in the grass."

Dominic had tormented Jane every day of school since September, and now he had the perfect opportunity to get her in trouble but he didn't take it. She looked over to his friends, now playing chase with other children, and she began to relax. She did feel bad for pushing Dominic, but she also knew that the stinging and welts would be gone by the end of the day. They'd have been gone by the end of lunch, had he used the dalken leaves.

Back in the classroom, Jane relaxed further; Dominic had gone home early. The teacher made an announcement about being careful around nettles and explained about the dalken leaves, making Jane smile. She slid her arm across his invisible line and smiled, hoping he'd leave her alone from now on.

She was knocked out of her daydream when Fr. Gilroy entered the classroom and announced himself in all his flamboyant glory.

"Good afternoon, boys and girls!"

"Good afternoon, Father," the class chimed in unison.

"Are we all ready for our First Confessions?" he asked the class.

"Yes, Father!" Jane looked around the class at the faces of all the other boys and girls and wondered why nobody else looked worried. She thought that she had time to prepare, to pick the three least or worst sins to tell him, and wondered would ten minutes be enough. While her mind was racing over the worst things she had done, she decided to omit that she had pushed Dominic today and opted to stick with the smaller ones.

Mrs. Doyle placed her third in line to go and confess her sins in the staff room. Jane stood in the hallway with her back against the wall, and her legs shook. Her mother was playing heavily on her mind and she wondered if she confessed her mother's sins instead of her own, would she be forgiven faster and stop drinking?

The boy ahead of her was out in a couple of minutes and Jane knew for a fact that he didn't tell the priest that he copied his desk-mate's homework the other day. She stepped into the staff room and sat on a cushioned blue chair, feeling as if she might sink right into it. Her legs barely reached the end of the chair let alone the ground.

"Bless me Father for I have sinned this is my first confession and I think I have a lot of sins to confess."

Fr. Gilroy, palms together and his head down, raised his greying eyebrows and looked up at Jane. "Oh, I'm sure you don't have that many, Jane. Just two or three will do. Go on."

In that split second Jane felt an ease and a comfort she hadn't yet felt with any adult, and when her mouth opened she found she was telling Fr. Gilroy everything. The tears began to flow and with each word spoken she felt as if a weight was been lifted off her shoulders.

She told the priest how her mother drank and got angry with her and Peter and sometimes slapped them or shouted and she was worried that her mother wouldn't get into heaven. When she was finally finished, she asked Fr. Gilroy a question.

"If I confess her sins and do her penance, will she be happier and nicer and maybe she'll get to heaven because I know she's worried about that and I don't mind not going? She can have my place!"

Fr. Gilroy looked at Jane with a smile on his face and it was clear that he was very out of his depth. He put his hand on Jane's head and took a deep breath.

"Your mother must hit rock bottom before she can seek help, but God will find a way, child. Have faith. Say three Hail Marys for your mother's soul."

Jane wiped her tears and slid down off the blue chair feeling as if she had wasted her time. She would pray for her mother's soul but she had lost hope at her getting into heaven. Her feet and her heart felt heavy as she walked towards the door.

The sound of her class reciting the Hail Mary could be heard ringing through the long hall as she dragged her feet along the tiled floor. The walls of the narrow hallway were adorned with photos of past pupils and class artwork.

She stopped to look at an old football team photo hanging over the 'My Family' drawings from her class and Peter smiled back, the captain of the team beaming as he held the trophy aloft.

He was much younger, but his eyes looked the same. Held the same worry. Jane looked down towards her drawing of her mother, Peter and herself and the rainbow she'd coloured in over their bungalow, all of their faces smiling. She remembered how desperately she tried to picture her mother smiling so she could draw a life that somewhat resembled those of her classmates, even with one person missing. Everyone else had drawn pets, too, their dogs, cats and some even had goldfish. Jane had drawn a magpie sitting on the wall beside her house. It was black and white in her drawing, but she knew it had sparkles of blue. She didn't want to be so different anymore.

❦

When the bell rang, Jane packed her bag and walked slowly over to the bike rack while others got into cars or waited on the bus to pick them up. Her bike was a lonely sight and the red frame made it stand out. She pulled the plastic bag off the saddle, shoved it into the front pocket of her pink school bag and clipped her backpack to the silver carrier over the back wheel.

The road outside the school was busy, and Jane had to focus while navigating the cars moving in and out. But when she turned right towards home, the traffic eased to nearly nothing and Jane let her mind wander as she cycled over the bumpy road, easing herself off the saddle every now and then.

The breeze had a bite to it; her hands became red and cold and her nose started to run as she pedalled along. Fully grown evergreen trees on the left shaded her from the sun and she slowed down when she saw a red squirrel running up a tree. Her teacher said that red squirrels were rare because the grey ones kept being mean to them, so she wanted to watch him scamper up the tree and giggled at how frantic he seemed.

On the right were huge open fields, some with sheep and some empty, and she reminded herself to ask Stephen where he put his cows in the colder months. When she turned right, the road for home became narrower and the potholes turned it into an obstacle course, with Jane weaving left and right to avoid them. She was concentrating so hard on not bursting a tire that she didn't notice the black mountain bike wheel sticking out from the hedge. When she turned the handlebar left to avoid a pothole, a blotchy, red face jumped out from the hedge and grabbed the handle of her bike, pulling her into the grass verge.

Dominic stood over her with his fists clenched and his eyes burning with an anger that she had only ever seen in adults.

"You hardly thought I was going to let you away with what you done?" he spat.

"Get away from me, Dominic! Just leave me alone!" Jane shouted. She was close to home, but not close enough that Peter would her hear her shouting if he were around.

Jane closed her eyes tightly and covered her face as Dominic pulled his leg back, ready to kick her. His leg was already swinging towards her when a hand grabbed him by the collar and pulled him back so hard he fell onto his back in the road.

"Jane? It's okay," Stephen said. He bent down and extended his hand to pull her up. She opened her eyes and started crying when she saw his friendly brown eyes. He took her hand and pulled her up, then he turned to face Dominic, who was sitting on the road.

"What in the name of God did you think you were going to do?" Stephen asked Dominic.

"She pushed me into nettles earlier," Dominic said, not looking up. Stephen turned to look at Jane, his forehead furrowed.

"Did you?" he asked.

"Yes, I did," Jane admitted. "I got angry. He said horrible things about my mammy and he... he called me a bastard."

"So let me get this straight," he glared down at Dominic. "You tease a girl, call her awful names, and when she fights back you think she deserves more torture?" Dominic sat with his arms wrapped around his knees, not looking up. "Jane. Go home. I'm going to walk this young lad home. I need to talk to his mother," Stephen said as he pulled Jane's bike from the ditch.

"No!" Dominic started to cry. "Please don't! I'll leave her alone! Please don't tell my mother!"

"Jane would never hurt a fly and *you* pushed her so hard she had to fight back and then *you still wouldn't leave her alone*," Stephen's voice was quiet but he sounded very angry. "You waited for her when you knew she'd be on her own, to do what, Dominic? No. You had your chance to learn from using hateful words. I'll be talking to your parents. I don't want to see you on this road again, and if you so much as look in Jane's direction - or anyone's for that matter - you'll be dealing with me. Do you understand?"

Jane listened to Dominic's pleas as she fixed her schoolbag onto her bike and her heart raced. She felt guilty at the thought of Dominic getting into trouble at home.

"Wait!" she cried. "I don't want Dominic to get in trouble from his mam! It's not fair that he'll get hit too, after getting in trouble from you. Don't tell his mammy!"

Stephen and Dominic turned to look at Jane, both with confused looks on their faces. Stephen removed his flat cap, rubbed his forehead and sighed. He was lost for words until the silence was broken by Dominic.

"My mam doesn't hit me, Jane. She'll ban me from watching telly."

Jane looked at Dominic, who now had a softer expression on his face, one she had never seen directed at her before, and she smiled.

"Well, that's good then," she replied, her hands resting on the handlebars, but unsure of why a silence had fallen between Stephen and Dominic.

"Dominic," said Stephen, "go on home now, but bear in mind I will be up to see your father later on."

Jane and Stephen made their way towards the bungalow, Jane happy to have Stephen walking alongside her, but still misunderstanding the silence.

"Jane," Stephen said, softly, "I have something to ask you, and you aren't in any trouble, but I'd like you to be honest with me." Stephen's reason for being there, erecting a memorial in the spot that his had wife died, no longer seemed important. But the answer to this question was.

"Does your mother beat you?" he asked.

"Beat me?" Jane repeated, looking up at him. When she heard the word beat, she thought of pools of blood and a person unable to move afterwards.

"Does she hit you, Jane?"

"Only when I've been bold. But she doesn't beat me."

Stephen suddenly recalled times at the bridge when Jane lay on her stomach instead of sitting, or just stood the whole time, and he felt sick. He couldn't imagine her misbehaving enough to warrant her mother raising a hand to her.

Stephen had begun the day thinking about how to make a memorial for his wife. He had designs and plans but those had changed now. His plans were now involving Jane and Peter.

# Chapter Nine

St. Patrick's Day came around, breaking up the monotony of the quiet time between spring and summer. Life had just started to bloom, but the unpredictable nature of the weather meant it felt like winter one day and spring the next. The trees were not yet in full bloom and sheep were ripe and round with lamb.

Jane liked every season, but she loved the comfort of winter. She loved the quietness of nature, how it took time out to rejuvenate before coming back fresh and new in the spring. She felt everyone should take that same time in the winter to sleep and rest and come back as new at the turn of the new season. We could all bloom like nature.

St. Patrick's Day was a family-orientated day with parades, carnivals and copious amounts of chocolate and sweets. Adults who had given up smoking for Lent could be seen chain-smoking the pack of cigarettes they bought as soon as the shops opened, and children were seen with chocolate smeared on their faces, hyper from too much sugar.

Everyone wore green, and pinned shamrocks to their clothes, and Jane hated the chaotic loudness of it. The whole world to her was like a minefield and instead of watching where she stepped with her mother, she had to watch everyone. Every single person was like a bomb waiting to explode. She felt she had nowhere to hide.

Peter, on the other hand, loved it. It was the one day that it was acceptable for parents to have a drink, even be drunk. It wasn't unusual to see children running in and out of pubs and up and down streets as if the whole town was their playground. This day, he and his sister were normal. He had earned extra money from helping Stephen on the farm and was looking forward to treating Jane to a fun day out.

Jane stood beside Peter, watching the Ferris wheel spin slowly round. She shielded her eyes from the low springtime sun and wondered what views could be seen from the top. She watched the bumper cars bounce off the walls and each other and the carousels bring little children in circles around on plastic ponies. The loud music and screams of young teens on the helter-skelter made her head throb, and she felt overwhelmed as people pushed their way past in a rush to get to the next thing.

"I think you're tall enough for most things now, Janey. What'll it be first? Will we go on the big wheel?" Peter's eyes were sparkling as he looked around, the inner child aching to be let out. He looked down at Jane and watched her eyes dart from one thing to the next, felt her move in a little closer as someone pushed passed them. Sensing her nerves, he gently pulled her in closer and bent down, looking her in the eyes.

"Jane, try and relax. Please try to let go and enjoy yourself. Not everyone is the enemy. Take a big deep breath... relax."

Jane inhaled deeply while staring into her brother's eyes. She wanted to be at home by the stream, listening to the babbling waters. This was too much for her, but she could see that Peter needed it, maybe more than she did, so she pushed her anxiety aside as much as she could and went with Peter to stand in the queue for the Ferris wheel.

It looked much bigger up close than when she'd stood on the street watching it. Her heart beat rapidly in her chest and she hoped she'd be too small to ride on it, but she wasn't. As she and Peter stepped into a cart, she could hear her blood rushing in her ears and her stomach turned. This would be her first time on a Ferris wheel and, if she had her way, her last.

When the door closed, it moved just a few feet at a time to let people get into the empty carts, and soon they were at the very top. She looked across the blue sky and could see the steeple from the church at the far side of town. Roads with cars going up and down looked smaller from where she sat, but over to her left the town stopped and the countryside began.

She noted how there seemed to be more birds over the fields. She watched the young swallows and blackbirds swoop and soar and she longed to be there. As she looked at Peter, she noticed seagulls over in the distance, their distinct call going unheard amongst the shrill obnoxious noise of the carnival, and she wondered why they were so far inland.

As the Ferris wheel spun round it felt as if they were transported into different worlds. The one high up above the earth, where she was close to the birds and away from the noise, made her feel at ease. The gradual descent towards the ground felt like a gradual descent into madness with the noises slowly getting louder and more intense until they came to a stop and it was time to get out, and they were yet again fully immersed in the bright lights and noisy crowds.

Next were the bumper cars, and they each had their own. At first Jane was consciously not bumping into anyone, until a car came at her from the side and pushed her into the barrier. Her whole body jerked to the side, and she looked over to see Peter laughing.

"You're dead!" she shouted over to him; as the car got moving again, she shunted Peters car from behind, causing him to bump into the one on front. But Jane too flew forward, hitting her nose off the steering wheel.

The pain made her eyes water as the burning sensation went through her sinuses and she put both her hands up to her nose, cupping it. She had no time to focus on anything else as a pair of hands grabbed her under her arms and pulled her out of the car and off the conductive flooring.

She knew the hands didn't belong to Peter and she started to panic. She was placed outside the metal railings and handed a tissue by the operator. She watched as Peter's face turned from a smile to a look of pure panic and he jumped out of the bumper car, running across to her, dodging other cars still in motion as he did. He hopped the railing and bent down to Jane.

"Jesus Christ almighty, you're some sight!"

Jane tried to squint her eyes in confusion to Peter's statement, but it hurt her nose as she put the tissue to it, feeling wetness. But it wasn't wetness from tears, it was blood. And it was dripping down onto her green t-shirt.

"Aww shit Janey, I think you might have broken your nose. We need to get ice on it or you'll have two black eyes in the morning. Wait here."

Peter went over to one of the chip vans and came back with an ice cold can of coke and handed it to Jane. The bridge of her nose was already beginning to bruise and it was quickly spreading towards her eyes. She gratefully took the can and opened it to take a long gulp.

"Ya eejit, you were supposed to put it on your nose to stop it swelling!" Peter laughed as carnival life continued around them. "We'll get some ice in the pub, c'mon." He grabbed her hand and led her out of the carnival.

He now felt the tension that Jane felt walking into the funfair, and he dreaded their mother's reaction to Jane's bloody, bruised nose. A part of him wondered if she would genuinely care.

As they tried to navigate the busy street, he picked Jane up and carried her to protect her nose from any further damage. She was beginning to feel heavier in his arms these days, and he knew the time was fast approaching where he wouldn't be able to carry her. When she wouldn't want him to carry her.

When they approached the doors of the pub, Jane sensed Peter's dread but could do nothing to comfort or calm him, because she felt the same way. The tall, nineteen year-old man still feared his mother.

They walked in and made their way through crowds of people standing in every available space, over to the table their mother had occupied since doors' opening. She sat next to Sean, her hand on his knee, surrounded by other regulars.

The table was covered in empty glasses and full ashtrays, and the pub's ventilation system was clearly unable to handle the excess crowd as smoke hung over every table. The pub was noisy, and children ran up and down the rows, leaving a trail of broken crisps and empty wrappers behind them. One small child bumped into a man about to take a drink from a pint, and it spilled down his shirt as he looked around angrily and the child ran off laughing. Older men sat at the bar, looking a bit worse for wear as they argued the merits of lent.

Their mother looked up to see her children walking towards the table and she nudged at Sean to get his attention. When he spotted the bruised, bloodied girl, he put his arm around her shoulders, pulled her in close and whispered, "Stay calm, keep it for home."

She took a deep breath before asking, "What the fuck happened?"

Jane sat next to her mam and Sean, and told them the story of the bumper cars, stating heavily that it was an accident, as Peter came over with some napkins and ice.

"Maybe you should take her to the toilets and clean up her nose?" Peter pointedly asked while wrapping the ice in the napkin.

"Why can't you?" she retorted. "You're her older brother. You can clearly mind her better than I can."

"It's fine. I can do it myself," Jane said, getting up to make her way to the bathroom. She kept her head down as she weaved her way to the back of the pub so nobody would comment on her nose.

Peter glared at his mother, her attention and conversation back to Sean. She'd already forgotten that her young daughter was in a pub toilet, alone, cleaning what might be a broken nose. His blood began to boil.

"Go and check on your daughter, for fuck's sake. Just pretend to have some maternal instinct, even just for one fucking day. Go and see if she's alright."

He wanted to follow up that sentence with more words of venom, fury and insult, but he knew he had said enough when his mother stood up, glaring as she stepped past him.

She bent down and whispered into his ear, "Your father would be disgusted to see how you turned out, talking to me like that."

Peter looked up and met his mother's furious gaze. He felt every muscle tense and he clenched his fists. She always knew the most spiteful thing to say that would cut him to the bone. Just when he thought she'd said it all and nothing could possibly hurt him as much as the last comment, she'd spew a new, more vicious, sentiment.

He prided himself on not being like her. Although he'd been very young when his father died, everything he did was with the intention of making him proud. He knew his father was a good man; he had heard the stories about him and, if he closed his eyes and pulled memories from the deepest corners of his mind, he could still feel the love radiating off him. But the fury he felt now made him wonder if he perhaps had inherited his mother's violent temper; briefly, he imagined pulling her back and doing to her what she done to him many times. In that split second, he wanted to return the favour.

Peter sat with his eyes closed, pinching the bridge of his nose, calming himself down. When he opened his eyes, he noticed Sean smirking at him as he took a drink of his pint.

"What?" Peter asked while raising his eyebrows.

"You're a good brother, that's all," Sean said. "She's lucky to have you." His eyes were darting in all directions as he spoke; these words felt genuine to him but they sounded condescending and Peter picked up on it.

"You're very patronising for a man who's having an affair. Fuck off, Sean," Peter replied as he spotted Jane making her way back through the crowd, alone. She was beginning to look as if she had been in a boxing ring.

"Where is she?" Peter asked as she got closer.

"Just using the toilet," Jane replied. "You can go now, I know you're meeting your girlfriend."

"No way, Janey, you and me are having a night in. We'll get chips on the way home. I'll ring Lucy, she'll understand. I'm sure you don't want to spend your night here anyway. No arguments, I'm taking you home."

As they drove off, Jane watched the dark clouds sweep in. They were moving in the direction of the town, slowly covering the blue sky. Every now and then there would be a break and a perfect blue would appear, but the low clouds and unusually heavy feeling signalled stormy weather. Maybe the storm was just moving through and they wouldn't get caught in it, but the closer they got to the countryside the darker and thicker the they became. Jane's head started to hurt.

In the distance the clouds looked like they were falling down, their blackness seeping out, and Jane was glad to be going home. She put her head in her hands as every bump in the road made her head throb dully. She wanted to sleep.

Peter looked over to her as they pulled in the driveway and noticed her rubbing her head.

"Jane, how bad is your headache?"

"It's a thunder headache. I'll be fine," she tried dismissing him but he kept staring at her.

"A what?"

Jane sighed as if she had spent her life explaining this to him. "The heaviness in the air from the thunder about to come gives me a headache. It always happens. It happens to my teacher too and she calls them thunder headaches. She says it's the only time she's ever right about the weather."

Peter sighed and opened the door of the car, now worried that Jane might have concussion. But as he looked across the fields and saw the black heavy clouds in the distance, he thought that she might be right. There was a strange heaviness in the air.

Peter gathered some paracetamol and a thermometer from the cupboard and a bag of frozen peas out of the freezer and brought Jane into his bedroom. He felt the frozen peas were now useless as the bruising had spread to both her eyes and the bridge of her nose was red, but he wrapped them in a tea towel and placed them gently on her nose. The bag more or less covered her small face as she laughed and lay back.

"We'll listen to some music, Janey, keep you awake for another while. Nirvana or Green Day?"

"I don't know, I don't mind."

Jane was now sitting in the bed with the frozen peas by her side as she took some paracetamol. "I really don't like your music," she said. "I'm very tired Peter"

"Nirvana it is then!" Peter said as *Smells Like Teen Spirit* started to play.

Jane rolled her eyes mockingly, but in truth she liked Kurt Cobain's melancholy voice and though the lyrics of his songs were depressing, she understood why Peter liked them.

They lay on the bed, chatting and laughing, Peter changing the music from time to time, alternating between old, traditional music and Nirvana and Green Day. Hours drifted past as the rain now beat off the window. There was no wind or breeze and it just fell straight and hard, pooling in the driveway outside.

The last song played, and Peter felt comfortable enough to let Jane drift off into sleep as a car pulled up in the driveway. He sighed, knowing it was his mother and Sean, and closed his eyes, silently praying for a quiet night.

He hated being home at the weekends. He hated the constant tension that hung in the air, and he hated the fear that his mother instilled in Jane – and, in truth, in him too. He knew he could physically stand up to her. He was taller, stronger and more than able, but something always stopped him. It was a mixture of fear, fear of not being able to control his temper if he did start, and the sense of 'respect thy parent' instilled in him from school.

He didn't respect her, nor did he like her, but she was still his mother and he knew no matter how much of a distance he put between them there would always be some strange cord that tied them. He wasn't going to cut it, not just yet, because it also connected him to Jane.

The car idled in the driveway a bit longer than usual, and Peter could hear his mother and Sean arguing even over the heavy rain. He stayed next to Jane, wishing he could just fall asleep and not have to intervene. When he tried to stop an argument between the pair, in one way or another the fury always ended up being directed at him.

As the arguing intensified, he gently eased himself away from his now sleeping sister and slipped his shoes on with another sigh. He was grateful that Jane was asleep.

He stood at the door, looking out, and could see his mother and Sean sitting in the back seat of the taxi with the back driver's side door open. They were arguing over who had to pay the driver.

"Will one of yas just pay him and let the man finish his night's work!" Peter shouted out the door. The driver looked relieved to see someone on his side and gave Peter a thumbs up, but Sean looked furious as he threw notes and coins onto the passenger seat, his temper clearly boiling as he glared at Peter.

"That lad needs to be taught a lesson in some manners," he said, pushing his mother to get out of the taxi quicker.

Sean, in his eagerness to unleash his wrath on Peter, wasn't looking at her bending down to pick up her bag as he pushed her out of the car. She fell out of the door, landing flat on her face. Even over the noise of the car's engine and heavy rain, Peter heard a loud crack of a bone breaking as she hit the ground with a groan. Sean's fury now turned to the injured drunk woman, lying flat on the ground in the rain.

"Get the fuck up! Jesus Christ, stop being so dramatic."

She tried to lift herself up but the pain in her chest spread through her as she howled. Peter felt like he had watched the whole thing unfold in slow motion, his mother falling headfirst out of the taxi. He stood still for a second and wondered how such a frail woman could have hurt him so badly over the years.

He felt anger bubble up inside him as he made his way to Sean. He had an overwhelming, perhaps misdirected, sense of needing to protect. He knew if Sean could so easily hurt the woman he claimed to love, without a second thought he would hurt her child as well. Peter angrily marched toward him, fists closed and jaw tense.

As angry as Sean had been in the car, he knew he was no match for the young man and instantly put his hands out.

"Calm down! It was an accident! I didn't mean it, I thought she was ready to get out!"

By this point, Peter was standing by the driver's door, blocking him from getting out to check on his mother, who still lay on the ground. The two men spat insults and fury at each other. Neither of them noticed Jane coming out the door and helping her mother off the wet gravel.

With a swing of his closed fist, Peter knocked Sean to the ground. Instantly his calm composure returned.

He looked at the taxi driver and said, "Would you take him home, please? The other one will need to go to A&E. I can't leave my sister alone. Sean will pay you double, won't ya Sean?"

He shouted the last question toward the ground, where Sean was nursing a bruised jaw and hurt pride. He stood up and stared at Peter before silently slinking into the back of the taxi.

Peter went back into the house where his mother was sitting at the table, very much sobered up now, holding her arm up to her chest. Her face was badly scraped up from falling on the gravel driveway. Peter almost felt pity for her as he helped her out to the taxi. He promised to call the hospital as soon as he could.

Peter had never lost his temper in that way before, but he felt satisfaction in punching Sean. He knew for sure Sean wouldn't hurt Jane now. And had seen his mother in a different light; she was more broken internally than she was physically. But the pity wasn't going to overcome the other strong feelings he had towards her. One night of sympathy would not make up for years of abuse.

Jane and Peter sat at the kitchen table, drinking mugs of tea into the early hours. When thunder began to roll across the sky and the lights began to flicker, Peter got some already used candles from the cupboard and laid them on the table.

"At least the electricity going out will be from the weather this time," Peter said as he fumbled with a lighter.

Jane smiled and stood up from her chair, opening the back door just as the next flash of lightning lit up the sky. In that moment, the field across the wall flashed a shade of electric blue and the clap of thunder was followed by the distant sound of dogs barking and cows lowing from the safety of their sheds.

There was a different feeling in the air now. The heavy rain felt cleansing as Jane stepped out into it, replaying the day in her head. Her nose still throbbed but her headache was subsiding as the air began to lift.

"Will you ring the hospital?" she asked, stepping back inside the door.

Peter could see the worry in her eyes. As he stood up to go out to the phone in the hall the electricity cut out. Jane's heart jumped into her throat and she ran to Peter's side, clinging onto his arm.

"Come on, Janey, we'll go and ring. See how Mam is. The phone should still work," he said, grabbing a candle that sat on a small plate and walking up the hall with one arm around Jane, who was shaking.

When Peter found the number of the local hospital in the phone book, he dialled and was instantly put through to the accident and emergency department. An out of breathe nurse answered the phone; Peter realised St. Patrick's Day was probably one of the busiest nights for the nurses and doctors.

He gave his mother's name and listened as the nurse recited off her injuries: a broken collarbone and fractured wrist. Peter sighed, thanked the nurse and told her he hoped his mother wasn't trouble for them.

"It's just going to be me and you for a couple of days," Peter said. Jane immediately burst into tears.

# Chapter Ten

THE RUN UP TO Jane's First Communion was filled with prayers, unblessed communion wafers, and excitement from all the other children over what kind of dresses they were wearing or where they were going to go afterwards. Jane's thoughts were filled with caring for her mother, who still had her arm in a sling; her Communion seemed unimportant.

She tried to avoid the conversations the other girls wanted to have with her. She didn't care about dress style or what she was going to wear on her head, because she knew her mother hadn't been working. Stephen had become a regular fixture, dropping off meals and food but never interacting with her mam, who always seemed to need a lie down when he knocked on the door. Nonetheless, the time to go dress shopping was fast approaching.

Peter drove them into the town and dropped them off. He dreaded leaving them alone, but Jane insisted, knowing it would be more tense with him there. She was also aware that he hadn't seen Lucy in the weekends since their mother's accident, and he was getting slightly grumpy because of it. Her mother was grumpy because she needed a drink.

The shop sat in the centre of the main street, and Jane looked at the wedding dresses in the window, sparkling under the bright lights on the ceiling. The glass was so clean she almost felt as if it wasn't actually there. She stuck her finger out to touch it, but stopped at the last second when she thought of a woman coming out to clean her fingerprint off.

Jane stood in the fitting room of the bridal shop wearing a white communion dress. The paper tag hung from a piece of white cotton thread attached to the zip at the side of the dress, and when she reached around to turn it over, she saw 'seventy-five pounds' written in blue ink.

She didn't notice the beading or the lace trim or the fact that it had a matching bag and umbrella but instead thought of the stash of crisps and chocolate her and Peter hid at the bottom of his wardrobe for the times when there was no food, and she felt guilty.

There were no mirrors in the fitting room, and Jane couldn't understand why. Outside, where her mother sat waiting, were wall-to-wall mirrors. As she stepped out from behind the fitting room curtain, she realised she could see herself from every angle. Her fingers gently touched the beads embroidered into the design on the front and then ran along the lace trim at the side. As the assistant placed the veil in her hair, she began to smile.

Jane felt pretty.

She turned from side to side, making the dress move with her, and under all the lights in the shop the beading looked as if they sparkled. Jane felt like a normal girl buying a communion dress with her mother, until she turned to her right and all of a sudden the tag seemed to be the brightest, shiniest thing on the dress. She stopped swaying side to side and walked quietly over to her mother, who she didn't notice smiling.

"I can pick a different one, Mam," she said quietly as she lifted up the tag and showed it to her mother.

"It's a special day in the eyes of the Lord, and if you're happy with that one, I'll get it," she replied.

Jane smiled and put her arms around her mother's waist. Though she was happy with her dress, a part of her felt guilty that her mother was spending money on something so expensive, considering she'd only be wearing it for one day.

"I'm glad you like it," her mother said as she placed her hands on Jane's shoulders, pushing her back. "Go and take it off, I want to talk to the lady."

As Jane was carefully unzipping her dress and trying to ignore the price, she overheard the lady and her mother talking. She didn't know what a deposit was, but she knew the dress was going to be hers after her mother made the last payment on it. She carefully stepped out of it and gently placed it on the chair. As she bent down to pick up her school uniform, she noticed the lace detail went further down that the hoop skirt that was under it and she smiled and ran it between her fingers again.

Every Friday, Jane would accompany her mother into the town to make a payment off the dress, usually driven by Sean while her arm was healing. And every week, as Jane was busy touching, feeling and memorising every detail on her dress, her mother walked out happy after being told a payment had already been made, followed by a celebratory drink in the pub across the road afterwards.

She wondered why her mother was celebrating, as she hadn't done anything, but as Jane watched her mother light a cigarette and take the first sip of her drink and sigh, she began to worry that the lady in the shop was making a mistake and they'd actually be stealing the dress. She didn't like the thoughts of telling Father Gilroy in confessions that she stole her communion dress. But surely God wouldn't mind, after all it was His idea for her to dress up so fancy for the special day.

When the big day came, Jane was nervous about doing the Our Father movements in front of a filled church, but she wanted to make Peter proud. Her mother fixed her up in her new dress and for the first time in her life she had new everything - even shoes. She felt like a princess.

As her mother straightened her headpiece, Jane looked up at her and realised that she looked happy.

"Mam, thanks for buying me this. I feel so special."

"You are special. In the eyes of God, everyone is special."

"Am I special to you, Mammy?" Jane asked sincerely.

"Well...yeah, course. Now go down and show Peter your new dress."

Jane stood up straight and walked down the hall to the kitchen where Peter was waiting. When she put her hand on the door handle, she paused and plastered on a smile as she opened it.

Peter's eyes lit up when he saw his little sister, and he stood up from his chair and walked over to her, grabbing her arm and twirling her around.

"Well don't you just look a picture? Absolutely beautiful Janey! I bet ya feel like Cinderella!"

"I do Peter, I really do! Wasn't Mam so good to buy this for me, brand new and all?"

Peter ignored the question and twirled her again. He had bought a disposable camera specially for today and stood back to take her photo. As he did, their mother walked into the kitchen, dressed in a flowery short skirt and matching top. The heels were far too high for her, and she stumbled as she walked in.

"What about me? Don't I look like a young one?"

Peter looked her up and down before glancing to the curtains and back again. The print on the curtains was similar to what she was wearing, and he imagined her blending in with them, almost like camouflage. He stifled a smile.

"I'll get a picture of you and Jane," he said.

"Yeah, then one of me on my own," she said. "I don't always look this well so I want to have something for a frame."

Peter bit his tongue, promising himself he wouldn't ruin Jane's special day by starting any kind of argument. He took the two pictures but covered the lens with his finger when he was taking the one of his mother alone.

Jane watched Peter glare at their mother, though she knew he thought he was being discreet, and as she inhaled to sigh she caught the smell of pipe smoke. She gently tugged on Peter's arm before she stepped outside. Her nose led her to the end of the driveway where Stephen stood.

When he saw her walking down the driveway in her dress, he removed the pipe from his mouth and allowed himself the broadest smile Jane had ever seen. His smile was infectious, and she couldn't but help to smile back, her cheeks blushing slightly at the attention.

"Well. My goodness, Jane. You look like an angel," he said, still smiling down at her.

"Oh yeah? And what about the brother?" Peter laughed, as he followed Jane up the driveway. Peter was dressed in a checked shirt not unlike Stephen's and navy chinos. He looked older than his years, and as Stephen opened his mouth to speak, he found no words came to his tongue. He felt pride surging through his veins, and he knew Jane would be alright with Peter looking after her. He pulled two envelopes from his back pocket and handed one to Jane and one to Peter.

"It's not me making my First Communion," Peter said, looking confused as he took it. He opened the envelope and gasped, looking back up at Stephen. "I can't accept this! A hundred pounds is an awful lot of money. Thanks Stephen, but I really can't take this," Peter said, swallowing a lump in his throat.

Stephen put his hand on Peter's shoulder and guided him away from Jane. Once they were out of earshot, he whispered, "That's for dinner after the Mass, if your mother doesn't have the money. If she does, no harm to offer her a small bit towards it and treat yourself and Jane to a day out afterwards."

Peter swallowed hard and hugged Stephen. "Jesus, thanks Stephen. Thanks so much."

While Peter and Stephen were at the wall whispering to each other, Jane opened her white envelope and pulled out a card with a picture of a chalice on it. Her smile turned to a look of astonishment when she saw a crisp new fifty-pound note and a crisp new ten-pound note sitting inside the card. She had never seen a fifty-pound note before and she felt rich.

She closed the card quickly and ran over to Stephen, wrapping her arms around his waist.

"Thank you, Stephen!" she cried. He looked down at her and opened the card, picking up the ten pound note.

"This is what you tell people I gave you," he said. He then picked up both notes together and said, "This is what I've really given you. Have a great day, Jane." He followed this with a wink and a smile. Jane held on to Stephen's hand.

"Step in for a photograph, Stephen," Peter said, winding his camera forward.

Jane didn't let go of his hand as they turned together and smiled for the photograph.

"Will you take two if you please? I'd like one too," Stephen asked as Peter began to wind the camera again, quickly taking another.

"Will you come to the church?" Jane asked, not letting go of his hand.

"Ah sweetheart, I can't, it's just for family and I have cows to milk."

"You are family!" Jane said, looking up at him and holding onto his hand even tighter.

"Agreed," Peter said. "No pressure, but you are welcome, and we'd love to have you there."

Stephen looked at Peter and then down to Jane and sighed and smiled.

"I'm not making promises. I'll try. But I don't think it'd be appropriate to sit in your pew. So if I'm there, I'll be at the back, and that's an 'if,' okay? If I get finished milking on time."

Peter and Jane's mother stepped out of the back door and watched her children with Stephen. She felt sick with jealousy, and wondered

117

if it was him who'd paid off the girl's communion dress. She wanted to run down and confront him, but decided against it, because it did mean she had extra money. She caught Stephen's eye and nodded her head in his direction. Stephen, always the polite gentleman, nodded back.

The church was already busy when they arrived; parents rushed about as boys dressed in suits with red badges on and girls in white dresses walked around the church grounds like lords and ladies. An excitement hung in the air as parents took photographs. Some had camcorders running, not wanting to miss a moment of their child's special day.

When they got out of the car, a lot of eyes were directed at their mother and her ridiculous outfit. She took this as a compliment and swayed her hips as she walked up the church yard. She was oblivious to the sniggers and took the whispers for compliments as Peter's face turned bright red from embarrassment, a feeling he was very used to around his mother. He put his head down as he walked up towards the door.

Jane stood in the church carpark and smiled as the other girls surrounded her and paid compliments to one another. She was, for the first time, an equal, and she relished feeling normal.

The seating in the church was assigned, and Jane's seat was in the middle aisle close to the back, which Peter hated because it would mean his mother having to walk up to the altar in front of the whole church.

"Hey, will I go up with Jane?" he asked her, leaning across Jane.

"No," Mother whispered back. "She's my daughter. I'm going too."

Peter sat back on his seat, sighing like a spoiled little boy who was refused an ice cream.

"You'll come up too, right Peter?" Jane asked with an air of panic in her voice.

"Of course, Janey. I'm not missing this for the world."

When the priest and altar boys walked out onto the altar everyone stood up and Peter realised he couldn't remember the last time he was actually in a church. He'd nearly forgotten when to stand and when to kneel. He was watching his little sister for the cues. He was faking excitement for Jane; Peter had said his goodbyes to the church a long time ago.

Boys and girls from her class brought up the gifts to the altar: a football, colouring books, a crested school jumper and a class photo to signify friendship. Jane wondered if God even knew that she didn't really have any friends up until today, and if He made the other girls like her because she was now nearly fully holy. She looked forward to going to school on Monday now that the other girls were being nice to her.

After the gifts, the boys and girls made their way up for communion, each family and pew at a time. Jane noticed that hers was the shortest line. There were no grandparents or aunties and uncles and no proud daddy holding camcorders. But she didn't mind that today. She was becoming holy, and God might like her enough to give her friends and make her mammy happy.

Jane walked up the aisle with her palms together and her mother beside her. She could feel Peter walking very closely behind her as she stepped toward Fr. Gilroy, who was holding a piece of blessed communion wafer over a gold chalice. When she reached him, she put one hand over the other and met his gaze.

"Body of Christ," the priest said as he laid the wafer onto her upturned palm.

"Amen," Jane replied, picking up the communion and placing it on her tongue. On her way back to her seat, she realised that it wasn't sticking to the roof of her mouth and smiled knowing it was because of the holy water. She bowed her head and felt happy.

At the end of Mass, her whole class stood up on the altar to sing the Our Father. Jane's stomach hopped and jumped with nerves. Even though she could sing it in her sleep, she wanted to make Peter proud.

From her spot on the highest step on the altar she spotted Stephen, standing at the back of the church with his cap in his hand. Her smile grew, she resisted the urge to wave down to him as the prayer started. Her eyes moved from Peter to Stephen and back again and an unusual feeling of happiness spread. She stood on the altar, smiling the biggest smile she had ever smiled in her entire life.

# Chapter Eleven

THE LITTLE GIFT SHOP had everything that Jane could possibly imagine. Candles in different shapes and sizes, books, t-shirts, toys, and the one thing she had been looking for: photo frames.

There was a whole wall at the back of the shop dedicated to them, and they came in every colour and size, but Jane wanted one that she wasn't sure existed. Her eyes began at the top shelf and scanned across the wall until she got to the next shelf and continued until she got to the bottom, sighing when she didn't see the one she wanted.

Over in the corner of the shop lay a wicker basket with a hand-written red sign hanging from the front saying, 'Sale: Half Price.' Curiosity got the better of Jane and she peered inside. The basket held small frames in the strangest of colours; in excitement, Jane began to flick through them. Close to the back, she spotted a very unusual green sticking out from behind the others. She pulled it up and gasped.

The frame itself was in the shape of an apple tree, the trunk being where the photo was inserted. It exceeded her imagination, and she looked through the basket in the hopes of finding a matching one, but contented herself with the one as she stood up and walked toward the cash register.

On the counter was a display of keyrings and the first one that caught her eye said 'WORLD'S BEST BROTHER.' She picked one up and put it on the counter alongside her frame. She turned the display and found one that said 'WORLD'S BEST MAM' and put that on the counter, too.

She was beaming as she reached into her little white bag to take out the crisp fifty-pound note. She didn't feel silly still carrying her white communion bag days after her big day; she felt grown up, and liked it when people asked her if she recently made her First Holy Communion.

When the lady started typing numbers into the till, she looked at the display again and staring right at her was another keyring that read, 'WORLD'S BEST DAD.' Jane frowned and twisted it away from her line of vision. She didn't want to start wondering again, so she pushed all thoughts to the back of her head and instead focused on who she was buying the gifts for.

"Would you like these gift-wrapped?" the lady asked, smiling down.

"No thanks, I have to put a photo into the frame first. Oh! Do you sell wrapping paper?" Jane asked, looking around.

"I'll tell you what...since you're buying so much, I'll give you a sheet of wrapping paper for free. I think one would be enough for each of them, but be careful with the scissors, okay?"

"Thank you!" Jane replied. Her excitement was rising with the thoughts of giving out her gifts. She relished the idea of being able to give something special to those she loved most in the world.

Jane handed the lady the money and almost walked out without getting the change. When she was called back, she worried that she didn't give her enough money, but blushed when the lady handed her back thirty-five pounds. It looked like a lot more money than what she gave her, but she quickly counted it and put it in her bag.

She stepped out the door onto the main street and saw Peter's car, still waiting for her in the same spot, and she smiled, watching him drum his fingers on the steering wheel and bob his head to the music on the tape deck.

As if he sensed that he was being watched, he turned his head to the left to see Jane smiling at him. She was holding a plastic bag from the gift shop, and her rosy cheeks showed dimples that he didn't see as often as he would like. He smiled back at her as she made her way to the passenger door.

"Jane, do you want to go into Dunnes and buy yourself a little purse and handbag? That white one will get messed up in no time, and it's not very secure holding your money with it only closing with a string."

"Am I allowed?" she asked as she buckled up her seatbelt.

"It's your money! You can do whatever you want with it!"

"I'd like to buy you a chipper. You're always buying them," she said sincerely.

"Ah Janey, I don't mind. But you might have enough for both. Do you want to go over now?"

"No, I want to go home and wrap up the presents, please."

She was eager to hand out the gifts she had bought with her own money and wanted to spend time wrapping them up properly.

"Okay," said Peter. "You know to hide that money, right?" He hated that he had to ask.

"I hid it under your bed. I hope that's okay?"

"Course it's okay," he replied, looking over his shoulder as he pulled out of the parking spot.

The scissors, Sellotape and wrapping paper were all laid out neatly on the kitchen table. Jane sat looking at the photo tucked away in the special tree frame she bought and smiled. Her heart felt funny, different and full when she thought of Stephen, and she was torn between keeping it for herself and wanting to see his reaction when he opened it.

She chose the latter and began cutting the wrapping paper. The scissors glided through the paper as she knelt on the kitchen chair, and she placed the frame in the middle. Wrapping wasn't as easy as she thought but she tried to figure out where the corners went and tried several ways to have them as neat as possible before she tucked them in under each other and Sellotaped them down.

It wasn't as neat as she wanted, but she was proud of her work as she grabbed the last remaining pieces and began wrapping the keyring for Peter. By the time she had gotten to her mother's, her need to have it neat was gone and she wrapped it quickly.

She neatly placed Peter's gift on his pillow and tried to figure out a good place for her mother's, deciding beside the kettle was a good idea. She left it there knowing her mother was either going to have a cup of tea after work or a different drink, and either way that'd be her starting point.

The bag swung by her side as she skipped towards the bridge to wait for Stephen. He was busier than normal, but always stopped by for lunch. Lately he had been driving instead of walking so he could get back to work quicker. She didn't see his land rover parked up by the gate, and wondered if he was at the bog or on the farm. She happily sat down on the stump to wait.

Jane's feet rubbed the ground where Stephen's feet rested daily. The grass didn't grow in that spot; he had made his mark on the earth. The grass tickled her ankles as she rubbed her feet over and back and she closed her eyes as a feeling of dread washed over her.

It wasn't like Stephen to be late, but it didn't feel right to be sitting in his spot either, so she moved down onto the grass beside it and looked for signs of ladybirds. When her feet started to go numb from sitting cross-legged on the grass too long, she stood up and picked up little twigs that had been dropped by the birds.

The back of her dress felt damp and she thought she might have been better off keeping the stump warm for Stephen. He always placed his jacket down for her to sit on, and on the wetter days sitting under their tree, she was able to wrap it around her.

Walking over to the bridge she threw in a twig and watched as the current pulled it away and then ran across the little lane to the other side waiting for it to pass, but it never did. In the water under the bridge, the little twig got caught between the protruding rocks and the bank. It was going to take a lot more water to push it onto its journey, and Jane didn't want to wait.

"Everything feels wrong today," she said aloud to herself as she walked back to the other side of the bridge and looked over the stone wall. A long sigh escaped her lips and she turned to pick up her plastic bag and walk home. The plastic bag didn't swing as it did on the way down. She was trying to ignore the quiet and lack of pipe smoke.

The grass in the middle of the road became like a balancing beam to her as she stretched out her arms and walked back towards the bungalow.

# Chapter Twelve

THE DUNNES STORES BAG was folded neatly and tucked under the seat of the tractor when Stephen stepped down with a jump. The bog was a sun trap, surrounded by evergreen 'Christmas trees,' as Jane called them. He inhaled deeply, clasped his hands on the back of his head and looked around.

The bog, untouched with the exception of cutting turf, was Ireland at its best. Each family rented or owned a plot and some cut turf by hand. Others used machinery. Here everyone was not only neighbours but friends. Families spent their summers here, footing sods of cut turf into piles and loading them into trailers when the stacks were dry. Picnics were eaten on blankets or the bonnets of cars and children played with cousins and friends while their parents shouted at them to help or not fall into a ditch. This was the place where people who lived miles from another person felt a sense of community, and nobody went without. But there was silence this morning when he stood at the top of his plot and he relished it; Stephen and a small number of others liked to get as much done as they could before the depths of the summer heat arrived and made the work unbearable.

Crows flew up from the tops of the trees in a wave and the heathers that grew wild rustled slightly in a breeze much too warm for the time of year. Cotton grass blew in between the plots and some of the stacks of turf, and suddenly this day didn't feel particularly right to Stephen. The silence gnawed away at him.

Pushing the bag in further under the seat, his thoughts drifted to Jane as he walked onto the plot to feel if his turf had dried, though he knew by sight it was. He enjoyed making extra meals for Jane and Peter and he noticed that over the last few months he too was eating better; he felt slimmer, quicker on his feet, while the brother and sister looked healthier. Less fragile.

A whole new routine had begun for him when he started driving along the country roads in anger, looking for the red car that had hit and killed his wife. In the midst of that fury, Jane sat beside him at the bridge and quelled it with her questions about birds, fish and anything that wasn't human. He wondered why she was so inquisitive about nature, and over time he realised Jane knew nature would never deliberately hurt her. His heart softened and opened up to her.

As the breeze picked up, blowing the smell of honeysuckle and dust in his direction, he realised that the trailer was close to full. His thoughts about someone else's children had distracted him from thinking about his aching back and he stood up straight with a moan.

Peter had never questioned why Stephen didn't speak with his mother, and his thoughts returned to that night. The night a garda named Chris called to the house, his cap in his hand. He didn't need to tell him what had happened; Stephen had already closed the front door behind him, ready to drive the route that he knew his wife walked. The night he lost the love of his life, but gained someone else's children.

The sound of another tractor pulling in dragged him from his thoughts, and Stephen turned to wave as his life-long friend pulled in. Not content to leave one stack left in the row, he bent down and picked them up to throw them into the trailer, but as he swung, Tom greeted him in a booming voice just as two stray sods took flight into the tractor, unnoticed by either man.

"Thank God I'm nearly done with this," Stephen shouted over. "Sure you're not too far behind me yourself?" He stood in between the tractor and trailer to lift the trailer up. But suddenly the tractor began to roll back. Stephen watched a parliament of magpies fly up from the trees, chattering, just as he felt the excruciating pain of the tractor crushing him.

*They're called a parliament of magpies because they're full of useless chatter*, he remembered telling Jane once. His thoughts flashed from Jane to Peter and to the red car. The red car that hit his wife while she was out for her evening stroll.

*One for sorrow, two for joy. Three for a girl, four for a boy. Five for silver, six for gold. Seven for a secret never to be told.* Stephen recited the poem to himself as his mind faded to black, taking a secret with him that Peter and Jane never needed to know.

※※※※ ※※※※

Night fell and Jane sat at the kitchen table with Peter. He smiled as he hooked his new keyring onto his car keys.

"Thanks Janey, I love it! I can't wait to show it to Lucy. Did you give Stephen his?"

"No, he wasn't at the bridge today, and he didn't call," Jane said as she twirled her t-shirt with her fingers.

"Hmm, that's unusual," Peter replied. "It's unlike him."

Just then there was a knock on the back door. Peter opened it to be greeted by a white-faced and red-eyed Tom, who held a flat cap in his hand.

"Lad... can I speak with you outside for a minute?" Tom asked, nodding towards Jane.

Peter looked back at Jane, who was staring up at their caller with a concerned frown, and he stepped outside, closing the door behind him. He followed Tom to the wall that overlooked the field and watched intently as he pulled the box of Majors from his pocket and lit up a cigarette while he hung over the wall, not wanting to make eye contact with Peter.

"I know he was desperate fond of you and your sister, so I said I'd call and make sure you heard it first and not off some aul' busybody up the road. But lad... *Jaysus*." He stopped and stood up, rubbing his hand across his six o'clock shadow and finally looking at Peter.

"Stephen had an accident this morning on the bog. The handbrake was knocked off by sheer fucking fluke and...Well. He got crushed between the tractor and trailer. I'm sorry lad. He didn't make it."

He slid Stephen's flat cap across the wall to Peter and stared out across the field. Peter clasped his hands on the back of his head and turned around, not quite sure how to process the news. He paced a few steps away from Tom, then a took a couple back. Before he could respond he was startled by a sob.

Jane stood at the back door, watching her brother trying not to cry. She had heard everything. The tears streamed down her face, her bottom lip quivered as she let out a wail, and the world stopped when Peter turned and ran to her, lifting her up and taking her in his arms. He had no words to say to his sister as she buried her head between his head and shoulder. He let his own tears fall and they clung on to each other. Feeling alone in the world again.

Tom kept his focus on the unusual sunset spread across the sky. The clouds, taking the sun's low rays spread across the sky, were the perfect pastel pink and blue of a small child's bedroom. He looked over his shoulder to see the brother and sister comfort each other over the loss of their friend. He felt a tear slide down his cheek quickly wiped it away. He knew there was nothing he could do in this moment to help in their grief; he stopped briefly, his hand on Peter's shoulder, and told him he'd be in touch with the funeral details before he walked down the drive and away.

Jane sobbed so hard her stomach heaved, and she didn't feel Peter carrying her inside and sitting on the couch. He wrapped his arms around her as he sat down and her sobs turned into shallow breaths that she couldn't control. Her whole being shook with each one, and she felt powerless over her own body.

"Jesus, what happened?" their mother asked as she walked in and sat in the armchair opposite.

"Stephen's dead!" Jane replied, turning around on Peter's lap to face her mother, her eyes red and puffy and the skin on her face becoming blotchy from the salty tears.

She got down and walked over towards her mother, her arms outstretched. The tears in her eyes blurred her vision, but she felt her mother put her hand out on her shoulder, stopping her from taking another step towards her.

"Let me get a drink and yous can tell me what happened." She stood up and walked out to the kitchen.

Jane's arms dropped to her sides. Her sobs stopped and her head dropped toward the ground. She felt empty and lost and looked back to Peter, who had his head in his hands. She didn't want to disturb him so she went to her bedroom and looked out the window. The normally bright, colourful front garden was shrouded in darkness, and a waning moon appeared from behind a cloud. More darkness was yet to come.

She took some deep breaths to stop more tears from falling, and returned to join Peter on the couch. Her mother was back in the armchair, a drink in her hand and a lit cigarette resting in an ashtray perched on the arm of the chair. Jane looked at her mother from the corner of her eye and wondered what kind of drink this was. She didn't look sad.

"What happened? Sure, he wasn't old?" she asked, taking a sip of vodka.

"He had an accident, that's all I know. Got caught between a tractor and trailer," Peter replied.

"I'd say they're still scraping bits of him off the bog. Shame. Nice man," she replied as she took another sip. "You'll miss him Janey, he seemed fond of you. I always thought it was a bit creepy myself, a man of his age taking an interest in a young girl, but you never complained so he must've been alright." Jane didn't understand what she meant but she knew it wasn't nice.

"That's an awful thing to say, or even think!" erupted Peter. "You're very fucking twisted if that's the first thing that comes to mind! He took an interest in me, too! He was a good man, a decent man, something you'd know absolutely nothing about because you're only attracted to fucking cretins!"

Jane was shocked. She'd never heard Peter speak to their mother in that tone, and her heart raced as their mother stood up, staring Peter down with a closed fist. Peter stood up and seemed to tower over her and he looked her square in the eyes.

"You can't possibly hurt me any more than I already am," he said. "So go ahead take your best shot. Go on! Or sit the fuck down and be nice for once in your life."

Jane sat and watched as her brother's face grew redder and his eyes bulged. Her heart raced in her chest and tears fell down her face. She had never seen Peter so angry before, and it scared her. But she couldn't understand why her mother wasn't at least a little bit sad about Stephen. Although she agreed with her brother, she knew she had to stop them before they came to blows.

The heaviness in the air grew as she stood up, and it felt as if she was wading through water when she moved toward Peter and grabbed his balled fist. With the gentlest of whispers, she asked him to come to the kitchen.

When the quiet voice registered in his brain, Peter broke his stare with their mother and looked down at his sister, gazing up at him. Jane pleaded with Peter without saying a word, and she led him out of the sitting room and into the kitchen.

They sat opposite each other at the kitchen table, silently wondering how they were going to get through a day without Stephen's presence.

"Ah, feck it!" Peter said, breaking the silence and running outside. He picked up the flat cap that Tom had left on the wall, and he held it tight to his chest and closed his eyes before coming back in to Jane.

Jane was resting her head on her folded arms at the kitchen table, staring at the clock. Her eyes stung. They felt heavy when she blinked so she tried not to, even though it made the burning worse. She had seen one a.m. on the clock before, but she didn't remember ever seeing three a.m. and her blinks got slower and heavier.

She Peter walk back in the door with Stephen's cap in his hand and didn't utter a word as he picked her up and carried her up the hall to her bedroom. His heart beat loudly in his chest beside her, but it was slow, and as she drifted off to sleep, she knew her brother's heart was sad like hers.

# Chapter Thirteen

THE BLACK PATENT SHOES felt hard and stiff under the soles of Jane's feet, but she could wiggle her toes which meant there was growing room. Her new black dress rested just below her knees but the shoulders kept sliding down, so she grabbed a piece of the material and tucked it in under the strap of her vest to keep them in place, running her hands down the front of her dress to smooth it out.

Normally getting new clothes was a treat, but this was a dress she never wanted to wear again and the black against her now pale skin made it seem whiter than ever. She sometimes forgot to brush her teeth or comb her hair but she never forgot to put on sun cream. Stephen would remind her daily and had given her a bottle of her very own which she kept beside her bed next to an aloe vera plant in a ceramic black and white striped pot. The plant was growing new leaves to replace the ones that had been cut; Jane cared for that plant as much as she cared for the ones outside.

Her shoes tapped on the linoleum as she made her way down the hall to the kitchen. Even through the noise of her shoes, a silence hung in the air. It was thick and heavy and it was as loud as the tension caused by her mother on a bad day. When she opened the door to the kitchen, she stopped to watch Peter shining a brand-new pair of shoes. His suit jacket hung loosely over his shoulders. The sleeves were too long and she thought maybe he had bought it too big because he needed growing room too as she sat on the chair beside him.

"Blessed are the dead that the rain falls on," Jane said as she looked out the window. She let out a deep mournful sigh and turned back, sitting heavily on the chair.

"Was that one of Stephen's too?" Peter asked, not looking up from the shoe he was polishing. He was keen to shine his shoes to the highest shine they could possibly be, even though they were new. Stephen always said, "You can tell a lot by a man from his shoes."

He wasn't sure if he agreed with this or not, but his friend had always had clean shoes. Even if he was wearing his working clothes, he would change from his wellington boots into a nice, clean pair of brogues. They never looked out of place on him, they were just a part of who he was as much as the pipe he smoked and the neat beard and flat cap he wore.

Everyone knew Stephen, everyone at one point or another had had a conversation with him, but no one really knew anything about him. He had a way of getting a person to talk about their deepest darkest secrets by making them feel safe and secure in his company, and he gave very little in return as he smoked his pipe, nodding along. Listening. He spoke little, but listened a lot, once telling Jane, "A shut mouth catches no flies."

"He said it once, when the Reynolds farmer died. It rained that day at the bridge, and he drove up because he didn't want to miss the funeral. I told him he didn't have to come. But he said he had beef sandwiches that he didn't want to be thrown out and I was doing him a favour. I don't know what it means, though. Is he happy to be dead because it rains?"

"Aw, who knows, Janey," Peter replied. "It's always raining in this country. Maybe it was made up to make family members feel better about burying someone in a wet grave."

"Well, he would've been happy with the rain today because he said it was too dry for too long and we needed some rain for growth. Who'll look after his cows?"

"Tom is for now, and Dominic is helping him. Apparently, Stephen has nieces and nephews who'll come out of the woodwork even though they only ever seen him at Christmas time. But it's nothing to do with us. Let them all tear each other to shreds over whatever they want."

"You mean to take his stuff? That hardly seems fair. Would they just not prefer to have him back like we do?" her voice broke as she replied.

"Ah, I'm sure they would, Janey. Don't mind me, I'm just cynical," he said, sliding his feet into his shining shoes. "We better get going. Are you going to be okay? You've never been to a funeral before."

"Yeah, I think so. Is Mam coming?" Jane already knew the answer, and Peter's raised eyebrows confirmed it for her. "Indeed," she replied to her own question, standing up and walking out the back door.

Jane walked down the driveway and into the front garden to look around at all the plants and flowers that only a few days ago meant the world to her. They had somehow lost their colour in the misty rain that was falling. Without Stephen, she wasn't sure if her garden would ever bloom in the same way again.

Crouching down by the buddleia, she picked two purple flowers and started to cry. More than anything she wanted to smell pipe smoke surrounding her, pulling her into a feeling of warmth and comfort. Remembering the last seeds she planted, she stood up and walked over to the wall to check on her sunflowers. What was once beginning to sprout through the soil now lay empty and bare.

The soil around the seeds had been dug up and all that remained were the empty casings where the seeds used to be. Jane sat on the damp grass, wrapping her arms around her knees, still holding onto the flowers, and she sobbed. The bottom of her dress began to get damp from the grass, but nothing could move her from that spot. She felt the tears would never stop, even when she felt Peters hand on her shoulder. He crouched down and pulled her into his chest.

"Jane, we need to go," he said, swallowing his own tears.

"Look, Peter," she sobbed. "I think the birds ate my sunflower seeds. I didn't plant them deep enough and the birds ate them. They were the last ones Stephen gave me and now all that's left is empty shells."

"What would Stephen say, Jane? He'd say, 'No worries, it's nature. It's what nature does.' Wouldn't he, Jane?" Peter couldn't help but feel guilty, remembering he was the one who dug the holes for her.

"But there's nothing left to bloom from him," Jane cried. "There's nothing left." She had forgotten about the bulbs hidden deep below the surface, biding their own time.

"He gave us so much, Jane, in a short space of time. And a lot of it can't be seen. But he loved us, and we loved him, and that counts for a lot. Now let's go and give him the goodbye he deserves."

Peter grabbed Jane under her arms and pulled her up to standing position before he led her to the car.

She sat in the front seat, clutching the flowers she had picked, and kept her head down looking at them. A single money spider emerged from between the purple flowers and crawled onto the top of her hand. She twisted and turned her hand as it crawled around her fingers and onto her palm.

When it reached the tip of her index finger, she pointed it towards the flowers, hoping it'd crawl back in. But instead it made his way toward her wrist. She put the flowers on her knee and used her right index finger to pick up the spider and place it back onto the flowers where it stayed until they arrived on the road close to the church.

Rows of cars lined both sides of the road far beyond the church and school. They were parked on the grass verge of the already narrow road. They were just on the outskirts of town but to Jane it felt a million miles away from the shops and pubs her mother brought her to.

Peter parked his small car behind a land rover that had seen better days, and Jane struggled to open the door because of the brambles and nettles that grew up, so she crawled across the driver's seat, the flowers still in her hand, and got out Peter's door, smoothing out her dress as she stood up.

The rain was misty and light which always seemed slightly wetter than heavier rain. Peter reached into the backseat and grabbed Jane's heavy, peach-coloured coat and handed it to her. She didn't want to wear the old coat over her new dress but put it on anyway, knowing today wasn't a day for arguing. She lifted the hood up while they walked quietly behind other mourners towards the church.

She looked up at the evergreen trees that grew as tall as the bell tower, and watched crows and magpies fly in and out from their nests, never going too far; she knew heavier rain was on the way. The birds seemed quieter than normal. When Jane and Peter turned into the church grounds, Jane was taken aback with the number of people waiting for Stephen's last trip to Mass.

They made their way up to the top of the church yard, close to the door, and watched as a hearse pulled in slowly followed by a dozen cars. Jane's chest jumped with each shallow breath and she held Peter's hand tighter and stood in closer to him. They watched the pine coffin being slid out of the hearse and onto the shoulders of six men who Jane didn't really know, apart from Tom. He looked years younger, freshly shaved and dressed in a suit, and solemn. His eyes were red and bloodshot, but he stood tall at the front of the coffin, looking fiercely proud to be carrying his friend on his final journey.

Jane stepped in to walk into the church behind the coffin, and Peter put his hand on her shoulder, holding her back.

"The family go first, Janey. We're not family."

She frowned as she watched Stephen's family walk in after the coffin, and she couldn't help but notice they didn't look very sad, with the exception of an older man who walked ahead of everyone else. She wanted to step in beside him and hold his hand and tell him that she loved Stephen too. But she waited for Peter to take her hand and they walked in with the rest of the mourners, taking their seat in the middle aisle, the very same pew where Jane had sat for her communion.

The air was different in the church as the congregation stood up for Fr. Gilroy's arrival. He was dressed in black vestments and had a quieter energy about him. She looked around at the different shades of black the mourners wore; though it was morning, the church seemed dark.

A choir opened the Mass with Amazing Grace, and Jane's eyes were fixed firmly on the coffin which now had Stephen's picture resting on top. She wished the choir would stop singing because every note and every word they sang made her heart feel sadder and she couldn't stop her tears from falling.

The priest talked a lot about Stephen's life, and Jane realised that she knew nothing about him, and this made her feel regretful. She wished she had asked him about when he was a boy, or where he grew up. With every new piece of information, she'd look to Peter who she knew was thinking the same.

She wished she had known that he loved hurling, and had played in a place called Croke Park, and wanted nothing more than to have him back sitting by the bridge so she could ask him. A wave of guilt mixed in with the sadness consumed her, and the smell of frankincense filled her nostrils. She liked the smell; it wasn't a sweet smell, it was hearty, like the pipe smoke she only ever smelled from Stephen. She wondered if he liked the smell, if he would be happy with it being sprayed on his coffin.

When the Mass ended, Jane and Peter waited in line to shake hands and offer condolences to the family. Jane thought this was a lovely idea and she wanted to meet his family, but it was so rushed that she barely got to put her hand in each family members hand before she was onto the next person. She wanted to tell them all that Stephen made the best sandwiches and he knew about all the flowers and that he made her feel less alone, but she didn't get the chance with the throngs of people all pushing through to be make their presence known. Jane imagined sitting there with all those people shaking her hand for ages before burying a loved one and suddenly didn't like the idea so much.

They stepped outside to a much less crowded church yard as the rain was now heavy. There was no breeze, and Jane noticed the smell of the earth with the fresh rainfall and smiled sadly, knowing Stephen would in fact be happy to see the rain.

Peter took hold of her hand as they walked over to the adjoining cemetery. The noise of the rain hitting off black umbrellas matched their footsteps and it felt like they were on a march towards the burial plot. They walked to the bottom of the graveyard, with Jane noticing some fresh graves with lovely flowers on them, and some unkept with grass and weeds growing high. She decided she'd never let Stephen's look like he wasn't loved.

She looked to her left and right, noticing names etched on the headstones. One of the names jumped out at her, and she wanted to ask Peter if he knew the man with the same surname as him, but the sight of the plot with a mound of freshly dug soil stole away the question.

Stephen's plot was slightly away from the others, close to the boundary wall and right under the shade of a big oak tree. It was the perfect resting place for him; close enough that he wasn't completely alone and far enough that he wasn't right in the middle of the business of the cemetery. Just as he was in life.

Jane and Peter were shielded slightly by the rain, as mourners on either side of them had umbrellas, and they watched as the six men carried the coffin down a gentle hill to the plot and rested it beside the gaping hole in the ground. Jane took a step forward to see how deep the hole was and, still holding on to Peter's hand, peered down. It looked as if it went on forever, and for a second Jane felt as if she was going to lose her footing and fall in, even though she wasn't as close to it as she thought.

Fr. Gilroy said a decade of the rosary and the mumbling of the mourners followed. It was nearly silent in its delivery, barely audible over the noise of the rain hitting off the umbrellas. The priest swung a thurible but the rain dampened the smell of the frankincense.

The same men who carried the coffin started to lower Stephen down into the wet ground. Tom looked distraught as he let the rope slide slowly through his hands, and he visibly tried to hold back his crying, but the raindrops that fell on everyone's faces hid the tears that flowed.

"Ashes to ashes, dust to dust..." Fr. Gilroy was reciting, and as Stephen made his final descent back into his beloved earth, a single magpie landed on a branch of the oak tree and quietly warbled before flying off.

Jane reached over and threw the now drooping flowers on top of the coffin and let out another sob before the mourners began to disperse.

Peter drove the car home in a silence was only broken by a sniffle from either him or Jane. The dark clouds hung low and made no sign of parting as they drove up the narrow road. As the car pulled into the driveway, Jane turned her head towards the bridge and knew she'd never see shiny, polished shoes from behind the ditch again. That eventually the grass would begin to grow over Stephen's spot.

They walked into the house and parted ways into their own bedrooms. Jane, understanding for the first time the selfishness that can come with the early stages of grief, was thankful Peter wanted to be alone as much as she did. She lay on her bed and pulled out the photo frame she had bought for Stephen and looked at it until the glass was wet with tears and she began to drift off to sleep with her belly rumbling.

# Chapter Fourteen

THE SMOKE-FILLED PUB WAS noisy with chatter from all the customers, mainly men with a few women sitting at the lower tables by the windows. Jane sat perched on a high stool by a pillar, her feet dangling above the footrest on the stool as she coughed and took a sip of Coke from a glass bottle.

The pillar had mirrors and shelves to hold drinks, and she was able to see the two women sitting at the tables behind her. She thought to herself how much they looked like her mother. They both wore ill-fitting fake leather jackets and A-line skirts and looked as if they had raided the same make-up drawer with blue eyeshadow and red cheeks.

Jane kept glancing from the mirrors to her own mother sitting at the bar across from her as she twirled the straw in her Coke bottle. A half-eaten bag of crisps lay open beside it, along with two empty packets and three empty Coke bottles. Her stomach felt full, but not of anything substantial, only fizz.

Her mother sat slouched at the bar, her jacket hung loosely over her frame. The shoulder pads amplified her bony shoulders. As Sean put his arm around her waist, pulling her in for a kiss, one of her flat black shoes fell to the ground when she tried to cross her legs.

Jane averted her eyes back to the mirror and looked at the other women who seemed to be as drunk as her mother, but they weren't kissing anybody. She swung her legs over and back and looked around at all the people chatting, listening to conversations about horse racing and football and felt boredom gnaw away at her until she heard the sound of music radiating from upstairs.

She could make out Madonna playing and stepped down off her stool to make her way through the pub, squeezing between those standing in groups and around those sitting on the low stools at the tables, no one even noticing the little girl passing through.

When she reached the other end of the pub, the air seemed clearer and she took a few deeps breaths. After being accustomed to the smoky air inside the pub all day, a breeze from an open window made her realise how nice fresh air was. She stood at the bottom of a wooden staircase adjacent to the toilets and, as she looked up, she could hear the music more clearly, along with people laughing.

Jane's heart raced as she took the first step up the stairs towards the music. The air felt lighter and cleaner with each step. She stopped halfway up to look back towards her mother who was still wrapped up in Sean's arms. When she got to the top, she stood at an open doorway and was amazed at how different it looked compared to downstairs.

There were two pool tables, a juke box, and seating all around the perimeter of the room. The atmosphere was different here, and so was the clientele. They were younger, not much older than Peter, and she couldn't help but notice that the cigarette smoke had a different smell... it wasn't unlike a turf fire. She inhaled deeply through her nose. It was a deep, dark, musty smell that made Jane think of warm fires and Peter being home.

None of the people seemed drunk in the way that the others were downstairs, but she noticed they were smiling and talking more. She took a step through the doorway. In the corner a young woman, dressed in fishnet stockings and black eye make-up, was sleeping and her boyfriend was trying to wake her by rubbing her legs and kissing her face. Jane felt uncomfortable watching this, and started to twirl the material of the bottom of her pink jumper around her finger. She felt uneasy; she had seen Sean so many times trying to wake her mother up in the same way when she had too many vodkas, but it didn't make her feel any better.

An empty chair sat in the corner beside the window and Jane moved quietly towards it, sitting crossed legged. Her already-too-small jeans rose far above her ankles to show her mismatched blue and white socks, and the waist band dug into her full and swollen belly, but she ignored the discomfort as she watched two men playing pool.

She liked the bar game and had watched it many times before, calculating the next move that should be made and often laughed when someone would shout, "We're not playing snooker, ya bastard!" if their opponent left them a tricky shot to remove themselves from. She knew the rules and swore to herself that she could play if she could reach the table or if the cue wasn't twice the length of her.

Jane pulled her feet under her on the chair so she could get a better view of the game and so far it seemed the man in the red t-shirt was beating the man in the checked shirt by three balls, but he overshot and watched the white ball bounce and go into the pocket, giving his opponent two shots.

"Ah, fuck it to hell!" the guy in the red shirt shouted.

Jane stifled a laugh as the other man stumbled forward to take his shot, trying with all his might to focus his eyes by blinking hard as he leaned down on the cue.

The man in the red t-shirt turned to Jane and said, "Aye lass, I don't think I need to worry. This lad couldn't see a car driving directly at him the state he's in. Almost makes me feel bad for taking his fiver. Almost." He winked when the other man cursed under his breath, and walked towards his drink, taking a sip as he watched his opponent pot the last remaining five yellow balls followed swiftly by the black, winning the game.

Jane was gobsmacked; for the first time since she set foot in the pub with her mother after Mass that morning, someone had spoken to her. She was used to being invisible and was shocked to be seen. But she still smiled at her new friend.

"You're a fuckin' shark. A shark. But here's your fiver. Shark."

"Hey, watch yer language, we have a princess among us! What's yer name, chicken?" the man asked, turning to Jane.

"Jane. What's yours?" she replied.

"I'm Joe. What age are ya?"

"Six and a half."

"Aye. The half is important. Do ye want a Coke with my winnings?" he asked as he waved the five pound note in his hand.

"No thanks, I have one downstairs."

"Is yer mother here, or did ya just wander in off the street for a quick pint and a game of pool?"

Jane giggled and shook her head. "Noooo! My mother is downstairs at the bar!"

Joe's friend stumbled to the chair next to Jane and sat down beside her, spilling some of his pint on his shirt.

"I think you're a secret fucking ninja," he said. "Ya came in so quietly I didn't even see ya. Do you work for the queen?"

Jane laughed again, her second time to laugh that day, and shook her head.

"I'm Alan," the man went on, "and you should let him buy you a Coke 'cause he's as tight as a duck's arse. Ya know he's rich? He doesn't ever buy anyone anything, so he must like you."

Jane laughed again. She didn't understand the expression and immediately tried to think what a duck's arse looked like, but she couldn't see the resemblance. She liked her two new friends and it felt like a different world upstairs. It felt lighter and friendlier, and she was no longer invisible.

Jane looked up and saw her mother leaning against the doorframe with a cigarette hanging from the corner of her mouth. Her heart started to race and she felt a flush of embarrassment as her mother stumbled toward the pool table, dropping her black handbag.

"Come on," she slurred. "We're going home."

Jane looked at Joe and Alan and gave them a small sorrowful smile. She started twirling her finger in her jumper as she stood up. She walked over and picked up her mother's handbag and put it around her neck. She wrapped her arm around her mother's waist, guiding her towards the door.

"Hold onto the banister tight," Jane said as they stood at the top of the stairs, which now seemed scarily steep as she put one foot down. One arm was still guiding her mother's waist and her other was stretched out to the opposite banister, her fingers barely grazing it.

Joe quickly appeared behind Jane and put her mother's arm over his shoulder. He was taller by at least a foot and one of her mother's legs was off the ground; he could've easily carried her.

"You go on ahead and mind your mammy's handbag. I'll get her down the stairs," he said, nodding at Jane to go on. With each step she took she looked back to make sure Joe was still holding onto her mother. Sean stood at the bottom, tapping his foot impatiently.

"The fucking taxi's waiting, come on for fuck's sake," he said as he grabbed Jane's mother and dragged her towards the door. Jane followed behind, still with her mother's bag around her neck.

Sean sat in the passenger seat of the taxi and Jane sat in the back with her mother who was slumped against the door, her face pressed against the window. Jane kneeled on the seat and leaned over, pulling the seat belt around her mother and clicking it into place. She was still in kneeling position when the car took off, almost knocking her onto the ground, but she steadied herself, settled in and fixed her own seatbelt.

She liked when they got a taxi home; it was a rare treat but she found it relaxing; it meant her mother was too drunk to drive home which usually meant a quiet night apart from her mother's silly squeaky bed which made a lot of noise when Sean was there. Peter had told her that it just wasn't used to having an extra person in it and that's why it made so much noise.

As the taxi rounded a corner, Jane heard the familiar clinking of bottles from the footwell and looked down to see a blue and white striped bag with two vodka bottles in it. Without even thinking about it, she slid down and kicked it under the driver's seat, all the time keeping her eyes on her mother who was now snoring beside her. With the bag tucked carefully under the seat and thoughts of a quiet night ahead, Jane allowed her eyes to feel heavy as looked up at the stars through the window.

When the taxi pulled in, her mother seemed to get a second wind and pulled herself from the backseat and in the back door of the bungalow. Sean paid the driver and Jane went straight up to her bedroom.

She knew her room would be cool, but she couldn't wait to wrap herself up in the warm duvet Peter had bought her last year. Even in the warm summer months, she wrapped herself up tight, ignoring the heat as she drifted off to sleep. Her jeans felt even tighter and smaller and as she grabbed them by the leg and pulled them off; she looked down at her belly and saw a deep red, itchy mark which ran the whole way around her back. She scratched it with her right hand as her left grabbed at her nightdress.

She pulled her duvet back and smiled as she put her head on her pillow, but knew her peace was short lived when she heard shouting coming from the kitchen. Her whole body tensed up as she listened to the words echoing up the hall. It was her mother, shouting back in self-defence.

Jane leapt from her bed, her bladder now suddenly full and her stomach crowded with nasty butterflies. She ran down the hall and into the kitchen to see Sean standing over her mother with his fist clenched. He had her cornered by the worktop and her mother was cowering, waiting for the blow that Jane had interrupted. She saw Jane come in and shouted.

"I swear to God it wasn't me! I thought you had them! It wasn't me! Ask Jane."

Sean swung around, his fist still clenched and looked at Jane, who stood at the kitchen door with her legs trembling as if they had a life of their own, and breathing as if her lungs couldn't get enough air.

"Did you see a blue and white bag in the taxi?" he asked, glaring at Jane. "I left it by your mother's feet?"

Jane looked from Sean to her mother, who was now standing upright, and back to Sean.

"No," she replied. She swallowed as she remembered kicking it under the seat. Her mind raced and guilt overwhelmed her as Sean grabbed the phone to ring the taxi company. He pushed Jane out of the way and walked into the hall. Her mother now seemed more sober than in the morning and was staring at Jane.

"Tell the fucking truth."

Tears streamed down Jane's face and she swallowed a hard lump, her eyes fixed on her bare feet on the floor. She looked up at her mother again who was glaring at her.

"Tell. The. Fucking. Truth. Jane," her mother demanded again through gritted teeth.

"I kicked it under the driver's seat," Jane sobbed. "I'm sorry, I just didn't want you to drink anymore. I'm sorry."

The tears rolled down her face, tears that were the product of fear. Her mother picked a knife from the butcher block on the worktop, and like an expert sword thrower flung it with a flick of her wrist. Jane was stuck on the spot, holding her breath, as she watched the knife come spinning directly towards her.

It landed in the linoleum flooring just in front of her big toe, sticking up. Another millimetre and it would have stuck in her foot, mere inches and it would've hit her face. Jane let out as gasp as the knife wobbled, and started to cry loud tears as her mother bound to-wards her, cheeks flushed with anger and eyes fiery with rage.

Jane's mother grabbed her arm, spun her round and slapped her hard on her backside. Jane let out a howl as three more slaps rained down on her. Her mother, feeling like it wasn't quite enough of a punishment, spun her back around and slapped her once across the face.

Jane's ears rang and her mother grabbed her chin between her nicotine-stained thumb and fingers, pulling her face close, so close Jane could smell the wild garlic of her breath.

"Look what you made me do, you fucking useless girl," her mother whispered harshly. "Don't ever fucking touch my drink again. And look, you've pissed yourself again! Go to fucking bed, I don't want to see your face!"

When she let go of Jane's arm and face, Jane turned and ran up the hall, past Sean, and jumped into her bed, pulling the duvet up over her head. She lay on her back first, but her backside stung so she rolled over onto her side and realised that her arm hurt from where her mother held her tight, so she rolled over again, facing the wall. She didn't like sleeping facing the wall because it meant she had her back to the door, but tonight she thought that the worst had already happened and she sobbed into her pillow.

After a while, she heard her bedroom door open and her whole body tensed and she held her breath, afraid to turn around. Her mother stood just inside the doorway.

"It's alright," Mother said coolly. "The taxi driver is bringing it back. It's alright, no harm done. See ya in the morning."

As she closed the door behind her, Jane wanted to vomit. The little contents in her stomach jumped up her throat, but she held onto it with all her might for fear of having to leave her room, and it passed. With no Peter and no Stephen, she felt lonelier than ever.

# Part Two

1997

# Chapter Fifteen

JANE STARED LONGINGLY AT the watch in the jewellers' window. The pink fabric strap with blue and white flowers sewn into it held a big watch face with matching flowers in the centre. It wasn't fitting for the new persona she let a lot of the world see, but it was a representation of the fourteen-year-old child she still was. She knew it was childish, but it reminded her of her time spent in the fields making daisy chains and picking wild bluebells and buttercups.

She'd allowed herself to become immersed in the countryside as a child, but she could slowly feel the town taking over. She didn't allow it to consume her and she still watched the birds and the weather very closely, but this watch would remind her of her home in the fields and by the river and sitting by the bridge chatting to Stephen. Every time she read the time she would remember where she really belonged.

She walked down the busy street towards the pub her mother was drinking in. It was nestled in an older part of the town up a lane off the main street. It nearly looked out of place on the cobbled street yet at the same time fit in perfectly to its surroundings.

On a warm summer day, picnic benches were placed outside and music from the jukebox was pumped out as people drank in the sun. It had a nice atmosphere to it and Jane liked it. It was a new hangout for her mother, frequented by a younger clientele and had live music playing at the weekends.

Jane's mother was too old for this crowd, but wouldn't dare admit to it, and Jane was still too young. No one had questioned Jane's age; her figure, though still transforming, was that of a much older teenage girl, and her maturity cemented the idea for a lot of people. She never volunteered her age either, and she liked people thinking that she was older. She felt grown up, a person of her own and not just her mother's daughter.

The fact she was the one to calm her mother down or knew when she'd had enough made her seem wise beyond her years. She had inherited Peter's ability to read both a person and the room at large, and often shook her head to the barman when she judged it was time to go home. It made her life somewhat easier when he complied, but neither he nor she refused if her mother herself argued too much.

Their odd ages made them both misfits, inbetweeners, so they kept each other company. Jane had begun to learn a lot about her mother on these occasions. She knew she hated being older. She felt her youth was wasted by raising children she didn't want and was trying to claw some of it back. She frequently warned Jane not to make the mistakes she did and not to fall pregnant unless she was married. She saw pregnancy not as a miracle but as a curse, and equally the children who followed.

Jane knew she wasn't a wanted child, but she didn't feel sad about it; she grew up knowing this fact and accepting it. She also knew her mother was desperately lonely and felt obliged to be her companion.

Jane sat up on the barstool next to her mother. The four empty glasses and full ashtray told her she had been gone longer than planned and her heart raced. But her mind was still on the watch.

"Where were ya?" her mother asked before taking a sip of her drink.

"I went for a walk up the street and I seen this watch in the jewellers, it's so pretty, it has flowers on it and its pink and I absolutely love it… it's only fifteen-pound, Mam."

Jane trailed off the last few words quietly, realising that fifteen pounds was, in fact, a lot of money to them. But something in her brain clicked as she looked at the empty glasses and pack of cigarettes on the table. Her mother had drank and smoked the price of her watch.

"I can't afford that. I don't have fifteen quid, forget it," Mother said as she lit another cigarette. Tears began to fill Jane's eyes as she felt pure, seething anger.

"You have money to drink and smoke though!" She had tried to say it under her breath, but the words came out through gritted teeth and full of venom. But as soon as she had uttered them, she knew she'd made a big mistake.

She watched in slow motion as her mother hopped down from the barstool. In one swift motion her hand connected with Jane's face so hard that it knocked her off the stool she was perched on. Both Jane and the stool fell to the floor. A loud gasp rang through the busy pub as everyone stopped to look over at the young girl sprawled on the floor with her mother standing over her shouting, "Don't ever fucking talk to me like that!"

Jane's ears rang as she laid there, embarrassed, humiliated and defeated. The tears rolled down her stinging red face and she made no effort to get up. She wanted the ground to open up and swallow her to save her from the watching eyes. She could feel them boring into her as she lay on the wooden floor. Her mother was now in the corner with another regular, crying and being comforted. Her words were loud, loud enough to travel through the whole pub.

"I'm just a single mother trying to do my best, and this is the way she talks to me."

Jane sat up but felt dizzy. She had banged the back of her head off the floor when she was knocked off the stool and she could feel a lump beginning to form already as she rubbed it. The heavy bar stool had fallen on her legs and her shin was screaming at her.

She didn't even notice Darren the barman kneeling down with his hand outstretched to her. His dark hair hung down over his forehead hiding his eyebrows, but somehow accentuating his blue eyes. He had a soft smile on his face as he looked down at her; for a moment she was reminded of Peter, and she felt an overwhelming sense of loneliness. She grabbed Darren's hand and stood up with a groan. She was glad to see that most of the customers were now focused on a football game rather than her.

"I turned on the big screen," he chuckled. "Football's more important to some people than a girl getting battered." Jane was grateful for this and she gave him half a smile. "I'm on a break. Come on with me," he said, grabbing her hand and leading her out the door.

She blindly followed Darren as he led her to one of the benches outside. They sat opposite each other and he handed her a glass of Coke with ice. The condensation ran down the outside of the glass and for a moment Jane watched it fizzing and bubbling, wondering how she had let her anger and desperation for a watch make her lose her senses. She had never spoken to her mother like that before but she had also never felt anger like she had in that moment. The watch had now lost all value to her, it had lost all meaning, and if it were ever to be on her wrist it would forever be a reminder of how she had angered her mother.

"Does stuff like that happen often?" Darren asked.

"No. I'm normally more careful in what I say to her. I just got angry and said something I shouldn't have. It's my fault, I'll apologise to her."

Darren looked at her, gobsmacked. "Why are you apologising? Jesus, Jane, you done nothing wrong!"

She looked over at him and noticed his tan lines creeping out from under the short sleeve of his t-shirt. With his blue eyes focused intently on her, she felt herself blush, but it was hidden by the redness in her cheek from her mother's slap.

"I have to apologise, whether I was right or wrong doesn't matter. She thinks I was wrong. She's the one feeling sorry for herself and if I don't apologise a lot then I'm in for a lot worse when I get home."

Darren looked at the young girl. He had never asked her age, but assumed she was sixteen. He liked her, she was down to earth and mature, sometimes even more mature than most needy nineteen or twenty year-olds he had met or been involved with.

"I have an idea... say no if you want, but do you want a job? It'll be just collecting glasses off the tables and washing them behind the bar, emptying ashtrays, that sort of thing. I presume you're too young to serve alcohol, but at least you can do that. It'll give you some money and you can keep an eye on your mother. Like, you'll be here anyway, right?"

Jane smiled the biggest smile that he had seen on her and her heart beat so hard in her chest that she was sure he could hear it. She allowed herself to relax in his company and almost felt the same way she did with Peter. But there was something different, a different feeling that she didn't understand, that was completely alien to her. She was developing her first crush.

"I'm way too young to serve alcohol, but I'd love to do the other bits. Thanks, Darren."

She still didn't disclose her age, nor was she going to. She liked having an older friend and she was scared that if he knew she had just finished primary school he would back off.

"We won't tie you to a rota or anything, just do it on the nights that you're in with her. You'll get paid, it won't be much but it's a start, and you'll be working with me. You can be my partner in crime and you'll be gaining experience from the best and most awesome barman in the town."

Jane felt a rush of blood making her blush from her neck up when he winked at her, and she was struggling to comprehend the feelings she was now experiencing. She liked him.

"So what kind of music are you into?" he asked, taking a sip of his Coke.

"I like Oasis and Alanis Morrissette, they're my favourites but I'm not fussy, I like a lot of the bands that play here at the weekends. There's always a fun atmosphere."

"Me too! See, I knew there was a reason I liked you Janey, we'll get on great. And I'll look after you as much as I can from your weapon of a mother! I have to go, though, my break is nearly over. I hope you're okay, do what you have to do with her, and I'll keep my eye on ya. Give me a nod if it's going to get out of hand."

He stood up and walked back into the pub, leaving Jane basking in the summer sun. She felt a new found sense of confidence. She was happy that she now truly felt as if she had a friend. An ally.

She took a deep breath as she lifted her leg across the bench and made her way towards the door. She realised she had left her glass on the table and smiled as she turned to bring it to the bar. It dawned on her she knew nothing about the workings of a bar, even how the glasses were washed, and nerves started to kick in. But when she thought of Darren the nerves turned to excitement. She was confident he would teach her well.

She noticed her mother sitting in the corner with her new friend. They were laughing and her mother's friend nodded his head to Jane as if to confirm that she was now in good mood. Another ally. This made Jane relax even further. In other pubs her mother drank in, she was just the annoying child who hung around her mother, but here... she was Jane.

Her stomach knotted as she approached her mother. She tapped her on the shoulder and her mother turned around with her eyebrows raised, practically demanding an apology.

"Mam, I'm sorry for what I said. It was wrong and I'll never say anything like that again," Jane said, her eyes looking at her feet. She stopped herself from adding 'out loud' to the end. She had to lay her apology on thick and seem genuinely ashamed or her mother wouldn't accept it. She could give no explanation, just an apology, and if there were tears to make the shame seem greater, then all the better.

"Jane, you know I do my best for you. Jesus Christ, I'm entitled to the odd drink. I'm allowed to have a fucking life. Darren told me you'll be collecting glasses... you'll be able to buy your own watch, and me a drink to celebrate!"

Jane felt empowered. The feeling of independence washed over her and she smiled like a Cheshire cat. She watched Darren behind the bar, pouring drinks and chatting with other customers. She watched him as he reached up for more glasses and she took note of where they were all kept. She found herself immersed in his movements and she was mesmerised at how he seemed at one behind the bar almost dancing along with the music that played.

He flirted with the women he served and chatted with the men about football or music, adapting perfectly to his surroundings. Jane could see that he too was reading the room, reading the atmosphere, and though he looked relaxed he was ready for anything. As she watched, he bent down to reach to the bottom shelf and Jane noticed how his jeans seemed to cling yet also hang loose, and she found herself blushing again but she didn't know why.

She took her eyes off his jeans and realised Darren had caught her with her head tilted, staring at his backside, and her gentle blush turned into a bright crimson neon face mask. He winked at her as he turned to serve another customer and Jane put her head in her hands, for the second time in hours wanting the ground to swallow her whole.

But her staring wasn't just obvious to Darren. Her mother grabbed her forearm and dragged her out the door.

"Where are we going?" Jane asked, feeling confused, as her mother never left a drink behind. Mother sat on one of the benches and ushered Jane to sit down next to her.

"I seen you staring at him." She took a deep raspy breath and closed her eyes before she continued. "Jane, I know you fancy Darren."

"I do not!"

"Don't fucking interrupt me! What I'm saying is, do whatever you want but just don't come home pregnant or I'll kill you, do you understand? I won't raise it. I'll disown you. Do not become a single mother, because he will fuck right off."

Jane sat looking at her mother in bewilderment. The girls at school had given her the only bit of sex education she had ever gotten and she wasn't even sure if it was true. It didn't sound like fun to her at all and she had no intentions of ever doing that. She had so many questions, but had no one to answer them. She wanted to know more, but her mother wasn't the right person to ask.

"Okay mam. I won't," Jane said, looking at her mother with a dwindling hope that there would be more to the conversation at some point. But there never was from her.

When Mother realised that Sean wasn't going to be joining her for the second Saturday night in a row, she decided it was time to leave. For the first time ever Jane was disappointed to leave a pub. But she wanted desperately to see Peter. She needed answers and he was the only person she trusted to give her them.

They travelled home in silence, Jane subconsciously rubbing her cheek as if her mother's hand was still connected to it. Her mind raced with the events of the day, and she didn't know how to process them. Peter's car sat in the driveway, and she was excited to tell him about her new job and her new friend and she hoped he'd answer some of the questions playing on her mind. The car barely came to a stop before

165

she opened the door and ran into the kitchen, stopping when she saw his face drop.

Peter took one look at Jane's raw cheek and his blood began to boil. He didn't need to ask who the perpetrator was, but he wanted to know what caused it. Jane's eyes begged Peter not to say anything, but Peter stood up in front of their mother and looked her directly in the eyes.

He stood tall over her as he stared her down. She took a step to the side to move past and he followed, never breaking eye contact, remaining in front of her the whole time. Their mother dropped her eyes to her feet, and Peter eventually stepped aside. A vein in his forehead bulged as he walked out the back door towards the wall overlooking the field, taking a box of cigarettes out of his shirt pocket and lighting one up. Jane followed him out and stood at the wall beside him.

"When did you start smoking?" Jane asked, shocked.

"Never mind that, what the fuck did she do? Jane, her hand print is on the side of your face... why didn't you ring me? You have my number, fucking ring me!"

Peter felt guilty that he hadn't been there to protect her. It washed over him like a tsunami and for a while he couldn't remember life outside this house. He had forgotten about his independence and his freedom, all he felt was soul destroying guilt as he dropped to his knees and began to sob. In that moment it felt as if all his beatings, all the times he stood in front of Jane, had come to nothing. He felt broken.

Jane knelt down beside him and threw her arms around her brother. He smelled of strong aftershave and cigarettes. She felt her shoulder get wet as he continued to sob into her arms, but she offered no words in that moment, knowing anything she could say would be meaningless. She knew that the sight of her being hurt had hurt him more than their mother ever did and she also knew that the last few years had come crashing down on Peter. She let him cry and she held him tight until he stopped.

"You hardly know much about sex, Peter?" Jane asked, both to lighten the mood and in the hope he would actually give her some answers.

He lifted his head from her shoulder and began to laugh the loudest, heartiest laugh he had ever laughed in his life.

"Are you serious? What kind of question is that? Oh my God is that why she hit you?"

"No, Peter! But I need to know because she told me not to come home pregnant. She thinks I fancy someone, but I don't. But it got me thinking, she keeps telling me not to make the same mistakes as her. I know what her mistakes are, I just don't know how not to make them."

In this very instant Peter knew his baby sister was gone and it was a young woman who sat before him, mature beyond her years and about to enter into teenhood without knowing the basics, which in itself could be a recipe for disaster.

Peter himself was woefully inadequate to be giving a girl the sex talk, but he knew the basics and that is what he told her and no more. They sat until night talking about the day, about how Jane's longing for a watch had caused a turn of events which led to a job.

They walked back into the house with the sound of their mother's snoring coming from her bedroom, and they both went their separate ways to their own bedrooms. Peter lay in bed trying to remember the last time Jane fell asleep in his bed. He tried to remember the last time he carried her sleeping into her own bed, and he felt sad. If he knew the last time was going to be the final time, he would have held her in his arms a little tighter and for a little longer. Peter now felt obsolete in the place he used to call home.

# Chapter Sixteen

JANE'S MOTHER WAS UP early and unusually cheerful as she packed a small suitcase. She hummed to herself as she packed her bootcut jeans and short skirts. She felt as if she could legitimately call Sean her boyfriend now since he had separated from his wife. Even though she found the word 'boyfriend' too young, she didn't like the word 'partner; either.

"Too snooty," she claimed many times, though always through a smile.

The brown suitcase had layers of dust on it that she wiped off with a damp cloth after she had finished packing. She was going to the UK to see Sean's new home and business. He was running a garage in the Midlands and, as far as she was concerned, she and Jane were moving there in a few months to be a proper family. Jane didn't object to aloud, but Peter knew she didn't want to go. She never felt wanted when Sean was around, and the thoughts of being away from her home nauseated her.

"There's food there, I actually done some food shopping yesterday, and sure Peter, you're an adult, you know what you're doing, so there's no point me dictating to you. It's not like you'll fucking listen anyway."

Peter didn't answer, nor did he look in her direction. There had been radio silence from Peter toward his mother for years and she had grown used to it. In her sober moments she was wracked with guilt. It ate away at her, gnawing at every thought in her head which was then followed by a craving. One always followed the other and she knew she started to drink to block out those feelings. Now she drank because it was how she survived. She struggled to care anymore about her reasons for drinking.

"Right," she said. "See yas." She waved as she carried her case out the door. Jane and Peter practically held their breaths until they could no longer hear her car, and then collectively let out a sigh of relief. It wasn't intentional, but it was the first time in years that they were alone for a full weekend. Jane felt tears forming in her eyes and she felt her muscles relax. She was happy to stay home and not worry about saying the wrong thing or looking in the wrong direction. She just wanted to be.

"Right. I have plans... we are going to have a great weekend!" Peter said, rubbing his hands together. He turned to look into the cupboard and stuck his head in. "Milk and bread is what she bought, fuck's sake! It's okay, I have money. We'll still have a great few days."

"I have money in my room, too," Jane said. "Darren told me to tell her I'm getting paid a tenner instead of a twenty so that way she doesn't take it all, and sometimes I get tips so we can use that. I have thirty pounds."

Jane ran to her room to grab her stash. Her fingers fumbled at the corner of the carpet under her bed, and she pulled it up. There she found the three ten pound notes and some coins and she felt relieved and also grown up because for the first time in her life she was able to pay her way. She grabbed them all and ran into the kitchen proud as punch, putting her money on the table.

"Will we start with burgers and chips? My treat, but no milkshakes, I'm not fecking made of money!" she said, laughing. Peter smiled up at his sister and marvelled at her sense of humour. He wondered when she stopped looking and acting like a child. Then he corrected himself: she'd never really behaved like a child. She was always older than her years. Just like he had been.

"Right, a night in tonight and a day out tomorrow? I was thinking it's about time you met Lucy? She's dying to meet you."

Jane knew Peter had already invited Lucy and she just smiled and nodded her head. She missed him coming home every weekend like clockwork, missed curling up at the end of his bed and sometimes still slept there if she'd had a particularly bad day. But she never told him because she didn't want to add any more guilt onto the mountain that he was already carrying around on his shoulders.

"What's the plans for tomorrow, then?" she quizzed.

"Well, I was thinking we could go to the cinema. When was the last time you went there, it must be years? Or have you at all?"

The thought horrified Peter that in her fourteen years on Earth she had never been to see a movie on the big screen, gorging on popcorn and a giant drink. He hadn't been that many times himself as a child or a young teen, but now it was one of his favourite things to do. He loved when the room went dark and the sound from the speakers surrounded him as he ate popcorn. He never minded what the film was about, he loved the feeling of being engulfed mentally and physically in someone else's story. An hour or two where he could forget his own. And he felt Jane deserved the same.

"That's what we'll do, we'll pick up Lucy and we'll go to an evening showing of whatever and maybe get some food and come home and chill."

Peter was happy with his decision as he stuck his head in the cupboard under the sink for cleaning supplies. He grabbed two sprays and two cloths and put one of each on the table in front of Jane.

"It'll be nice to have a clean house, even just for a weekend. We'll get on top of it now."

Since moving out, he had kept his space clean and liked knowing where everything was at all times. He was incredibly organised, but also found it a way to avoid studying. As soon as he sat down to study, intrusive thoughts battled their way into his mind and he was finding it harder and harder to focus. But Peter was like a sponge, and absorbed whatever he needed to in lectures and cramming before exams worked for him. The cleaning bug hadn't bitten Jane yet and she rolled her eyes. She did agree that the house needed to be cleaned, but it didn't bother her as much as it bothered him.

"Will we each do a room, then?" she asked, getting up from the table.

"No way are you doing a half-arsed job," he replied, "We'll do each room together and do them properly and we'll have them done in no time."

Jane felt as if she was losing hours of her life cleaning, but they chatted the whole time. Every now and again after she had remarked about something or other she'd find Peter staring at her. It was, in truth, the first time they'd had a proper conversation without an underlying fear that their mother would hear or enter the room in a foul humour. They relaxed into each other's company, feeling as if they were getting to know each other for the first time as siblings and not siblings who were afraid of their mother.

As the last load of washing was taken out of the machine and the last room was swept, Jane felt a sense of accomplishment and peace. She liked that her home no longer looked chaotic and untidy and she marvelled at how in a few hours Peter had turned her into a neat freak. She felt her thoughts began to clear and she enjoyed her surroundings.

There was still plenty of light left in the day and as they started to drive Peter remembered a promise he'd made to Jane one dark night when she was a lot younger. He passed through their local town and kept going.

"Eh, you're long passed the chippers, Peter!" Jane laughed.

"I know! I'm keeping a promise. I'm not even sure you remember but I want to show you I'm a man of my word."

He drove for an hour, passing through little villages and towns, each one reminded Jane of the town she now spent her weekends in. She took in the beautiful scenery and ached to be back out in the fields. She took mental notes of the fairy rings the farmers avoided and noticed each tree, some perfectly symmetrical and some growing in a way that looked to be against nature itself. She longed to be back watching birds.

Eventually, she could see it in the distance: a tall, grey stone lighthouse that looked both a little out of place among the green fields. The Spire of Lloyd, the inland lighthouse, stood tall and proud and incongruous, miles from any ocean.

It was magnificent. Tall and defiant. The car drove up a little lane and parked in a small car park in full view of the tower, yet not obtrusive. A stone wall ran around it and a playground sat on the grounds.

They walked up the steep stone path towards the tower, the trail lined with sycamore trees, offering shade without blocking the view.

The trees, full bodied and lush, sung the gentle song of the summer breeze but only if one stopped to listen. On the left, in the middle of the long grass, stood stone remnants of what appeared to be a shrine, but without a statue and devoid of religion. Jane wondered if a statue of the Virgin Mary at one point sat looking down on the children's playground. It seemed like a fitting place to look down upon children.

Another stone wall circled the grounds of the tower. Peter and Jane walked towards the tower itself, in awe of its sheer size. Steps spiralled around the outside of the lighthouse, leading towards a locked door.

"It's only opened on bank holidays," Jane shouted down at Peter, but as she looked away from him, she caught sight of the view. In front of her, in hundreds of shades green, fertile fields cascaded downwards towards a road. In the distance stood a spire from a church and a round tower from the nearby town. Beyond that she could see mountains belonging to other counties.

Jane walked down the steps and climbed up the wooden fence, letting the beauty of the view wash over her. She let her thoughts drift as she watched the swallows swoop and dive, the practically cloudless blue sky a perfect backdrop for their shimmering colours. She watched as their streamers looked tangled for a split second as they flew in unison yet alone. Jane felt at peace.

"There's the graveyard I told you about," Peter said, instantly regretting breaking Jane's trance.

She swung herself around on the fence and jumped down, walking over to the entrance to the pauper's graveyard. There stood a rock with a poem carved into it to explain that this unmarked piece of land was in fact a mass burial site from the famine. The path was designed in the shape of a Celtic cross, and in the middle sat a stone cross marker, the words on it barely legible, ravaged as it was by the elements and time. At the top of the path stood a stone altar.

The sand-like gravel on the path made a louder sound underfoot than Jane expected. The crows cawed in the trees, their noise their only giveaway.

Without the altar or poem or cross, this would have been just a normal piece of land by looking at it, but Jane could feel that it was different. When she stood in the pauper's graveyard the outside world drifted away and all sounds quietened. Jane stood at the altar, looking down the path with the cross and lighthouse in full view. Her thoughts began to unravel and she knew Peter felt the same as he stood over to the left staring at the view.

She walked out of a little gap in the stone wall over to the green area, the noisy gravel giving her footsteps away to Peter as he followed. More remnants of a stone wall lay on the ground with mature trees growing from them. Jane loved how a place in which religion had tried its best to conquer had been won over by mother nature; this place was rightfully hers and she had reclaimed it beautifully.

The children's playground lay at the bottom of the hill. It seemed morbid to Jane to erect it beside a mass burial site, but then she thought perhaps the sound of children laughing and playing might help to dry the millions of tears and drown out the anguished cries from grieving mothers and fathers who soon followed their children into an early, unmarked grave. Lloyd had a peace about it, as if in a way all those years ago it had become the final destination for people's pain and suffering, and Jane felt she could let some of hers go, too. It now belonged to the hallowed ground.

She felt tears fill her eyes as she sat on the bench and felt a wave of emotion. She let her tears flow freely as she felt a sense of serenity wash over her. She wasn't crying from sadness, she was releasing years of hurt and tension and heartache and though her heart still felt heavy, her mind became free.

Peter put his arm around Jane's shoulders and took a deep breath. He too felt overcome but couldn't make sense of the power this place had. He couldn't put it into words, but he knew Jane understood. She was always at one with nature and the land, but he could see that Lloyd spoke to her louder than any field at home ever did.

"Next time we'll bring a picnic and stay longer," Peter said to break the silence, without taking his eyes off the view in front of him. In every direction there was a view that took his breath away. "But we'll need to go before it gets dark," he said, nudging Jane gently with his shoulder. "We're still an hour from home and you're treating me to a chipper, remember?"

"Yeah okay, let's go. Peter, thanks for bringing me here, it's been..." Jane trailed off, swallowing a lump in her throat. There seemed to be more of a release needed than she first thought, but for now it had to be swallowed down. They walked back to the car and, before setting off, took one longer look at the Spire of Lloyd watching over the village of Kells and its surrounding areas.

When they arrived home with their chips and burgers, Jane felt drained. She ate and chatted with Peter, but in truth she was happy to go to bed. Once her head hit the pillow, she was asleep and slept what was perhaps the best sleep of her young life.

Jane slept with the window open, even in winter. She loved the feel of fresh air hitting her lungs as she woke and the cold air in the winter made her bed feel extra warm and safe.

In the summer months she woke early, the early morning chattering from the birds upon sunrise her alarm clock, but not this morning. She slept well past sunrise and into the morning. She was woken today by an unfamiliar young woman's voice coming from the kitchen, and pulled the covers over her head with a sigh. She liked having Peter to herself without the fear of their mother coming home, and she just didn't feel ready to share him. At least not for this weekend.

A pang of jealousy hit her right in her solar plexus and she rolled over in bed, ignoring her bladder and mustering the courage to meet the other woman in Peter's life when a knock came on the door.

"Are you awake?" Peter whispered. Jane groaned a response and Peter laughed. "Is this the teen years kicking in now or what, you always had me up at the crack of dawn. I've never known you to sleep in! Come through, I want you to meet Lucy!"

Jane could hear the excitement in his voice. She pulled the covers down off her face and looked at her brother. His excitement was sweet and new and she never noticed his eyes to sparkle quite as much as they did in this moment. She rolled her eyes playfully at him and said, "Right, give me a few minutes please, I better make a good impression for the girlfriend!"

Peter left her room, chuckling like a schoolgirl at Jane's sarcastic response. Jane pulled out her best pair of blue jeans and a navy hoodie. She noticed how tight it had become around her chest, but decided to go with it anyway. Once her face and teeth were clean and she had applied her sun cream, she walked down the hall. She paused at the door, took a deep breath, smiled and went in the kitchen.

It seemed Peter had undersold Lucy's beauty to her; Jane was gobsmacked but hid it well. Lucy sat at the kitchen table with her long, straight blonde hair draped across her left shoulder. Her eyes were a blue that almost shone and her skin was flawless. She was radiant; she was gorgeous.

"Wow, you're far too pretty to be going with my brother!" Jane said.

Lucy laughed but didn't blush, and hooked her arm into Peter's. Lucy eyed Jane up and down. That made her feel uncomfortable, and she started to regret wearing her tight hoodie.

"Peter told me you were fourteen?" Lucy asked.

"Fifteen in a few weeks," Jane replied, still pulling at the bottom of her top. She felt uncomfortable and wasn't sure why. She felt as if Lucy was reading her... or trying to.

"Jane, you'd easily pass for eighteen, there's no way I'd believe that you were just fourteen. Jesus Peter, you said you had a baby sister! I wasn't expecting a gorgeous young woman!"

Lucy playfully slapped Peter on the arm, but she never took her eyes off Jane.

"It's nice to meet you Jane. I've heard so much about you, and I really hope we can become friends. It'd be nice to have another girl to chat with and give out about Peter's bad habits!"

Jane looked over to Peter and smiled a sly grin as he put his head in his hands in a mocking way and realised she had never seen Peter so happy. She let the pang of jealousy go.

The threesome sat at the kitchen table for what felt like hours, relaying stories about each other, both Jane and Lucy finding out new things about Peter. They never spoke about their mother though; there was an unspoken agreement between them to redirect the conversation should the topic arise.

Finally, Lucy spoke up. Peter watched her as if he was seeing her for the first time and he was clearly in love with this girl. Her body language, directed all at him, told Jane that she felt the same. It was nice, but she knew her days of having her brother all to herself were now at an end. It made the evening trip to Lloyd all the more special and poignant.

"Peter, I'm taking your sister for some girlie time in town. You can do whatever you like, but for a couple of hours it's a man free zone."

Peter's heart swelled with pride and love at the thought of his two favourite people bonding and he could have danced on the spot. He looked to Jane, who was blushing, and realised that she'd probably never had what Lucy was offering. When Jane went to the bathroom, he handed Lucy some money.

"Get her what she needs, and thanks for this. It never dawned on me there might be stuff she needs that I can't get for her, or even know where to."

Jane and Lucy spent the day in town. They bought make up and clothes and Lucy took Jane to get fitted for her first proper bra, a trip that was overdue. They laughed and joked and let the hours roll past, enjoying each other's company. Jane felt grown up and spoiled and every second sentence from her mind was expressing gratitude to her new friend.

She felt so grateful that it seeped from her whole body but she also felt guilt every time Lucy told her to put her money away, calling each thing "an early birthday present." She could understand why Peter loved Lucy; her bubbly, positive personality was catching, and her kindness was unlike anything she had experienced. She was radiant and it made her external beauty glow more.

When the car started to turn for home, Jane got a familiar uneasy feeling. Her stomach lurched as Lucy navigated the winding roads and fear and panic rose in her body. Lucy sensed the sudden change in Jane's mood and asked her if she was feeling alright.

"I think she's home."

She began to take deep breaths to control the panic rising higher the closer they got to home. Lucy parked in the driveway in silence.

"Stay in the car, please?" Jane pleaded to Lucy, forgetting the bags in the back as she turned to get out.

"Jane, I know," Lucy said, gently grabbing onto Jane's arm. "Peter told me everything. I already know that your mam drinks."

Jane turned and looked at Lucy's kind eyes pleading with her and replied, "No Lucy, you don't know, and I know Peter would not want you to come in. Your opinion of us will change and I don't want your pity. Neither does Peter. We want your friendship. Stay in the car."

Jane had never taken control like this. Her tone was commanding, and feeling strong and courageous she stepped out of the car like an adult ready to take charge of the situation. Perhaps the break had been what she needed; for two days she'd felt like herself without the burden of her mother.

She walked in the front door and found Peter at the kitchen table, his head in his hands. Jane walked over and gently removed his hands to check for any marks.

"I'm okay," he said softly. "I'm fine, but she's not. Jane, it's bad."

Jane silently left the kitchen and walked up to her mother's bedroom, opening the door, and what she saw saddened her to her soul. Her mother was laid on the bed, a shell of her former self. She was black and blue all over. Her eye was swollen shut, her lip was burst, caked in dried blood. Her good eye was so red and puffy from crying that it was almost as swollen as the bruised one.

She was sobbing an almost guttural cry. Jane sat on the bed beside her and rubbed her head. She didn't need to ask what happened; she knew this was Sean's handiwork. She had seen the marks through the years but never this bad.

Suddenly Jane saw her mother not as an alcoholic but as a deeply flawed, broken human being who needed and wanted to be loved. In that moment, Jane decided she would be the person her needed. She would overlook every word that had cut her in the past and had already forgiven the future ones. She knew she needed to be her mother's rock.

She rubbed her mother's head gently and looked into her sad eyes and said, "Don't worry Mam, I'm here. We're best friends, remember?"

It was in this moment that their relationship changed. Her mother's attitude changed. She no longer viewed Jane as an inconvenience to her life, she viewed her as her only friend.

Back in the kitchen, Jane boiled the kettle and popped painkillers out of the box as Lucy left the bags at the door. There was an unspoken sadness between the trio as if they sensed the shift in Jane, and they knew there would be unspeakable changes. They could see and sense the determination in her: she was now her mother's carer.

"Come and stay with us at the weekends?" Peter asked, putting his hand on Jane's shoulder.

"Who'll mind her?" Jane asked, nodding toward the bedroom. "No, I can't. Anyway, I can watch her when I'm working and Darren will help me. It's grand Peter, you've done your bit. Your job is done. You minded me and took beatings for me. I'm taking over now."

Jane could see Peter had reached his limit; she preferred losing him to Lucy and a life of happiness rather than watch him succumb to the misery of the life he had already led twice over. She needed to let him go, for him to release himself of the responsibility he could no longer carry. He knew it too, and though it was the end for him and his mother, there would never be an end for him and Jane.

# Chapter Seventeen

THE LAST BOX PACKED and taped up, Jane and Peter stood in the now bare kitchen of their childhood. Peter placed his arms around Jane's shoulders and sighed. The pea green kitchen, untouched since the '80s, looked worn and dated, its walls carrying the stains of bad memories that Peter felt could never be washed clean or painted over. They were now ingrained in the very fabric of the whole house in the same way they were part of his and Jane's DNA.

"That's an awful ugly colour," Peter declared. "I never want to see anything green again as long as I live."

"Yeah, I'm not exactly fond of it myself," Jane replied. "If this kitchen could talk?"

"It wouldn't talk, Jane, it would fucking scream. Please come and stay with me and Lucy. You can keep your job for pocket money, and I'll make sure you're alright in school. Please, Jane?"

Peter was now leaning on the kitchen table looking at his sister, his eyes begging with her to change her mind. But she wouldn't make eye contact with him, ignoring the question until he straightened up and sighed.

"Who'd mind her?" she finally said. "Who'd make sure she gets up for work on Monday when she's hungover or that she doesn't throw up in her sleep?" Jane was trying to busy herself but there was nothing to fidget with, so she eventually stopped and met Peter's gaze.

"It's not your job or mine to mind her, Jane. Fuck's sake, she's a grown woman and she needs to sort her life out. It's not for you or me to do!"

He threw his hands up in frustration and ran his fingers through his brown hair which now carried highlights from the sun. The sleeves of his t-shirt rose when he did so, revealing toned biceps and tan lines. He looked healthier and stronger than ever. He was no longer a thin little boy and Jane noticed it.

"Are you playing football again or something?" Jane asked, picking up a box to carry to Peter's car. "You look different."

"Running a bit. And the gym helps fight the demons in my head, that's all. The physical side of things is just a bonus."

"You're a poser who stands on front of the mirrors flexing! If you were a bar of chocolate, you'd eat yourself!" Jane laughed as she walked out the door, but she couldn't help but wonder about his demons. Were they the ones created in this house, or created by his own mind? She worried that she hadn't been fully introduced to her own, yet, and she closed the back door of the car.

"Thanks for the compliment, Janey!" he shouted out the door to her. "Have we any more room in the car?" Jane ignored the empty footwells and the fact that she could probably carry the last box on her lap.

"Nope, wouldn't fit a field mouse in here now," she shouted back as she put her seatbelt on.

Peter instantly knew she was lying, her voice too high, but he didn't mind. He knew why she wanted one last trip. As they drove the winding roads, Peter broke the silence while keeping his focus on the road ahead.

"Do you really think an apartment over a pub is a good idea? Jane, will you please think about this for a minute... it's going to be a disaster and you'll be right in the middle. Please come and stay with me and Lucy. Please Janey, I'm begging you."

Jane sighed a loud breath of air that felt warm on Peter's cheek, reminding him of the nights he carried her into her own bed, merely a child himself with the responsibilities of a man, and his heart ached for the childhood they both lost.

"It's close to her work, it's close to school, it's cheaper..."

"More money for her to drink," Peter interrupted as he rolled his eyes.

"Maybe, maybe not. She only drinks at the weekends Peter, always did. Why will that change? An alcoholic drinks every day, she doesn't. So just stop. She just gets a bit nasty when she's drunk."

"Nasty when she's drunk," Peter repeated. "And hungover, and hungry, and sober..."

Peter trailed off but Jane had stopped listening. She was watching the tree line fade away as they came into the town. She didn't want to move away from the countryside, didn't like the hustle and bustle of the town, especially at the weekends, and she hated crowds and loud noises. Her escape from it all was down by the stream, alone. She was now losing a big part of herself and she was scared. But she had no choice.

The older she had gotten and the more times she made this journey, she had come to realise it wasn't as far away as she used to think. The trips in the car when her mother was drunk felt as if they went on forever, but still without transport she had no way of coming back here.

They carried the boxes up a side street nearly hidden in the middle of the main street and into the building's side entrance and then up a flight of stairs. The door was open and their mother was unpacking cups and plates, placing them in the cupboard over the white electric oven. She was humming to herself and smiled when Jane and Peter walked in.

"What do you think, Petey?" she asked.

Peter frowned. She hadn't called him by that pet name since he was a small boy, and it stopped him in his tracks. He felt a pang of emotion that he wasn't quite able to pinpoint, and his heart ached as a memory of her kneeling down kissing his grazed knee and rubbing his head came flooding back. He knew she wasn't always bad, or wasn't bad in her entirety, but in the years that followed the goodness was overshadowed. He had only been home on the weekends since he left for college, so in previous years he had only ever seen her drunk, and he felt he was looking at his mother for the first time since becoming an adult.

"Em, yeah, good. Nice. Where will you park?" he asked, unsure of what to say to the stranger in front of him.

"I sold the car. I needed the cash for the deposit, the social only help with so much. I won't need it anymore, sure, everything I need is here."

She in this moment realised she was looking at her son through sober eyes and felt the stinging of tears as she blinked them away. It had been over three weeks since her last night out because she was saving for the apartment. She didn't like sobriety. She didn't like the flashbacks she got, and she didn't like the ache in her heart and the heaviness in her head. She felt sad all the time and seeing her grown son, unfamiliar to her, was too much as she brushed past him, making her way down the stairs.

Peter took a moment to compose himself before calling out for Jane.

He walked up the hallway towards Jane's new bedroom, stopping to look out a window on the way. There was nothing to look at except a concrete roof with skylights looking down into the pub. He couldn't envision Jane being happy here, away from the nature she loved and knew so well. Jane stood at a bedroom door on the left watching Peter as he gazed out the window.

"Nothing much to look at, huh?" she said with a tone of sadness in her voice.

"Ah, a couple bird feeders and it'll be like you're at home," he said, following her into her new bedroom. The view from her bedroom window made him feel angry. It was a brick wall. He walked over to the window and opened it, reaching his arm out the narrow gap and touching the building opposite. "Jesus. This is very different to what you're used to. It's not you."

"I hardly had a choice. So I can sulk or I can make the best of it. Maybe it's time to leave the little country girl behind completely anyway."

Peter stared at his little sister and wondered how she had become more mature than him already. She seemed to take everything in her stride, where he let it weigh heavy on him. He didn't mind helping out with the move, but he couldn't bear to see his mother drunk or bruised or abusive anymore, so he had stepped back, a lot. Jane understood, more than he did, accepting it graciously and moving on, bearing no ill towards him. He was constantly in awe of his sister.

"One more trip home?" he asked, throwing his heavy arm around her shoulders again.

As they walked down the hall they were greeted by their mother, who stood with a familiar looking glass in her hand. A tall slim glass, with vodka, a dash of 7-Up, ice and a lemon. She looked immensely pleased with herself as she held it up smiling.

"Handy, isn't it?"

Peter and Jane glanced at each other before Peter glared at his mother.

"Ya couldn't wait 'til the last box was unpacked and maybe Jane was settled in bed? Fuck's sake mother, is this it now? Just saunter down to the bar anytime you feel like a quick one? You'll have a path worn in the stair carpet in no time, so."

He looked towards Jane again who now wore a look of disappointment on her face and again asked her to change her mind about staying with him.

"She's not going anywhere," their mother cut in. "I'm her mother, how fucking dare you? You don't show your face in months, and now you come in here trying to take my daughter away from me?"

Jane stepped in front of Peter. "Mam," she said gently, "I'm not going anywhere. He only meant for a sleepover. Isn't that right, Peter?"

Peter realised that all he was doing was making Jane's life more difficult. Where he could just walk away, she couldn't or wasn't ready to yet, and he needed to control his anger around his mother.

"Yeah, that's all I meant. A sleepover every now and then. Maybe during midterm or whatever." He said this through gritted teeth and knew it was the last time he'd be seeing his mother because he could no longer control him his temper in her presence.

"Oh. Right. Well, go get the rest of the boxes then." She turned to another half-emptied box and continued unpacking while sipping her vodka.

They drove back to the old house in silence, Peter wishing Jane was young enough to just take with him and Jane wishing Peter would just let it go. She watched the birds in flight and the breeze blowing through the trees and wondered when she would be able to watch the trees as closely again, watching for the change of season, or to see a magpie protecting its young in the undergrowth. A lump began to form in her throat.

Two boxes sat in the kitchen, waiting to be packed, and Jane walked past them and took one final tour of the bungalow with Peter following her. They both stood at Peter's old bedroom door and it was then he realised what he had left was gone.

"Where's my stuff?" he asked, looking at Jane.

"It's in those boxes in the kitchen. I kept your posters to put in my room, if that's okay?"

The Green Day and Nirvana posters were snippets of the comfort he gave her on dark nights, a reminder of a boy who had left home and the man who never returned.

"Yeah, of course you can have them," he said, smiling. "I have a present for you too. A housewarming."

Peter went outside to the little shed on the side of the bungalow and grabbed the box he had hidden earlier and carried it back into the house. Jane was now back in the kitchen and beamed a huge smile when she saw the picture of the CD player on the box.

"Oh my God, is that for me?" She was excited, already planning where it might go in her new bedroom.

"Yeah, I know you used to like music when I was home, maybe you've actually got some taste and won't play Take That on it?" he joked, but was happy to see Jane excited.

She put the box on the ground and threw her arms around him.

"Thanks, Peter! It'll kinda feel you're still with me. I love it. Em, can I leave you to pack these up? I want to go for a quick walk."

"Sure," he replied. "You want company, or will I leave you alone?"

"Follow me down. You know where I'll be," Jane answered as she walked out the door.

She walked down the road and tried to memorise every single leaf on every single tree, the different colours of each as the tree readied itself for winter slumber. She inhaled through her nose, smelling the country air as if it would be her last breath for the rest of her life.

Crows circled low around the trees and she knew rain was on the way but today she didn't mind. The fresh autumn air didn't feel cold as she closed her eyes and let herself feel the change in season.

As she kept walking, she could hear the gentle murmur of the babbling waters that ran around the field, and she stopped to look over the stone bridge that had stood there for centuries. She looked down into the clear waters and watched as fallen leaves floated with the flow of the water. Some were momentarily caught on protruding rocks but the persistent flow of water eventually set them free to continue their journey onwards.

Jane felt like a fallen leaf beginning its unknown journey, but she wasn't withering and shrivelling like them. She was more like the tree itself, shedding the old in preparation for the new. But the tree knew what was coming after a long, hard winter... she had no idea what kind of transformation she was going to come after her winter.

She climbed down onto the ledge that sat just below the bridge. Many times had Peter lifted her up onto it to avoid the cows in the field or to wading through knee deep muck, but she was now tall enough to climb up herself. The water below, waist deep in her younger years, would sit just above her knees today.

She let her legs dangle, but her feet didn't quite reach the water like she had hoped. An unusually dry summer had made the water levels low, and she felt sad that she couldn't dip her feet one last time. She rested her head against the stone bridge and closed her eyes, letting the tears fall freely.

"Goodbye, bridge. Goodbye, river. Goodbye, trees. Goodbye, cows. Goodbye, Jane."

Peter sat on the road with his back to the bridge, listening to his sister bidding farewell to her old self. He wrapped his arms around his knees. She didn't hear his movement over her own cries, and he decided to sit for a moment longer so as not to disrupt her train of thought. He felt as if he was intruding on her private moment, but he also knew any sudden movement would interfere with what she needed to do.

He listened to her sobs and cried silently himself, knowing that starting a new school and moving house was a lot for anyone to bear, let alone alongside the responsibility of caring for an addict. He wished for her to change her mind about living with him, but knew she wouldn't. He felt nauseous about what lay ahead for her.

Peter's guilt erupted from him in the form of a deep, mournful sigh. This was enough to get Jane's attention as she sat on the ledge beneath him. She climbed up and sat down beside him, putting an arm around his shoulder.

"I can see why you loved it here. It's peaceful," he said, keeping his gaze straight ahead.

"Peter," said Jane, "I know why you can't stay with me, we've had this chat. Please let go of the guilt. You've done your bit, let it go and go and live."

As Jane sat with her older brother, she could see how vulnerable and fragile he really was; she worried he might be closer the breaking point than even he realised. She vowed to not let another thing from home weigh on him.

"Come on, let's go," she said, standing up with her hand out-stretched to Peter. "I'm sure you need to get back to Lucy anyway." He looked up at her with a knowing smile and grabbed her hand.

As they walked away from the bridge, Jane stepped away from Peter and went over to the stump, now overgrown with grass. Jane parted the long grass and looked down at Stephen's spot, turning and sitting down as she did. A broad smile spread across her face when she put her feet down and heard a gravelly sound underfoot. She leaned over and started to move the grass aside with her hands, and there it was: two patches of earth where Stephen had once rested his feet.

"He made his mark here too, it seems," Jane said with tears rolling down her face. "I just lost interest in flowers after he died. Do you think he'd be disappointed in me Peter?" she asked, not looking up.

Peter crouched down and put his fingers under Jane's chin, lifting her head so her gaze met his. "Jane, it would be virtually impossible to be disappointed in you."

She smiled at her brother and put her arm around his waist as she stood up, mentally saying goodbye to Stephen, knowing if he was hanging around anywhere it'd be here rather than a graveyard.

With their arms around each other, Jane and Peter walked up to the bungalow in silence, for the last time.

# Chapter Eighteen

JANE SAT DOWN IN the back row of maths class and made herself as small as possible in the plastic chair. She lowered her head and hid behind one of the taller girls, praying Mr. Fenton wouldn't notice her or ask about the previous night's homework. She was sure she had gotten every answer wrong and she didn't want the shame of the teacher pointing out her mistakes in front of the whole class again.

"Jane?" Mr. Fenton called, seeking her out around the other girls. "How did you get on with last night's homework? Have you got it there to show me?"

Jane's cheeks flushed red and she sighed a quiet sigh, wishing the bell would ring, as she rubbed her palms together feeling them sweat. She hated maths; she found it so difficult, and even though Peter had tried his best to explain things to her with the time he had, she still struggled.

"Em, well, em, sir, I done it but... I actually left my copy at home," she said, not even looking at him.

"Give me your journal. A note's going home to your mother and father. You'll need to be more organised if you're going to get on in life, Jane."

Second year in high school was proving to be a lot harder than first. The sheer amount of homework in the evenings was impossible for Jane to keep on top of, and maths was by far her worst subject. With no help from anyone, only criticism, she soon lost interest and hope in ever doing well.

On some weeks the notes came hard and fast, on others she sat unnoticed at the back of the classroom, desperately trying to focus her mind enough to retain some of the information. It seemed that no matter how many notes she took, by the time her mother arrived home in the evenings Jane would've completely forgotten how to do the equations. Her main concern was survival: how she answered, in what way she looked at her mother, and the egg shells that she tried to avoid treading on like a gymnast. The mental load of that alone was more important than any x or y but she hadn't even realised it. It was just life.

Jane exhaled through her nose in a quiet snort, followed by a smile. She was trying to not let on that neither parent was interested in her journal. Her mother's hand had become so shaky, it had become very easy to forge her signature for convenience's sake. But her heart still sunk when she heard the title 'father.'

She pushed the chair back, grimacing at the noise it made, and walked up the middle row to the teacher's desk with her mauve A4 journal in her hands. She kept her head down, not wanting to meet the gaze of any other girl, but she could feel them watching her all the same.

Mr. Fenton wrote a barely legible note in the teacher's comments section and handed it back. The only word Jane could make out was 'unacceptable.' Her heart raced while she made the walk of shame back to her desk. The bell rang as soon as she sat down and she let a sigh of relief so hard that she felt as if she had been holding her breath for the entire class.

Her last class of the day was religion, which she looked forward to for several reasons. She loved the teacher, Mrs. Clarke, and she loved that she had the chance to learn not just about one God, but many gods, and all the different cultures that went with them. It was also one of the very few classes where she, Ruby and Niamh were together.

The three girls had gelled quickly and had become nearly inseparable. They didn't fit into any of the other categories that brought other groups together. There was the popular group, with the girls who clung on for dear life, hoping to be popular by association. There were the sporty girls, some from the same football team or basketball team who always seemed to be in their sports uniforms. Then there were the bookworms, who felt they were more intelligent than anyone else and often hung out together outside the library or the science room. They were all, in their own way, exclusionary. Neither Jane nor her friends fit into any of these categories, but they were happy with one another.

Ruby sat down beside Jane and flung her straight blonde hair over her shoulder.

"Well, guess what? Connor said he'd meet us in the usual spot, can ya come?" Ruby smiled a broad white smile and put her palms together in a praying position, pleading at Jane to say yes.

"Please come with us, it won't be the same without you!" Niamh said, sitting down on the opposite side of Jane, clasping her hands in the same attitude. Both girls stared at Jane with big, toothy smiles.

Niamh's dark hair was tied up in a ponytail and the waves were clear at the bottom. She never wore her hair down, but having it up made her brown eyes more visible and, mixed with her dark eyebrows, gave her an intensity.

Ruby, with her long blonde hair and blue eyes looked to be Niamh's opposite in almost every way and their personalities were different, too. Ruby had a desire for a boyfriend and every male in the town her age was a potential. Niamh, on the other hand, watched sports and the only time she looked at boys was from the sidelines. Ruby, of course, accompanied her, most of the time not even knowing what sport she was going to see.

"Oh good, girls, you're already praying, I see," joked Mrs. Clarke as she sat on the empty desk in front of the girls. "I'm so glad you're getting into the spirit of it, as it were!" Her ankle length skirt rose up to show her pale shins and open-toed sandals. She smiled at the girls and asked them about the last class.

"So, ladies, what did you think of the discussion we had last week? Did you think any more about it?"

Jane was the first to answer. She loved how Mrs. Clarke allowed her to voice her opinion and always engaged with her, and her relaxed teaching style meant the girls could speak their mind, within reason, and have actual discussions.

"Yeah, I still think they are essentially all the same, give or take a few minor differences. God may be called different things, but his rules still apply, and no matter the culture, they'll still fight over it. One believes the other is wrong and will kill to defend it even though it goes against their god's will. It doesn't make sense to me."

Jane sat back in her chair, crossing her arms. She felt empowered by this teacher, and though Jane normally hated anything religious, she respected Mrs. Clarke's beliefs because she was one of the first religious people she knew who treated her just as she was and not a product of what her mother had done.

"I see your point, Jane, and it's very, very valid, but have you ever wondered why people are so quick to defend their belief system or why they're willing to die for them? Is it because certain cultures have been supressed?"

"But aren't religions themselves oppressive?" Jane replied. "They try to supress people and, in some ways, normal human nature, don't they? Believing is fine, but when it means one type of people are shunned because of it then maybe it deserves to be supressed. I think they're all the same bar a few minor differences. But each religion seems to hate equally."

"Okay, can we leave the religious wars and fights out of the situation for a moment, and think about this," Mrs. Clarke said. "Take away the building and the priest and all of the things you associate with God, and what have you left?"

"Mother nature," Jane replied quickly, sitting back with a smile on her face, sure she had just converted her religion teacher to her way of thinking.

"Isn't it the same thing? Call it what you will, but it's a belief in God. Call it mother nature, the universe, Allah or Buddha, it's all the same. When you go for a walk in the woods and breath in the fresh air or lie on the grass with your eyes closed, isn't that a form of prayer and meditation?"

Jane looked at her teacher open mouthed for a moment before she smiled

and rolled her eyes. "I'm never going to win with you, am I?"

Once Mrs. Clarke moved on to another group of girls, Niamh turned in her chair and said, "I wish you wouldn't entertain her. Just nod and agree and we can get back to making our plans!"

"Course I'll see yas, usual spot, usual time?" Jane said while opening the chapter on Buddhism just as the last bell of the day rang. The easy-going thirty five-minute class was now to be swapped with the bedlam and scramble for lockers and girls rushing to get buses home or just to get out the doors, but Jane wasn't in a rush for any of that, so she took her time and watched the other girls run past, arms laden with books or gym bags.

Jane's friends had lived in the town all their lives, so they already knew most of the local lads. Connor had grown up a few doors away from Ruby. They had a brother and sister kind of relationship, and were very protective of each other. Connor didn't play sports, and in the boy's school if a boy didn't play hurling or football it was hard to fit in, but he was a very gifted guitar player and his guitar and stereo went everywhere with him.

Jane liked Connor, liked that he was different to the other boys her age. She sensed an anguish in him that only appeared in his music. She would sit in Ruby's bedroom listening to Connor play and sing, and often found herself staring at him, lost in the words and notes that seemed as if they were coming from someone much older.

Sitting with her head resting on her palms, she'd imagine him singing on stage for hundreds or thousands of people and it annoyed her when Ruby or Niamh told him to stop. It made her sad that even his parents would have preferred if he played sports, and she made sure Connor knew that she was his biggest fan. He'd get as lost in his music just as she used to get lost in nature, sitting by the stream. Some days she felt pangs of envy that she didn't have her escape anymore, but she had learned to let the music transport her back.

When Jane was with her friends, she adopted the persona she had while working in the pub, and they liked her for her confidence and bubbly outlook. They didn't see the anguish she carried around and in moments laughing with her friends she sometimes forgot about it. The little girl who cried with relief at school on Monday mornings was gone.

The gang hung out in a local park that had a big river running through it, and Jane loved it there. Though it was busy with runners and walkers it was still the most peaceful place in the town. It reminded her of home, and she would always be the first one of the group to arrive. She'd just sit by the river listening to the flow of the water. She had never attempted to so much as dip her feet in it, because it was bigger and the current was much faster than the little stream by the old bungalow. Even though her friends hung out here many times before, it took Jane's knowing eye to find 'their spot.'

This was a place hidden from the business of the park. A small gap between the bushes and brambles opened up into a clearing hidden from view from those who had stopped looking at the world around them. Small children frequently stuck their heads in and gasped in awe at the room created by nature because they were still seeing, still curious and taking in every inch of the world around them.

The clearing, about twenty feet in width and length, sloped onto the banks of the river and had a perimeter of trees which all intertwined with each other, making a canopy overhead, hiding the sky and shading them from the hot sun on summer days. When the trees were in full leaf only a few beams of sunlight could penetrate the roof of greenery; it made Jane think of cats chasing a light up a wall and she imagined many cats here playing with the light on the forest floor, amusing themselves with sunlight.

The floor of the wooded area looked fake in the summer months; it was entirely clear of weeds and grass with the occasional clump of moss growing from the bottom of trees. The roots of the trees formed steps towards the river, and from a distance one would think the area had a low pile, beige carpet. During the autumn months a whole new carpet was laid; leaves of different shapes and colours, creating noise and texture, adorned the area and they practically stayed crunchy until they disintegrated because even when it rained, the perfectly interlocking trees held onto each other like fingers and created a sturdy shelter.

They made this area their own just by their continuous presence alone. They often brought drinks and junk food. Connor would bring his guitar and stereo that ate batteries quicker than he could replace them, and vowed every single time to always have a fresh set, but never did. In truth he was happier playing his guitar, and Jane was too. There was less noise from the acoustic guitar and she found it easier to concentrate on the words and the melody without other instruments interrupting it. It accompanied the sound of the flowing water beautifully.

When Connor played here, the sounds of nature became his band. Jane would close her eyes, lean against a tree, and wonder if he was aware of this.

Stephen played on Jane's mind when she sat here. On one of their first occasions hanging out, she pulled a faded Quinnsworth plastic bag out of her pocket and uttered the words, "Leave no trace. Mother nature was good enough to create this space for us, let's not ruin it," and though the others laughed at her sentiment, they followed suit. There was never a trace of the group after they left, only their footprints and the sounds of laughter etched into the root of every tree.

# Chapter Nineteen

As PETER ATE HIS cereal, he became very aware of the ticking of the kitchen clock. It seemed to get louder with every minute that passed; soon he felt as if the noise was echoing around the room.

The rattle of his cup and spoon being washed in the empty sink then being dried and put away didn't dull the noise. He felt as if the ticking was boring into his head and he couldn't focus on anything else. He wondered if the clock was broken as he walked out of the kitchen towards the front door.

Peter's daily routine didn't differ much from day to day. He felt less anxious once he knew what his day entailed, and it made him more capable of dealing with any unknown surprises that might arise, as they often did when it came to his mother and Jane. Enough chaos came with them.

He laced up his runners and, as he closed the door behind him, noticed the date on the calendar marked in red. A sense of guilt washed over him; he had nearly forgotten his father's anniversary and knew his normal running route was going to change. He stepped to be greeted by the weary autumn sun beginning to rise.

The sunlight reflected off the windows of the other houses in the estate, and Peter thought they looked as if they were on fire. The morning illuminated everything in a perfect glow, and he felt grateful to be watching it. As he took off into a gentle jog.

He took a left out of his estate and let his mind drift as he increased his pace. Running helped him unravel his thoughts, which seemed to tangle very quickly throughout the day, allowed him to pull on the loose threads and untie the knots. Some days his thoughts seemed as regimented as his routines; he'd start thinking about work and lay to rest any lingering anxiety from the day before. He'd replay conversations he had with his co-workers while wiring a house or replay a joke that was made to make sure it was a joke. Peter spent his time overthinking, when he wasn't occupied with reading a room or body language. His fear was always that he may have missed something.

As he ran through the empty streets, he noticed signs of life beginning in some shops. He could feel the tension from early morning staff preparing for the day ahead just as he could smell the fresh bread. He cast his mind back to his time working in a newsagent's while he was in school; he could still remember the codes for the newspaper returns and the feeling of ink on his fingers as he finished unbaling them and putting them away. He loved being an electrician, but some days he missed the hustle and bustle of a busy morning or evening. He felt sometimes it was easier to deal with lots of people in shorter interactions than to spend his days working with the same people. It was easier to deal with a foul humour if the customer was only in for a few minutes.

He kept the pace until he got to Main Street, slowing as he came closer to the pub his mother and Jane lived above. He looked up the alleyway at their door and then up towards the living room window, trying to ignore the empty vodka bottle on the sill. As he averted his eyes a vase filled with dying flowers on the bottom windowsill transported him back to a day many years before, back to the bungalow to a time long before Jane.

"Mammy, why does the water need to be changed?" he asked as he followed her into the kitchen.

"Well, Petey, I want them to last as long as possible, so it's important to keep the water fresh." As she spoke, she pulled one of the carnations out of the vase and wrapped it in a piece of kitchen roll, gently patting it dry.

"Why are you drying that one Mammy?"

"I'm saving this one," she replied with a smile. "I'm going to dry it and put it in a book upside down and then I'll have it forever. By the time you're a grown man like your Daddy there might be a whole bunch of dried flowers, like memories you can hold."

Peter's dungarees were still a bit too big and his mother bent down, tightening the straps on his shoulders and kissing him on the forehead

"You'll grow into these in no time," she said, walking back down the hall to replace the flowers on the windowsill. She hummed as she poked at the embers on the fire and made space for more turf. The smell radiated through the whole house and it reminded Peter of their neighbour who took his lunch to the bridge on sunny days to sit, watching the birds as he ate and smoked his pipe. It was the same kind of hearty smell.

Peter picked up the pace as memories came flooding back - for a second, he could almost smell the turf fire in his nostrils as his breath quickened. He ran through the town and over the bridge, passing the park, and came to a stop at the graveyard, which lay outside the town, where he and Jane had gone to primary school.

The stone wall was a dirty grey from the cars passing, and the leaves from the trees across the road lay piled at the feet of the black metal gates. He leaned against the wall, waiting for his breath to return to normal, and stared in at the hundreds of graves with very little space between them. Every year he came, the graveyard had expanded. Amongst the black and grey headstones were splashes of colour, flowers and wreaths places by loved ones, which did little to dull the bleakness inside the stoned walls. The gate opened with a stereotypical creak and he began his ascent down the path.

"Who's at the door at this hour?" his mother had asked as she placed the last sod of turf on the fire. That's the last sentence he remembered his mother speaking that day, but he remembered the blood curdling scream she gave as two Gardai stood at the door, hats in hands, explaining that his father's body had been pulled out of a wreckage.

"We think he fell asleep at the wheel," were the only words Peter remembered. He was young, younger than Jane had been when he went off to college, but he was old enough to know what it meant when the Garda explained that his daddy was dead. He was old enough to know that life would never be the same again.

In the days and weeks that followed, neighbours and friends called and offered sympathy and help. Many were armed with pots of stew and apple tarts which kept them fed for a while. But soon enough, everyone else got on with their daily lives, forgetting about the grieving widow and her young son. As the flowers began to die in the window and the last of the yellow water dried up, Peter's mother started to drink.

The memory made his heart beat as fast as the run did, and as he walked down the gravelly path and towards his father's grave he noticed a lone figure kneeling by the headstone. A fresh bunch of yellow and white carnations lay in the middle of the plot and his mother was pulling up the weeds that grew up around the headstone. Peter was just about to turn back when she spotted him and stood up.

He looked at his mother: a pitiful, thin-looking shell of a woman, not the mother of his memories. As he looked into her gaunt face, he wondered if his memories were a figment of his imagination. But as she smiled sadly and he saw his father's name etched on the headstone, he knew that at one point she had been a good parent. He took a deep breath and walked over to the grave to have his yearly civil conversation with his mother.

"You're here early," he remarked. As he got closer, the smell of stale alcohol hit him and he knew that perhaps she was there early because she hadn't been to bed yet. He wondered what kind of night Jane had had with her, and made a mental note to check in with her.

"I prefer to be here when its quiet, before all the aul' ones come and start bothering me," she answered as she bent down to pull at more weeds. "How are you doing? You and Lucy happy?"

"Em, yeah," he replied. "I suppose. Yeah. We are." He was thrown by the question; he couldn't remember the last time she'd asked after his wellbeing. "You? How are you?" She seemed equally shocked by his enquiry as she stopped what she was doing and looked up, still kneeling on front of him.

"He'd be fucking disgusted at me, wouldn't he?" she said. "It wasn't supposed to turn out like this, Petey. He'd hate me for this." She turned her back to him as she sat on the edge of the grave and put her head in her hands. "Hell. I hate me."

Peter didn't move to comfort his mother as she sat crying by his father's grave, couldn't muster even a shred of forced, fake sympathy for her. He muttered under his breath,

"I hate you too."

He turned and walked back up the path. When he reached the gate, he began to jog, stopping only for a second to watch his mother's shaking shoulders. His heart longed for just a second to comfort her, but his anger stopped him from turning back, and he took off into a sprint back to town.

Sprinting so soon into his run left him breathless by the time he reached the pub on Main Street. His legs ached and his mouth felt like sandpaper. Though he had given up smoking not soon after he started, when he got breathless he wondered if he had done long-term damage to his lungs. Quitting was easy when he realised he was taking up one of his mother's habits.

He looked up to the window and noticed the curtains open and the vodka bottle gone from the windowsill. Jane was up. Turning up the alley he noticed his mother had left the downstairs door unlocked and rolled his eyes as he opened it and made his way up the stairs, knocking on the door at the top.

Jane opened the door barely a crack and looked out.

"Peter!" she shouted, throwing her arms around his neck. "How did you get up here? Did she leave the door unlocked again? And why did you knock? You don't need to knock! Ah *Jaysus*, you're all sweaty. Where were you?"

"Out for a run. Can I have a glass of water? I'm gasping."

He turned towards the cupboards but stopped when he realised he didn't know where anything was kept. Jane laughed when she saw his hesitation and reached up, pulling out one of the many pint glasses that had found their way into their mother's handbag and filled up a glass of water, pouring in a dash of MiWadi from the fridge.

"The bar skills are coming along nicely, I see?"

"Hardly! A pint of water isn't exactly a pint of Guinness, but Darren did show me a few times how to pull a good pint. He lets me, the odd time, especially if it's busy. I just don't actually hand them to the customers," she said proudly.

"So you like it then? Do you ever get a weekend off? Me and Lucy want you to come over for a weekend, we'll go to the cinema and maybe go shopping? I haven't seen ya in ages Janey. I miss ya." He continued before she could answer. "How are things here with her? Did you get the call card I left in the letterbox? You don't even ring anymore. How much do you have to save for a mobile phone? I'll give you whatever you need, then at least I don't have to wait for you to call to let me know you're okay."

"Peter, all the questions!" said Jane. "Jesus Christ. No, I don't really have weekends off. I've thirty pounds left to save but I'll manage it myself, thank you though. It's fine, it's okay. She's okay, she kind of stays out of my way these days."

She wasn't lying but she was omitting a lot. She didn't tell him about the different men she brought home on the weekends or the strange faces over breakfast on Sunday mornings. She didn't tell him that she caused so many rows in the pub, but it was true that she did leave her alone, mostly. Peter was like a wound-up spring ready to snap at any time and Jane could see it very clearly.

"Maybe, me and Lucy will go for a few drinks there some night, meet this Darren lad. I'd like to see him, is there any night she's not in there?"

"Saturday nights she's started going to the bar downstairs. I think she made a new friend and he drinks there instead. But only on Saturdays."

"Right, that settles it so. Can't wait to see you all grown up behind the bar, but are ya not wrecked doing these late nights? How are ya coping at school?"

"Fine. Grand. School's just fine," Jane replied, not making eye contact. Peter instantly knew she was lying and added that to his list of things to check up on.

"Right, I'm off home again, lock the door after me and I might pop in tomorrow. Or will you at least ring me from the payphone? I worry about you."

They hugged each other at the bottom of the stairs and Peter went jogging up the street towards home. Once Jane had locked the door, she took the stairs two at a time. She could see how worried he was and she vowed to ring him more often.

Jane didn't particularly like ringing Peter too much because he was very school focused. To him it didn't matter if she had friends or was liked; all that mattered was results. She didn't have the heart to tell him that she couldn't understand any of the maths questions and as soon as she got home, she had forgotten what the teacher had told the class.

It didn't make sense to her because there was no reason for it, no reason to why she was learning it and no reason for finding the answers. Her maths teacher called her analytical which would be good for maths if she wasn't so focused on the 'whys.' During one lesson when he was explaining equations to the class, Jane asked,

"But why, why do we need to do this?" and when the class and teacher collectively sighed and she got no answer, she stopped asking... but also stopped trying.

History gave her the answers she desperately sought. Wars, famines, risings, all had a why and she devoured her history book and enjoyed writing long-winded essays on whatever the topic was. She loved the teacher, but seemed to be the only one who did. He was a small, older man with greying, curly hair that resembled Einstein, and he always wore a grey suit and stripey tie. He terrified the other girls and Jane had witnessed him throwing a duster at a girl at the back of the class for talking too much. But she was in awe of his knowledge.

Mr. Desmond didn't read from textbooks and gave information in a way that was far more entertaining to her than just reading it aloud. He talked of things not in their books and amazed her when he picked apart her favourite film, Michael Collins. Though some things were historically inaccurate, according to him, it was still her favourite. She loved how someone could hold so much love for something that they were willing to die for it.

Mr. Desmond held no prisoners when it came to late homework or messing at the back of the class, and as soon as the other girls realised lunchtime would be spent in detention, they stayed quiet and handed their homework in, but Jane put the most effort in for this class.

Some days, if Jane had nothing for lunch and no money, she'd forge her mother's signature and go home to raid the cupboards, knowing full well there would be as little there as there would be in her lunchbox, but it was an excuse for her friends. She'd tell a lie and say her mother had some stew on or a big pot of vegetable soup with brown soda bread left over that she couldn't wait to get into her stomach. It was better than telling the truth, that she might have some crisps stashed away in her bedroom and if she was really lucky there'd be a slice of bread left over that had blue mould on only the corners that she could pick off.

These days weren't as often as they used to be, when they lived in the countryside, but they still happened enough for her to be an expert at her mother's signature. When Jane thought about this, she always marvelled at how well her brother looked and knew he was eating every day. There were two or three days running where she had nothing to eat and contemplated using the call card to invite herself over for dinner, but she didn't want an argument or more begging to move in with him, so she stayed quiet and let him live his life as best he could.

"What he doesn't know won't kill him," she often muttered to herself when she'd be on the verge of telling him something. Those days she avoided her friends after school too, because Jane often got emotional when she was hungry and didn't want to explain her tearfulness. And anyway, it's very hard to tell your friends that you're crying because you've only eaten crisps the last two days.

She grabbed another pint glass from the press and filled it with ice from the freezer. If there was nothing else in the fridge, there'd be ice and lemons. *The lemons never go mouldy*, Jane thought as she walked towards her bedroom.

She opened her wardrobe and pulled out a can of Coke she had hidden under a pile of clothes. She had started hiding some of her fizzy drinks because if her mother had a visitor over he may prefer vodka and Coke, and Jane got fed up sharing with strangers of the night. It was always a good sign when her stash of chocolate bars and crisps was building up as it meant there was plenty food in the cupboards.

The Coke fizzed up as she poured it into the glass, gradually, like Darren had showed her. She pressed a button on her stereo. As Oasis started to play, she sat down on her bed and wondered where her mother was.

She had opened the bedroom door softly, as she did every morning, noticed her bed hadn't been slept in and began to worry, wondering where she'd spent the night or if she had an accident.

Jane tried to pull her mind away from whatever gutter her mother may be laying in and started thinking about the silver Motorola she was going to buy. Thirty pounds and it was hers. One more weekend at work, but then she was starting from scratch with her savings and she argued with herself over whether to buy the phone or some new clothes. She wanted to take Peter up on his offer, but felt that he had given enough over the years. She reasoned with herself that if he offered one more time, she'd gratefully accept.

Jane got a familiar feeling of dread in her stomach and picked up the remote, turning her stereo down to zero. She laid so still she could hear her heart beating in her ears and it raced faster as she heard the keys rattle in the door followed by a raspy cough.

It was strange to feel a sense of relief and a sense of dread at the same time, and she waited to make sure there were no other voices before she ventured out of her room. The clink of ice into a glass could be heard up the hall as she opened her door and her heart sank. Ten in the morning was early, even for her.

Jane opened the door to the kitchen as the vodka was being poured. Her mother was still in the previous night's A-line skirt and flat shoes.

She looked sadder than usual. Her eyes were red and puffy, and for a second Jane was unsure if they were bruised or she had actually been crying. She took a silent, deep breath and slid into the chair across from her.

"Are you okay, Mam?" she asked, hoping she'd be told to fuck off, but she knew that she'd be here for a while, listening to how she ruined her mother's life by being born.

"God, Jane. How the fuck did I end up like this? I didn't want to be like this. I don't want to be like this. But the sadness, oh God." The last two words sounded almost guttural as if she was in physical pain.

"What sadness? Sean?" Jane asked. She reached her hand out to touch her mother's, but stopped when it got halfway across the table. She pulled it back down to her lap and started twisting the bottom of her jumper.

"No, not that cunt. Well maybe a bit. But no, you wouldn't understand sadness. You haven't lived the life I have. You wouldn't understand. It just eats at me. Drink used to kill it, or numb it. If I cried at night while I was drunk I'd have forgotten the next morning that I cried. I could mourn without remembering. But a bit stopped been enough."

"Is that why you drink all the time?"

"I'm not a fucking alcoholic, Jane! Fuck off. You wouldn't understand, you're only a fucking child."

"But... I do understand. I know sadness that sits in your bones. And I know when it feels as if your blood has been replaced with it. I know." Jane was looking into her mother's blue eyes, eyes that never shone with joy or happiness, but a flash of anger was after coming into them and she knew that her time at the table was short. She tried to decide if it would be best to get up and leave, or wait to be told to go.

"What the fuck would you know about sadness?" Mother snarled. "What the fuck, Jane? And all I do for you? Paying stupid money for uniforms and books so you can go to school and you're telling me you're sad? You're ungrateful! Please fuck off out of my sight."

*Gladly*, Jane thought, happy to leave and let her mother wallow alone. She stood up and went to her room, grabbing her call card and taking her money from her school blazer pocket. The blazer she never wore that apparently cost her mother fifty pounds, but had a rip under the arm. She needed a phone to contact her friends on days like this when she needed to be out of the flat, and she was going to take Peter up on his offer.

But she stopped in her tracks, not wanting to leave her mother alone. If she went downstairs, or somewhere else, who would mind her? She sighed as she sat on the edge of her bed, wondering what to do. But her decision was made for her as she heard her mother go into her bedroom and get into bed.

Jane's mood had soured as she opened the door onto the roof of the pub to check the weather. The breeze was cool and she could feel winter approaching. She stepped out onto the wet roof and walked slowly across to the green skylight looking down into the pub. The sound of horse racing on the television could be heard with the clinking of glasses. She imagined the sad faces of men who had lost a week's wage on bets and had to come home with faces full of apologises to their wives and kids.

The sound of muffled snoring could be heard coming from her mother's bedroom as she walked over to where the two buildings met and sat on a ledge. She tried to like sitting there, high up away from the world, but it wasn't home. There was no changing of the seasons living here, no subtle changes which told her another one was coming. Everything was just... grey. The sky even seemed to lack birds, or any colour; it all blended in with the buildings. Her life had become bleak and grey.

If she sat on the windowsill inside, she would sometimes notice the change in people. The woman who walked that street to work every morning starts in a jacket in spring, shedding clothes as the seasons go on, only to wrap up warm again.

Jane made her way inside and locked all the doors before heading down to the street. She felt a sense of freedom and relief knowing her mother was asleep and out of harm's way, and inhaled some of the cool air deeply as she turned for Main Street. A car with a bad exhaust backfired just as she did so, which led to a fit of coughing.

*Bloody town. I can't even fecking breathe here*, she thought as she walked towards the phone box on the corner, pulling the call card out of her jacket as she did. She stepped into the phone box, put the card into the slot and dialled Peter's number.

"*Jaysus*! You actually called! Oh god, is everything alright?" Peter asked immediately.

"Hello, Peter. Yes, everything's fine, she's in bed asleep. Fancy a guest?"

"Absolutely! Call over, we're here!"

"Right, I'll be an hour. I'm going to go around the shops first."

"Great! See you then."

When Jane put the receiver down and turned around towards the door, she nearly jumped out of her skin to see Darren with his face pressed up against the glass. She screamed and then laughed.

"Arsehole!" she shouted as she opened the door, playfully hitting his arm.

"I already told you I was an arsehole... just a nice one! Where are you off to, going to meet the boyfriend?" he asked.

"Hardly. I'm going to my brother's house for a while. What are you at?"

"I'm at a bit of a loose end, actually. Fancy a McDonald's?"

Jane realised it was closer to lunchtime than it was to breakfast and her stomach was starting to rumble a bit at the thought of it.

"God yeah, I'd love one."

They both walked up the street towards the newly opened McDonald's. The exterior was barely recognisable as a fast-food restaurant, but the interior was bright, spacious and modern. It was still a novelty in the little town and had become a haven for teens to gather after school with six sitting around a table envying the one who could afford a sundae or a milkshake.

But it was particularly quiet when they stepped in. They ordered and when Jane tried to give Darren the money for her food, he threatened to fire her. She laughed and said thank you before calling him an arsehole for the second time that day.

They sat in a booth in the corner by the window overlooking the main street, and if Jane really craned her neck, she could see the pub she lived over. But she didn't want to look, her eyes were on Darren who was listing the bands that would be playing over the coming weeks in The Hive. The conversation flowed smoothly and easily between them; she talked about school and he talked about their shared interest in music and it felt easy for both of them

"Right, do you want an ice cream?" Jane asked.

"Oooohh I'd love a caramel sundae," Darren replied as he handed her a tenner across the table. Jane very quickly slid out of her seat and went to order without taking the money. She stood at the counter watching the girl pump caramel into the cup and over the ice cream, and Jane smiled to herself and sighed. It was nice to be with Darren outside of work and she was glad to see that they still got on so well without the common interest of customers.

The other seats started to fill and they had both been sitting over empty ice cream containers for over and hour. Jane looked at the clock on the wall and realised she'd left Peter waiting far too long.

"Shit. I better go, he'll kill me!" she said, getting up and putting her jacket on.

"Ah you're a big girl now, surely he won't be that annoyed? I'll walk a bit with you," Darren said. He was already putting his own jacket on when he realised Jane wasn't stopping to answer.

"He worries, that's all," she said as she walked fast up the street, towards the bridge to bring them to the estate. "It's the estate across from the park, me and my friends hang out in there sometimes, it's nice."

"I'll leave you here then," said Darren. "See you tomorrow?"

"You know it," Jane said as she kept walking. When she glanced back, Darren was still standing there, watching her walk in to the estate. She took into a jog and ran the rest of the way to the end of the cul-de-sac where Peter's house was.

# Chapter Twenty

By the river, Jane heard a rustling of crunchy leaves underfoot and instantly knew it was Connor. He was always first of the group to join her, and in recent weeks had started to show up earlier and earlier, much to her annoyance - it was interfering with her alone time. But he seemed to enjoy the quiet as much as she did and they often both sat in silence with their backs against trees overlooking the river. Connor would gently strum his guitar, lost in his own thoughts as much as Jane; they enjoyed each other's company in the moments before the noise.

At the sound of rustling leaves and Ruby chattering, Jane and Connor's gaze met and Connor rolled his eyes skyward. Jane laughed. Ruby's chatter reminded her of the magpies warbling in the morning; though loud and incessant, it was one of the sounds in her life that had become her favourite.

Connor placed his guitar back in the case and pulled a CD out of the front pocket. He put it in his stereo and Oasis started to play quietly. Ruby was pulling junk food out of her bag, humming to herself as she reached in again and again, pulling out Taytos, bars of Cadbury and a big bottle of Coke. She looked like a magician pulling a never-ending coloured scarf from a hat. When she was finished pulling the treats out of her bag she looked up, saw the others staring at her and laughed.

"What? Mam done the shopping yesterday and it's my brother's birthday so there was extra!" Her laugh was loud and contagious; when she laughed everyone else laughed or smiled.

Niamh pulled out the contents of her bag and pulled out a stash of junk about half the size of Ruby's and put them together. She still had a green lollipop in her mouth, now the size of a marble, and sat back down, quietly shrugging her shoulders. Niamh lived in a bigger house just on the outskirts of the town and was the first of the group to have a phone. She never seemed to be without anything, but never bragged about it either.

"So, what's the plans for the weekend anyway, peeps?" Ruby asked, to no one in particular.

"Working tonight and tomorrow, as per usual," Jane replied.

"You're not working Halloween night are ya?" Niamh asked.

"No, I only work Friday and Saturdays, when Darren is on. If he's off, so am I."

"That's such a weird set up," Niamh said, looking down at her phone. "Why are you working anyway, and why only with him?"

"What's it to you?" Connor asked, noticing Jane's cheeks flush. Jane just looked at Niamh, who didn't seem all that interested in the answer but lifted her head from her phone at Connor's reply.

"I'm just saying, it's weird. My mam would never let me work in a pub."

"Your mam wouldn't let you work anywhere because you don't have to. Mind your business, Niamh," Connor snapped back. Normally quiet and reserved, this was as outspoken he had ever been. Jane watched his neck get red as he stood up for her and she didn't know what to say, so she just tried to redirect the conversation.

"I have to head u and get ready for work. I might get a McDonald's," Jane said, before she remembered something. "Oh, shit! The Hive is having a fancy-dress party for Halloween, and Darren said we should dress up. I have nothing to wear. What should I dress up as?"

"A sexy nurse?" Connor replied. All three girls just glared at him.

"Do you have anything at all? Even something from last year we can jazz up a bit?" asked Ruby.

"I've, um, never dressed up for Halloween before," Jane confessed.

"Ever?" the other three asked, nearly in unison.

"No. We lived in the middle of nowhere. Trick-or-treating's hard when your closest neighbour is four miles away."

"But what about Halloween parties as a child, Jane?" Connor asked.

A redness began to form on Jane's neck, spreading up towards her cheeks. Her palms felt sweaty as she looked at her three friends and struggled to find the words to explain her situation. Ruby spotted Jane's red cheeks and quickly jumped in with a solution.

"It doesn't matter," said Ruby. "We'll get you sorted. We still have, what? A few hours? Niamh, I'll go home and grab some of my sister's costumes from last year and we'll meet at yours. Jane, go get food and come to Niamh's in an hour. We'll make you look class!"

The three girls turned and looked at Connor, who took a step back with his hands in the air. "This is far too girlie, even for me. I'm not participating in a makeover or whatever yous are doing. But I'll see yas Halloween night," he said, packing up his things. The batteries in his stereo had long since died.

Jane felt excitement like she never had before. She had never dressed up for anything other than a funeral and her First Communion. This was a whole new experience for her.

"Oh goodie! A makeover!" Ruby squealed as she started to pack everything back into her bag. "Come on, Niamh! Jane, go get some food! We'll see you in an hour!"

Jane turned to Connor, who gave her a smile as he packed up the rest of his stuff. The colour in his eyes was intense but there was a gentleness there she had never seen before. When he stood up, she put her arms around his neck and whispered into his ear.

"Thank you."

Connor didn't reply but he put his arms around Jane's waist and hugged her tight, letting his head rest on her shoulder. He was much taller than her, and broad, but they fit together perfectly. Their hug was broken by the sound of Ruby screaming at Connor to hurry up, and they both laughed and broke away from each other.

"Enjoy your girlie stuff, see ya on Halloween," he said as he stepped out of the clearing.

Jane walked down towards the bank of the river, holding onto tree branches and watching her step as she used the roots to secure her footing. She climbed down the steep incline, now damp from rain the previous night, to stand briefly beside the water. She closed her eyes, listening to the flow of the water and the crows beginning the call of the evening. She took a deep breath before she turned back, climbing back and leaving the clearing, leaving the quiet, as she made her way back into the busy town towards McDonald's.

Two hours in Niamh's house went past in the blink of an eye. Jane had laughed so hard her ribs had hurt at some of the costumes they had found from their childhood, and the masks made from hard plastic with an elastic band at the back. The edges were so fine it wouldn't have been hard to cut your face with one.

Niamh's bedroom was huge in comparison to anything Jane had ever seen before, but it was inviting. The white double bedframe and pink bedding didn't seem like anything Niamh would've chose for herself, though, and the white dressing table and huge mirror looked like it belonged to someone else, too. The only part of the room that seemed to bear Niamh's mark was the desk next to the wardrobe which had Trolls lined up at the back, each with a different hair colour and expression. A poster of the Spice Girls adorned the wall behind. Jane thought was the only corner of the room where Niamh had free expression.

"I think we've found the one!" Ruby said, clapping her hands as Jane stepped out of the bathroom. She was wearing a black all-in-one jumpsuit with a long black tail hanging from the rear. A hair band with two cat ears finished off the costume.

"Is it not a bit tight?" Jane asked as she ran her hands down her abdomen.

"It's meant to be tight, you look class!" Niamh replied as she rummaged through the dressing table drawer for some lipstick. Ruby was drawing on a black nose and whiskers with her eyeliner.

"I wish I had boobs like yours," Ruby laughed suddenly, cupping her breasts with her hands before the mirror. "I have two backs. I don't think mine will ever grow. Yours are huge. It's not fair!"

Jane flushed when she stood in front of the full-length mirror. The jumpsuit clung to every inch of her body and accentuated her newly formed curves, ones she hadn't paid much attention to before. Niamh applied bright pink lipstick to finish her costume. Jane was pleased to see you looked older.

"Thanks so much guys!" Jane said. "I better go. I'm really nervous!" She grabbed her bag and stuffed her normal clothes into it, rushing out the door while looking at her watch.

Jane was met by whistles from the regulars when she walked into The Hive. She saw her mother at the bar, hunched over beneath a plastic witch's hat, a cigarette hanging from her mouth. The whistles drew her attention as well as Darren's and they both looked towards Jane at the same time.

Darren grinned as he called over, "Meee-ow!"

But her mother's expression was a different one, one she had never seen before, and she instantly knew that her reaction wasn't going to be a good one.

"What the fuck are you supposed to be and where did you get that?" she spat as she looked her daughter up and down.

"It was Ruby's from last year," she replied quietly, hoping that would be the end of the conversation, but knowing it wasn't as she slid in behind the bar beside Darren, who was still looking her up and down.

"You look great," he said. He suddenly seemed unsure whether or not he should be looking at her at all, and turned to the customer waiting to be served.

Jane cleared empty glasses from the tables, the jumpsuit helping her move with ease between each table and customer, sometimes placing her hand on someone's back as she leaned in to pick up and empty glass. Throughout the evening, she could feel her mother's eyes boring into her, and she tried to not make eye contact. With each vodka she drank, she would sigh a little louder. If someone paid Jane a compliment, she'd mutter to herself; Jane could feel the venom from across the room.

As the last person left to go to the club, the only person left sitting at the bar was Jane's mother. She had drunk over a half bottle of vodka, but she seemed to kept upright by pure spite. As Jane wiped down the last table and Darren left to clean the toilets, she heard her mother's words.

"Bitch."

Jane swung around and looked at her mother, wringing the cloth in her hands.

"Mam? What's wrong?"

"You. Wearing that."

Jane's heart raced as she stood looking at her mother, who stared at her with a look Jane couldn't fathom. It still scared her, not knowing exactly what her mother was feeling.

"You... don't like it?" Jane asked quietly.

"Parading around the pub looking like that. Showing me up!"

When the cloth dripped onto the floor, Jane realised she was wringing it harder and harder; she tried to comprehend what she had done wrong, what crime against her mother she was guilty of, as her bladder felt close to exploding within her body.

"Mam, I don't know what you mean. Did... did I do something wrong?" Her mother stepped down off the barstool and took a few steps towards Jane, her eyes unfocused and full of rage. She swiped the cat ears off Jane's head and threw them nm the ground.

"Showing me up!" she repeated, her voice raised now. Jane stepped back just as her mother lifted her hand and Darren stepped out of the toilets, a toilet brush in one hand and cleaning spray in the other. Without saying a word, he quickly moved to step in between Jane and her mother, waving the wet toilet brush in her mother's face.

"What is wrong with you? Go home! If you make one move towards her or say one more word I'll bar you and I'll make sure you're barred from every pub in town! Do you understand?"

Jane's mother muttered under her breath as she grabbed her bag and her jacket and stumbled out the door. Darren locked it behind her. He looked to Jane, who was still standing in the same spot, looking confused.

"You okay?" he asked, going behind the bar to grab two Cokes. He filled up two glasses with ice and lemon but quickly took the lemon out, remembering Jane thought they ruined the taste of the Coke.

"I don't even know what that was," she said when she eventually sat down.

"It's a thing you have to watch out for, Jane. Jealousy. Every compliment you got fuelled her anger more. You're welcome to sleep on my couch tonight if you don't want to go home."

"No, she'll be asleep soon, and I'll sneak in and go straight to bed. I just don't understand. I didn't do anything."

"Jane... you're gorgeous and it's killing her." He picked up her cat ears from the floor and gently placed them back on her head, his brown eyes shone and her heart skipped a beat. He leaned over and kissed her on the cheek, just like Peter used to. She missed her brother.

# Chapter Twenty-One

THE RIVER DIDN'T HOLD the same peace for Jane she had felt sitting by the old bridge. The noise of the town travelled in and started to clutter her mind. She didn't feel the same comfort from her friends that she felt when Stephen sat beside her in silence, and she found herself pining. She adored her friends but something was missing and she felt it deep within.

She watched a fisherman sit patiently on the opposite bank with a rod in hand, wondering how he could quiet his mind enough to sit for so long, waiting for a trout to take a bite. She envied the purpose he seemed to have as she twirled her school jumper between her fingers. The fabric was getting worn, a small hole appearing where her thumb constantly caught it, and she unconsciously moved her hand to another part of her jumper.

Two birds caught her eye and she watched as they swooped to feed on insects from the water, the fisherman letting out a frustrated sigh as their presence scared the fish away. They looked like swallows, with their long tails streaming behind them, but their red faces told her otherwise and she longed for Stephen to break the silence by naming them.

She looked to her right, the side he used to sit, and half-hoped to see a pair of shiny shoes. The sound of footsteps crunching on dry leaves made her heart sink - though she was lonely she wanted to be alone - and she turned to see Connor stepping in.

"Did you mitch today?" he asked as he stepped under a low branch.

"No, I was in school. I just didn't go back after lunch."

"So, you mitched?"

"I suppose I did. Anyway, I was just about to leave. I don't think the others are coming today?" Jane asked, hoping she could just go. She'd feel guilty leaving him on his own, but she didn't want company.

"Jane, what's wrong? The girls said you were quiet in school today. Is everything alright?"

"Nothing is wrong. I'm just tired, that's all, and wasn't bothered going back after lunch. I promise. But I'm going home now. It's getting dark and I think I'll just eat and go to bed."

"Okay," said Connor. "But can I walk with you?"

"Sure," Jane shrugged.

Jane parted the bushes so gently it almost seemed as if she just appeared in the spot opposite them, whereas Connor made so much noise and grunted with every move she thought he'd uproot something. Her frustration grew slightly. *Leave no trace*, she thought to herself, and knew that soon enough, with him trampling in and out in that manner, a gap would form in the bushes, making their private little spot not so private anymore. She decided to look for another way in the next time she was down.

They made their way over a little stone bridge and out onto the street where it seemed brighter and instantly louder as they walked towards the town in silence. Every so often, Connor would glance down at Jane with a worried look on his face. He had never seen her so downcast. Jane could sense him looking at her, but she kept her head lowered and watched their feet walk in unison.

The darker evenings seemed to draw a different type of crowd into the town. These people were more subdued than those making their way to the beer gardens, and more focused as they went about their late-night shopping. There were very few small children in tow and Jane wondered if the bustling women were busy mothers trying to get some Christmas shopping in while their boys and girls lay warm in their beds.

Although there wasn't as much noise and chatter as there was on summer nights, Jane could still feel the business in the air, and she stopped looking at her feet and began people watching.

When they got to the entrance to the alley down where Jane's front door was, she noticed something hanging outside the garden shop on the main street and turned to face it.

"Come with me for a minute," she said to Connor as she began to walk ahead. He shrugged his shoulders and caught up to her with a couple of long strides, bumping into her as she came to an abrupt halt outside the garden shop. Jane looked at the metal cylinder with a yellow lid on top with her head titled. The yellow lid had imprints of birds pressed into it and a hook at the top. She picked it up and held it over her head by the hook, looking to see how the lid opened.

"A bird feeder," Connor said. "My mam has a few around the back garden." He wondered why Jane was taking such an interest.

"I thought that's what it was alright," she replied, still looking up at the lid.

231

AMANDA GILSENAN

"Have you never had one?" he asked. Jane stood up straight, focused on Connor properly for the first time that day and smiled.

"I lived in the countryside," she said. "I didn't need bird feeders to attract them because they were already there. I lived amongst them. There were swallows and thrushes... and magpies, they were my favourite! We even had a little robin that hung around all year round. You know they are very clever, especially crows, but I don't love them. I mean I don't mind them, but magpies and the smaller ones are my favourites. I used to watch them all day long."

Jane's eyes were glowing as she spoke, and her face lit up as she recollected sitting in the sun, watching the swallows fly in and out of the gable end of the bungalow where the pointing and tiles needed to be replaced.

"Did you learn the names of them in school?" Connor asked, happy to see Jane coming back to herself.

"No. Stephen was teaching me. He was teaching me about plants and flowers too. I had a lovely garden thanks to him," she replied.

"Do you still get to visit Stephen?" Connor asked, sensing the change in tone to her voice as she moved back to looking at the bird feeder.

"No. He died after my Communion. He had an accident and didn't make it. I miss him so much some days it hurts."

"Aw, Jane I didn't know, sorry," Connor said, putting his arm around Jane's shoulder. She wasn't sure she wanted that and immediately stepped forward to hang the bird feeder back, removing herself from his arm.

"It sounds like you prefer being in the country?" Connor asked as they walked back up the street.

"Yeah, I loved it, but the town has good parts too. I'm close to all of yous," she said as she playfully shouldered him.

Connor threw his arm around her shoulder again and pulled her in for a hug once she reached the alley. Some days she ached for physical affection, a hug just like she was getting now, but she noticed that when she did it felt so unfamiliar and strange to her that she almost didn't know what to do. How long should she hug for, should she be the first to break away? She didn't even hug Ruby or Niamh. She closed her eyes tightly and pulled away.

"It's nice to get to know you a bit better, Jane. Go to school tomorrow, the girls missed ya."

"Even Niamh?" she asked.

"Ah, pass no heed to her. She gets like that with everyone. She's insecure as fuck and she can't help herself sometimes. It's no excuse to be a bitch, but ignore her when she gets like that. The sarcastic side is a cover, Jane, that's all."

"Yeah, maybe you're right. I might see ya tomorrow. Thanks Connor," Jane said as she turned to walk towards her door. She reached into her skirt pocket for her bunch of keys and realised Connor wasn't all he seemed, either. He was far more mature than he allowed himself to be around the other lads and seemed to read people well.

But she started to worry about what she had told him. She took the steps slowly and tried to pull her thoughts away from her friends talking about her and thinking she was the sad little country girl and began to wonder what kind of mood was behind the door.

The door was locked, and Jane fumbled in her pocket for her keys again; the top one was never locked when her mother was home, which she should've been by this time. As she opened the door and stepped inside she knew her mother hadn't been home since she left that morning. There was no lingering smell of smoke, or empty glasses by the sink, and the curtains weren't pulled over. The room, lit by street lights, had a very empty feel to it.

Jane wanted to enjoy the moments there by herself, but she worried about her mother. She took a deep breath as she walked over to the windows and pulled the thick, heavy, green curtains closed.

A layer of fine dust came off them followed by a stale musty smell and she wished she could take them down and wash them, but she knew they'd never fit in the washing machine and the pelmet that bordered the top would've been off-colour if she did.

Her thoughts were jumbled as she walked towards her mother's room and opened the door slightly. She knew it was empty, but was so surprised to see the bed made and the room tidy that she took a step inside. It was like a different room. The ashtray beside the bed wasn't overflowing, there were no empty glasses lying about, and it smelled fresh and clean.

The window was open at the top, and Jane walked over and looked out. The light from the skylight of the pub below shone green from the colour of the glass. It looked wrong to her and she looked up towards the dark sky and squinted in the hope of seeing a star or two. She could hear the mutter of people downstairs and she wondered if her mother was there.

The silence in the flat left Jane feeling odd; there was often silence, but there was always a presence, and she turned on the CD player in her room to drown out this particular quiet. Nirvana played as she took her uniform off, throwing it in a corner and picking up her pyjama bottoms but she felt uneasy and couldn't understand why. She had been alone many times before, but tonight felt different.

She grabbed her beloved Adidas tracksuit bottoms and slid them on. She didn't feel the need to wear shorts under them on this occasion, none of her friends being around to rip open the buttons which ran down the side, and she pulled on a grey hoodie before slipping the call card from Peter into her pocket.

# Chapter Twenty-Two

BACK ON THE STREET, the uneasy feeling began to slightly dissipate and she crossed street to the phone box. The smell of urine hit her as she stepped in and she tried to not hold the receiver too close to her face as she inserted the card and dialled Peter's house number.

"Hello?" Peter answered instantly.

"Jesus, it hardly rang, Peter! Were you sitting on top of the phone?"

"Not really. Is everything alright? You never normally ring at this time, or any time lately. What did she do?"

Jane sighed and wanted to hang up the phone and go back into her room and listen to music and enjoy the rare peace, but instead took a deep breathe before replying, "She hasn't done anything. She's just not here and looks as if she hasn't been all day. I've no clue where she is. The Hive isn't open tonight so she's not there. Will you help me look for her? I'm worried." Peter sighed down the receiver and before he got a chance to reply, Jane spoke again. "Its fine. Don't bother. I shouldn't have asked. I'll find her myself."

"Wait!" Peter said quickly. "I'll be there in five minutes. Go back upstairs. I'll be there in five minutes."

"I'll leave the bottom door unlocked," Jane said and hung up the phone.

She pulled the call card out and stepped outside as quick as she could, deeply inhaling the damp night air, trying to get the foul smell from her nostrils. She remembered Darren telling her if she blew her nose it'd release the odours trapped in the small hairs, removing it from her nostrils, but she had no tissues.

When Peter walked in the door, Jane burst into tears. She was relieved to see him and felt overwhelmed. She didn't move from the armchair, just wiped the tears from her eyes.

"Jesus, I don't know what's wrong with me today. I don't normally mind being alone. I just, I don't, I don't want to be here when she comes home. Not tonight. Just for tonight. I'm so tired Peter. I'm just tired."

The tears that fell down Jane's cheeks were silent but plentiful, and Peter knelt down in front of her.

"Go to your room, grab your pjs and whatever else you need. I'm not taking no for an answer on this, grab your things. You're staying with me tonight."

Jane nodded her head and went to her room.

Peter straightened his back and looked at the porcelain masks hung over the fireplace. Three painted white faces with black eyes and ribbons hanging from them. They seemed pointless and dead as he tilted his head to look for signs of life. He paced over to the window, held one of the curtains aside and looked out.

The wide sill made it a perfect seat to people watch or sit and read. When he looked up and saw the yellow stains on the top of the window, he knew Jane wasn't the one who sat here. He wondered what his mother thought as she sat on the windowsill, looking down at the street. He wondered if she thought of him.

"Right. I think I'm ready. I'll leave a note for her and let her know where I am," Jane said, interrupting his thoughts.

"It'd be fucking nice if she gave you the same respect!" Peter replied, suddenly feeling the familiar anger towards their mother. Jane sighed, remembering why she hated asking Peter for help. His view of things was always clouded by his own emotions and though she knew his concern for her was coming from a good place, he could be selfish in his delivery. She felt tired of always trying to calm him down.

"Can we not do this anymore? The bit where you get pissed off and I try to tell you it's okay and calm you down? I'm sick of eggshells. I'm always treading, Peter, and some days I just want to walk."

"I'm sorry," he said, smiling. "I suppose I'm as bad as her in a way. I'm sorry. Let's go home."

Jane slid into the passenger seat of Peter's now old and battered Renault Clio and rested her bag at her feet. She smiled, remembering the bags of chips eaten in that very seat. They drove in silence through the town until they arrived at the housing estate on the outskirts.

"God, I didn't realise you lived so close to Ruby."

"Who's Ruby?"

"She's one of my best friends."

As the car pulled in the driveway, Peter realised he knew nothing about the teenager sitting beside him, and he felt a pang of sadness and guilt considering he once knew her every move.

Jane looked out into the front garden; even in the dark, she could see colours of autumn shrubs and flowers coming into bloom. Without a word she stepped out and over onto the neat grass. The garden was small compared to the one she used to tend, but it was beautifully kept. The buddleia bush in the corner, days away from going dormant for the winter, made her smile. She turned around to see Peter leaning over the roof of the car, watching her.

"Do you approve?" he asked, smiling.

"Well, it's beautiful, Peter. Really gorgeous. Is this your handiwork?"

"You know Jane, most things I do are with you in mind. I just wish you'd call more. I could do with a hand with the back garden in the spring." He unlocked the front door, nodding at her to go in.

Stepping inside, Jane was immediately hit with a smell of vanilla from a candle burning on the hall table, under a matching white mirror. The carpet in the hallway led up the stairs. It was high piled and gave the feeling of warmth; Jane could feel her body relaxing until another smell hit her and her stomach started to loudly rumble. Cottage pie. It was unmistakeable and smelled exactly like the one Stephen used to drop down to them, a favourite of Peter's.

"I'm in here!" Lucy shouted from the kitchen.

Jane followed Peter up the hall and into the kitchen, passing the sitting room on the left and a small bathroom nestled in under the stairs on the right. On the walls were framed photos of her and Peter and some with Lucy and Peter together. It felt like a home.

"It took years to perfect this, Jane," said Lucy. "I hope you're hungry!"

"I didn't think I was but I'm starving. I haven't had cottage pie in years. Thanks, Lucy. I hope you didn't go to this trouble for me?"

"It's nice to have us all together. Sit," Lucy said, gesturing to one of the chairs. The kitchen was big, but it was homely and warm and it was one of the cleanest kitchens Jane had ever seen in her life. There wasn't a thing out of place except for what Lucy had used to cook dinner and she watched as Peter moved to start cleaning and tidying the work-top. He filled the sink and started washing up the utensils and pots that Lucy had used as she finished dishing up the massive meal onto plates.

As they ate and reminisced about trips to the chippers and to the inland lighthouse around the kitchen table, Jane couldn't help but notice Peter cleaning and tidying everything as soon as they were finished before rejoining them again. She could see him trying to control the need but failing and watched him every time he got up, but Lucy managed to distract her with questions.

"Any boyfriends, Jane?"

"Lucy!" Peter gasped. "She's far too young to have a boyfriend. Jesus Christ."

Both Lucy and Jane looked at Peter with smiles on their faces. "What age were we when we started going out, Peter?"

"That's different," Peter said as his face flushed. He left the kitchen for the bathroom.

"How is he, Lucy, really? What's with the cleaning?" Jane asked.

"Oh. He's always been like that Jane. Sometimes it's worse than others. It gets worse when he's worried about you, actually. It's under control at the moment, but some days it's really bad. This is a good day."

"I had no idea. I don't know what to say," Jane replied. It felt as if another weight had just been dropped on her head, and this one was heavier than the last.

"Just call him more. Call over more. I know you're looking after your mam but he has suffered too, and he absolutely adores you, Jane."

Peter walked back in and smiled at the two girls sitting at the table. He struggled to see Jane as anything but the little girl asleep on his shoulder, but appreciated she was now a teenager.

"Lucy, it's midnight," he said, looking at the clock over the window. "I think it's time to give Janey her birthday present?"

Jane burst into tears and put her head in her hands at the kitchen table. Peter quickly sat beside her and put his hand on the back of her neck, rubbing it with his thumb. He could feel the ball of tension sitting under the skin and he knew she was at her breaking point.

"What's wrong?"

"I thought everyone had forgotten. I know mam has. I thought she'd be home," Jane sobbed while letting her head rest on Peter's shoulder.

"Right," Peter replied. "Tonight you don't think about her. We're taking tonight and tomorrow to celebrate you turning fifteen and we'll enjoy it. We'll deal with Mam after, and I bet she hasn't forgot." He rose from the chair and pulled Jane up to standing position with him.

"Your present is on your bed. Come on," he said, guiding her up the stairs.

The second of the three bedrooms was one Jane had slept in before, on an air mattress that had deflated all throughout the night, and Jane had avoided any more nights like that because it hurt her back. But when Lucy opened the door, Jane was greeted to a freshly decorated room with a wooden double bed in the middle. It was covered with a thick duvet with a crisp white cover, and it reminded Jane of one of the beds on display in the fancy furniture shops.

To the left of the bed was a small dressing table and mirror with a stool; on top sat a small, neatly wrapped gift. There were matching lamps on either side of the bed, giving off a warm glow that made it look like the most inviting, warm, cosy bedroom she had ever seen. She truly couldn't wait to get into bed. Jane squeezed Peter's hand as she stood at the door, taking it all in, and couldn't muster a word as the lump of emotions in her throat grew.

"I... is this...?"

"Sweetie, this is your room," Lucy said. "You are welcome here any time. So are your friends. I know you feel obliged to mind your Mam but you need an escape too. This is it." She grabbed Jane by the hand and led her into the bedroom. She opened the drawer of the dresser and showed her some fancy toiletries she had put inside before they both sat on the bed.

"We're forgetting something," Peter said as he picked up the gift and handed it to Jane. "Happy birthday, Janey," he said and kissed her on the forehead.

"The room was enough," Jane said through tears. "You didn't have to do all of this for me. I'm so grateful. Thank you."

She carefully began to unwrap the gift. She gasped and then jumped up and threw her arms around Peter's neck when she saw the brand-new silver Motorola phone. She then turned to Lucy and did the same.

"Oh my god! I can't wait to ring Ruby and Niamh! I can't wait to use it! Thank you both, so so much. This is too much, but thank you." Jane couldn't stop smiling at the box.

"Well, you're not calling anyone at half one in the morning, so plug it into the charger and it'll be all ready for morning," Peter said. "I've taken the day off, we'll spend it together. I know you're working hard at school so one day off won't kill you. We'll have a great day."

They exchanged hugs and Lucy closed the door with a smile on her face.

Jane put on her pyjamas in record time, and smiled as she watched her new phone light up. She switched off the lamps and slid into the most comfortable bed she'd ever lay in. It had no springs sticking up, no musty smell, and her body sunk into the soft yet firm mattress. As she drifted off into the longest and best sleep she ever had, she decided not to tell Peter about her struggles with maths.

# Chapter Twenty-Three

THE MORNING SUN HADN'T fully risen. The warm glow spreading across the horizon didn't bring a whole lot of light to the sky, but the streetlamps on the quiet street were switching off with an audible click as Peter stood at the top of the dark alley.

The bins at the other end were overflowing, and the smell of days-old rubbish and stale beer from the bottle bin made his empty stomach heave. But he took a deep breath, held his shoulders back, and walked towards the door, right down the middle of the alley. He was holding a pink and gold gift bag close to his chest, not wanting to near the urine-soaked walls, and he hoped the comfort of a new bed and freshly decorated bedroom would win Jane over. She didn't belong here.

Peter fumbled through his sister's keys, trying three in the lock. He felt his hands shake and heart race faster the closer he stood to the rubbish. The third key unlocked the door, but it wouldn't budge even when he put his weight against it. A small, green Heineken bottle crate sat at the side of the door, and he rested the gift bag on it to use both of his hands to push the door. Still it wouldn't budge.

"Fuck's sake!" he said out loud as he took a step back and ran towards the door to push against it harder. As he did, he noticed a small brass yale lock positioned high up on the door, and he smiled; the crate was for Jane to stand on to reach it. He put in the matching key, opened it, and made his way up the stairs.

The anxiety he felt standing next to the dirty bins was being replaced with anger with every step he ascended, and he played an imaginary conversation in his head for those few seconds until he felt as if his blood was running hot through his veins and fire was burning in his stomach.

He didn't fumble with the keys at the top door; he unlocked it quickly and stepped in, looking around the corner to be greeted by his mother sitting at the kitchen table cradling a cup of tea and smoking a cigarette.

"Do you know what day today is?" Peter asked.

"Tuesday, and how the fuck did you get in?"

"Its Jane's birthday! Jesus Christ. Did you even wonder where she was last night?"

A look of confusion quickly swept over his mother's face, followed by a smirk so minute Peter missed it in his anger.

"I just thought she had stayed the night with Darren," she said, picking up her mug and taking a sip out of it but never taking her eyes off Peter.

"No, she stayed with me. She stayed with me because you didn't come home. Why would she stay with Darren... isn't he like twenty-two?" Peter asked, his anger quickly dissolving into confusion.

"I dunno. They get on very well in work, always eyeballing each other. Anyway, she stayed with you? Right. Grand. Nice birthday treat for her. She'll be home tonight, I take it?"

"Hopefully not. I want her to stay with me. She's had enough of your poison over the last fifteen years and the fact that you've forgotten her birthday again is just sickening."

"Excuse me! Peter, I'm a single mother. I can't afford these things. It's alright for you, you don't have a child to look after. And anyway, Jane is happy with her lot."

"I'm not getting into your 'woe is me' act because I don't have the time or the patience for it. As you're so broke I'm assuming you didn't get your daughter a birthday present, so here. And for the record, just because she doesn't require a lot to be happy doesn't mean she deserves the bare minimum," Peter said, placing the gift bag on the table on front of her. "You can pretend yet again that you actually give a shit about her." He turned to leave.

"Where do you get off talking to me like that?" she replied. "You turned out alright!"

Peter wanted to turn around and smack her, shake her, scream in her face that there were days where he felt far from alright, days where his thoughts got so out of control that they seemed to take over his physical being. There were days where he couldn't think straight.

"Please just give that to Jane. I won't say anything. You can take the credit, just like you did for her Communion and every other birthday. I don't care, as long as she's happy. She'll know in time what you're really like without my interference."

Peter's hands firmly gripped the steering wheel and he let out a loud guttural scream as his knuckles turned white and his body convulsed. The days where his hatred for his mother took over were now few and far between, but when it did happen there was no stopping it. He kept it at bay by running; when he ran it never bubbled over. He took a deep breath and looked down at his runners and then checked his watch; he had just enough time.

The street was still empty, just how he liked it, but he didn't care if he had to trample over hordes of people to get the anger and frustration out through his feet. The slow pace didn't feel enough, and he wanted to stamp his feet like a child during a tantrum, so he sped up. A name started pushing its way into his thoughts until it was all he could think about.

*Darren. Darren. Darren.*

The name and the anxiety grew and rang with every step he took. Who was this guy, really? Jane knew nothing about him, only what he had told her and who knew if any of it was true? He knew Jane was soft, she saw the best in people and gave far too many chances to those who didn't deserve it. He wondered how she kept going. How did she manage to find so much trust to give people when she had been hurt so many times?

He decided on a loop around the small town that would bring him back to the car. He had all but forgotten about his mother, now worried about his sister and her crush on an older man. Maybe there was nothing to it, but he needed to find out.

He drove home past weary-looking commuters waiting at bus stops, stifling yawns in silence. There was no chitter chatter from anyone as people kept their distance from each other, some with newspapers or books and others just staring off into space. The cool autumn air felt refreshing as it came in the car window and Peter felt goosebumps erupt onto his skin. He liked the frosty mornings; the thought of the ice killing all the germs made him feel more at ease and he seemed to come to life more in the wintertime.

There was no fumbling with keys at his own front door, and even after years of not living at home he still closed his eyes, inhaled through his nose and smiled, knowing there would be no tension or bad atmosphere. He dropped his keys on the hall table and called out for Lucy.

"Shhhhh," she replied from the sitting room.

Peter stuck his head in the door and smiled at Lucy; even in her pyjamas she was the prettiest girl he had ever seen in his life.

"Is Jane still asleep?" he asked as he sat down beside her on the couch.

"Yeah, that's why I didn't start making breakfast. She obviously needs it. Did you see your mam?"

"Yeah. I don't know how Jane tolerates her. She's a selfish bitch. She did say something strange though. She said she thought Jane stayed with Darren last night. They're hardly... you know? Surely not?" Peter asked. Lucy's worried expression made him worry more as he realised he wasn't overreacting. It also made him relax a bit, for the same reason: he didn't feel crazy.

"Do you want me to talk to her? I don't want to overstep but I will if you want?" Lucy replied, resting her head on his shoulder.

"You're not overstepping. I'd be so grateful. It's very hard to talk to your older brother about boys. Or men, in this case. God, I hope she's wrong." Peter rested his head on hers.

"You're a great brother Peter. I'm sure it's nothing. You know what your mother is like."

The smell of cooking slowly started to creep under Jane's bedroom door. As she lay half asleep, her stomach began to sing a similar tune to the one her bladder had been crooning for a half hour or more, and she finally sat up in the bed and let her feet touch the floor. In her haste to get into her pyjamas at bedtime, she hadn't notice the fake sheepskin rug under her feet, and she looked down and let her toes curl around the pile.

There were new levels of comfort here she had never experienced before, and she didn't want to leave the bedroom. She stretched as she walked towards the door and felt her feet go from the mat to the carpet and onto the lino of the bathroom. She felt comfortable in her surroundings, but it still didn't feel like home. It was missing something, and she couldn't figure out what it was as she stared at her reflection in the mirror.

Some days she felt so out of place that it was as if she had been dropped right in the middle of someone else's life. She often wondered if she would always feel that way. The Hive felt more like a home to her than most places, but even at her young age she knew that wasn't normal. Her thoughts were interrupted by the smell of sausages and bacon cooking downstairs and her mouth began to water.

The banister felt smooth under her hand. With each step she took, her feet felt as if they were experiencing freedom for the first time since she moved into the town, and it felt as if her toes were wiggling all on their own. Being barefoot in the river or on the grass was always a pleasant experience, but lately she was even wearing socks to bed. The feel of the sticky stains on the carpet at home was unbearable to her so she was very rarely without socks and shoes.

"Here's the birthday girl!" Peter said when she walked into the kitchen. He wrapped his arms around her. Jane closed her eyes and let the feeling envelope her. The smell of breakfast cooking was now lost as the scent of shower gel and deodorant invaded her nostrils. It was different, it was like smelling a different man, but underneath it all Peter was still there and she squeezed tighter.

"How did you sleep?" Lucy asked as she started dishing up breakfast.

"Oh God, like a baby. I think it's the best night's sleep I ever had. Thank you. Em, did Mam ring?" she asked, looking to Peter.

"Jane, she doesn't know where I live, let alone my phone number, but I was out for a run this morning and the lights were on. She's home."

Jane immediately relaxed and sat down at the kitchen table. Lucy placed a full Irish breakfast in front of her. In the middle of the table was a big silver pot of tea neatly sitting on a cast iron coaster beside a side plate filled with homemade brown bread.

Condensation filled up the window and when Peter opened it a crack, Jane felt the cool autumn air around her neck. It was brighter than it usually was when she got up for school, but the day looked dark and dull. There was a warmth in the house that she didn't feel in the flat, that she had never felt it in the bungalow either for that matter. But she had felt it with Stephen. It was a warmth that she felt from the inside out and she closed her eyes and let herself feel it.

"This looks lovely, Lucy. You sure are spoiled, Peter!" Jane said as she started cutting into a sausage.

"Excuse me, but I helped! I'm not useless!" he replied through a mouthful of sausage.

Jane looked at the white pudding and cut a sliver off it and delicately put it into her mouth. When the salty, savoury flavour hit her tongue it was followed by an eye-widening, "Mmmm, this is delicious!"

But the gritty, strong-tasting black pudding wasn't to her liking. She didn't utter another word as she ate her breakfast, occasionally looking up from her plate to smile at Peter and Lucy who were eating what looked to be the most satisfying meal they had ever eaten. When she was finished, she sat back on the chair and rubbed her stomach.

"That was the nicest breakfast I've ever had in my life. I won't need to eat until tomorrow!" she declared happily. She looked up at the clock. "I take it I'm not going to school then? I've already missed English and geography. I'd be half way through maths by now."

"How is school going anyway, Janey?" Peter asked as he poured tea into the mugs. Jane regretted even mentioning school and sighed. "What subjects are you doing the best in, and are you struggling with any?"

"Well. I love history. My last essay I got a B, but I like the way Mr. Desmond teaches. It's different, but I seem to learn easier. I don't like maths, Peter. I just don't."

"You can't like everything and I'm sure you're doing great," Lucy assured her before taking a loud sip of her tea.

"No," said Peter, "but if she needs help then I can organise grinds or something. It's no big deal."

"Yeah, but other things are important too, Peter, not just results. Did you ask her if she likes school, about her friends? It's not just about results."

"Yes it is, Lucy. It is if she's not going to end up like our mother, working dead end jobs and drinking herself to death then it is important!" Peter answered in a slightly raised voice.

Jane put her face in her hands and closed her eyes. A tension had begun to fill the room, not as bad as the one her mother created, but enough for the knot in her stomach to return.

"Will yous please stop talking about me like I'm not here?" she said, not removing her face from her hands. "School is fine. I have friends. Life is great. Drop it, please!"

Peter and Lucy exchanged glances and both of them moved their chairs either side of Jane and sat in close.

"How are you feeling, Jane? Really?" Peter asked.

Jane felt like the walls were beginning to close in on her; she felt trapped. She was caught in a conversation that she didn't want to have and there was no way out.

"I'm fine. I'm really, really fine. I'm just tired. Please stop questioning me all the time. I have nowhere I can breathe, can I just breath here please?"

When she lifted her face from her hands her face was wet with tears. Peter put his arm around her shoulder and pulled her in close.

"I'm sorry, Janey. I didn't mean to put you under more pressure than you already are. Can I ask the question once more though?"

Jane started to laugh. She knew Peter meant no harm and only wanted the best for her, but she did feel under pressure. Some days her brain felt as if it was going to explode.

"No, I'm not moving in," she said. "But, I will stay more often if I get a breakfast like that and the odd day off school!"

"No chance of another day off! But that breakfast will be on the table for you every time you stay. Will you stay tonight?"

"Ah, I'll have to head back to the flat at some stage. I'll hang around for a while though," she said as she finished her tea and stood up to start clearing the plates off the table.

"It's fine Janey, I have a system. I'll do it," Peter said quickly.

Jane looked to Lucy who rolled her eyes. "He really does have a system. Leave him at it. Come on, we'll go into the sitting room."

Jane watched as Lucy grabbed two cans of Coke from the fridge and walked into the sitting room. Peter was already in a little world of his own, but he seemed happy in it no matter how odd it seemed to her. She watched as he washed the heavy pots and pans first and then drained the sink. He used fresh water for each different item of kitchenware and scrubbed and wiped and rinsed each item before placing it on a draining board. She closed the door behind her and he looked back with a smile, peering out from whatever world he was in for a brief moment before he was pulled back in.

Lucy was curled up on the couch with a can of Coke in her hand and another on the cushion beside her when Jane walked in. She lifted up the Coke and stretched her arm out to Jane, offering it to her.

"Thanks. I'm thirsty after the breakfast," Jane said, taking the can and sitting on the arm chair opposite.

"Yeah, the salty pudding would do that. How's work going?" Lucy asked.

"Yeah, really good. I love it there. It's good craic and the money is handy." Jane took two big mouthfuls of Coke and smiled at Lucy. "Go on," she said. "There's more. What does Peter want you to ask me?"

Lucy started to laugh. "Am I that obvious? Ah look, we were just wondering about Darren, that's all."

"What about him?" Jane asked, but she could feel her face blushing. Straight away knew she was giving away more than she wanted to without uttering a word.

"Is there something going on between you two? Look, you can tell me. I don't actually tell Peter everything, because... well, you can see how he is when he gets anxious, but I'll help you in any way I can, Jane," Lucy said, unfolding her legs from under her and resting her elbows on her knees. She had lowered her voice not quite to a whisper, but enough so Peter wouldn't hear from the kitchen.

"No! God no! We're just friends, that's all, we work together. I think I've seen him outside work a handful of times. Where is this coming from?" Jane asked.

"Alright," said Lucy. "That's fine, I'm just concerned, that's all. Do you like him though?"

"Fuck's sake! The whole point of being friends with someone is actually liking them. Lucy, he's looked after me when mam was... in a bad mood. I promise, that's all."

"You know what I mean! Relax Jane, I'm only trying to get to know you."

"I'm going up to get dressed," Jane said, standing up and walking to the door. As she walked up the stairs, her feet hit each step angrily. She went into her room and closed the door behind her, letting out a sigh as she walked over to the window and opened the curtains. She was so used to being independent when she was with her mother that it was hard to adjust to being the little girl she'd always be in Peter's eyes.

The day was dull and damp, making the bright splashes of colour in the garden stand out. Jane was impressed with Peter's placing of all the shrubs and flowers; he'd remembered that particular ones needed shade and some preferred sun. They were perfectly placed with the same amount of space between them and there wasn't a weed in sight. She thought that daffodils and tulips would look lovely in the spring time, coming up between the shrubs, but she knew Peter probably had another system for the garden as well as the inside of the house.

She turned to make her bed and sat on the side of it and picked up her new phone, turning it on. She smiled when the welcome message appeared on the screen and winced slightly at the loud sound it made. The box had an instruction manual and her new phone number printed on the side, along with a PIN and ten pound welcome credit.

She had no idea how much credit she'd need or how much phone calls cost but she felt like she had won the lotto as she lay back on the bed and read the instructions. It was simple enough to use and she got the hang of it very quickly, inputting Peter's number first because it was the only one she could remember by heart. Her friends' numbers were written in a little address book in her dresser at home.

She dressed quickly and packed everything into her bag, ready to go back to the flat. Not knowing how her mother was going to react to her staying the night with Peter had her feeling unable to relax, and she needed to know one way or another. But she would make sure to apologise to Lucy before she left. It was bad enough wondering what kind of mood her mother was going to be in without worrying about Lucy, too. She knew she didn't mean anything by her questions... Jane just wasn't used to someone caring.

# Chapter Twenty-Four

As soon as Jane got to the bottom of the stairs, she knew her mother was home. She couldn't explain how she knew; it wasn't hearing footsteps or movement, she could just sense her presence. It was heavy and thick and never pleasant, but it was still her mother, and she was relieved to know she was home, regardless of the mood that came with it.

"Did you have a good time in Peter's?" her mother asked from her spot at the kitchen table as Jane opened the front door. Her usual glass was replaced by a mug, but Jane wasn't sure if there was tea in it or something else as she dropped her bag and shook off her jacket.

"Yeah, it was nice for a change," Jane said, not wanting to give too much away until she knew what kind of humour her mother was in.

"There's something for you there on the couch," her mother said, nodding back towards the faded fabric sofa. Jane hated the old piece of furniture, it smelled musty and looked dirty and wasn't very comfortable unless she brought all her pillows from her bedroom to cushion the wooden armrest.

Jane's eyes lit up. She moved over to the couch and sat down beside the gift bag, marvelling at how expensive that alone must have been. She opened it up to see a black handbag sitting inside it. The front had purple butterflies embroidered into it and the back was plain. It had two short straps and was designed to be hung over the shoulder.

"I love it Mam, thanks so much!" Jane said, getting up to put her arms around her mother, who didn't move from the position she was in to reciprocate. She sat with her legs still crossed and her hands still on the mug as her daughter wrapped her arms around her. It didn't last long, but long enough for Jane to realise that a proper hug would've been more appreciated than a handbag.

"I know how hard it is for you to buy things Mam, so I appreciate this. Thank you," Jane said sincerely.

"Did your brother get you anything?"

Jane took the mobile phone out of her pocket and put it in the middle of the table, feeling as if she had stolen it, unsure of how her mother would react to such an expensive gift. As the scowl spread across her mother's face she knew it'd be in her best interest not to mention her new bedroom in Peter's house.

"What do you need a phone for?" she asked, picking it up and turning it around in her hands. "*Jaysus*, Peter must be doing very well for himself if he can afford something like that for you. And he wouldn't even think of throwing his mother a few pound. You can write your phone number down and stick it on the fridge. It'll be handy been able to ring you wherever you are."

Jane suddenly saw a downside to having a phone that she hadn't thought of before. She didn't want her mother contacting her all the time, didn't want to be so easily accessible to her. She knew that there'd be no escaping anyone from this point on. As if on cue her phone lit up with a text message from Peter.

*Now I don't have to worry about popping call cards in the letterbox! I can send you credit whenever you need it. It'll be nice to have a way to chat with you more! Hope everything is okay there? Peter*

Jane smiled as she read the text and realised she wasn't very sure how to reply; she put it back in her pocket to figure it out from the comfort of her bedroom. Which, after spending the night in Peter's wasn't at all comfortable, but it was hers.

"I'm meeting my friends later on, are you going out again mam?" Jane stood up, put her new handbag back in the gift bag and picked up her backpack to go to her room.

"I might. I don't know yet. I have work in the morning so I might just go to bed early."

Jane walked up the three steps towards her bedroom and on the way looked out at the bleak, grey view from the hall window. It was a far cry from Peter's beautiful garden and it was depressing to look at.

She walked into her bedroom and turned on the light. The curtains were never open because no light came in the window. She opened the window to let out the smell which never seemed to leave the dark room. Jane figured it was from the carpet which looked like it was laid when the building was first built. She had never minded her room until she had spent the night in Peter's; now she longed for natural light coming in the window and the sound of birds singing, rather than lorries passing at five a.m., rattling the windows and door frames.

Pushing the thoughts aside, she sat on her bed and took her new handbag back out of the gift bag, folded it down flat and put it in her wardrobe with the rest of the items she deemed special enough to keep. She had a shoe box full of smelly notes and pieces of paper torn from copies and scribbled on that her friends had written her during class.

Looking back on some of them she had no idea what they were about, but they made her smile and the smell of the scented paper that always hit her when she opened the box reminded her of swapping paper with Ruby and Niamh at school.

She kept everything from little stones she found down by the river that reminded her of the first time she brought her friends there, to a bottle cap from the first time they ate out together. She tucked the gift bag in behind the battered shoe box and sat down on her bed to look at her new handbag.

"Butterflies!" she chuckled to herself as she opened it up.

It had a small fabric compartment in the middle, and when she opened it there was a white envelope in the inside. Her mother never wrote birthday cards because she thought they were a waste of money, so her excitement grew thinking her mam had written her a heartfelt message. Even to see the words 'happy birthday' written by her would've made Jane happy.

She carefully opened the envelope, already thinking about where in her shoebox the card would go. When she pulled it from the envelope, she laughed out loud; pink, glittery butterflies emblazoned the front of the card, swarming upwards from a birthday cake. Jane laughed at how little her mam actually knew her.

The times when she was little, running into her mother's legs and trying to hide from a butterfly flapping its wings had obviously slipped her mind. But she didn't care, it was still special; a gift could easily be bought, but to sit down with a pen and write a note or a message for someone you loved was more special.

Jane opened the card to read the message inside.

*To Jane, Happy 15th Birthday! Have a shopping spree on me! Lots of love, Lucy xxx*

Jane's tears fell onto the card, blotting and blurring the ink. She let the bag drop to the ground and lay down on her pillow, trying to stifle her crying. She couldn't understand the rejection she felt, why the one person in the world she wanted love from didn't care for her in the slightest. Her lungs felt as if they were going to burst and she couldn't catch her breath. Every time she tried to inhale, her body convulsed.

She sat on the side of the bed and tried to slow her breathing, but the shuddering continued so she walked over to her window and opened the curtains, pressing her palms on the glass and closing her eyes. She imagined the sound of the babbling stream and the birds singing and her breathing slowed enough for her to inhale deeply.

Once she had gathered herself enough, she turned around. On the floor beside her bed lay a crisp fifty-pound note. It had slid out of the card unnoticed when she was reading the message. She picked it up.

Her mother's footsteps on the creaky floor made her dresser rattle, and she quickly shoved the note into her pocket and slid the card back into her handbag. She wiped her face on her sleeve, took her phone out of her pocket and lay back down on her bed, ready to be attempting a text if her mother should walk back in.

She rarely did; most nights she didn't even say goodnight to Jane. She'd either stumble into bed and start snoring as soon as her head hit the pillow, or shout at Jane to turn her music off as she was passing her room, but this was too early for bed and Jane was wondering what she was up to as she walked straight past and into her own room.

The need to know where her mother was, who she was with and if she was safe was like a little mouse nibbling away at her intestines.

Some days it felt as if there were a family of them in there. The only time Jane truly relaxed was when her mother was in bed asleep, and even at that she listened out for noises in case she was vomiting and she needed to turn her over or clean her up, which happened frequently.

She put her phone down and listened to the sounds coming from her mother's room. When she heard the chest of drawers opening, she knew she had changed her mind about going out tonight and she wondered why.

Jane was sitting up, listening, when the door opened.

"Did you get any birthday money off anyone?" her mother asked.

Jane felt for the fifty-pound note in her pocket and felt a surge of anger flowing through her. Many times before she had handed her mother ten pound or sometimes even twenty if she had it, knowing it'd be spent on drink. But she felt so betrayed and angry that she no longer cared what kind of mood her mother would be in.

"No. Peter bought me the phone. Where are you going?"

"Well since it's the day I gave birth to my only daughter, I thought I should celebrate. If you're going out with your friends, I'll meet mine. What's good for the goose is good for the gander."

"Don't you have work tomorrow?"

"Don't you have school?"

"I'm not going to be drinking, and I'll be home early," Jane replied quickly, keeping her tone as neutral as she could. Considering she wanted to shout at her mother, it wasn't easy.

"I'll be in work tomorrow. It's midweek, there won't be many out, and I don't have too much money so it'll only be a few. I'm celebrating my daughter's birthday. See you later." She closed the door abruptly behind her.

Jane waited until she heard the door to the apartment close before she sighed and pulled the note out of her pocket. She walked over to her wardrobe and hid it inside her blazer pocket with the rest of the money she had earned from working. A thought popped into her head that she should spend it soon, before her mother found it and spent it on herself, and that thought stayed in her mind as she sat back down and started to reply to Peter's text.

*all good here she was home when I got in and looks like she settled for the nite its hard to text*

Within seconds of it sending, Peter replied, and Jane rolled her eyes and began composing a message to Niamh.

*1st text yay are you meeting me outside*

Like Peter, Niamh had long ago mastered the art of texting, and Jane received a quick response.

*Yup, see you outside at 5!!*

Jane played around with her phone for another little while, figuring out how to add full stops and question marks to messages. With a few hours to spare before meeting her friends, she decided to listen to some music.

Jane was set in her taste with music. She liked songs and lyrics rather than the actual melody and that's what won her over every time. Oasis was her favourite, but she was in the mood to listen to the angry vocals of Alanis Morrissette and fed *Jagged Little Pill* into the stereo. She needed to release some of the rage she felt towards her mother. She didn't want to be carrying it with her when she met her friends.

The aloe vera plant's leaves had dropped and grown brown over time. No matter where Jane placed it in the bedroom, it never thrived in the dull environment. When she first moved into the flat it was green, full and healthy, but with the lack of sunlight it had failed to grow and Jane watched it slowly die.

She lay on her bed and looked at it sitting on the dresser, thinking about putting it out on the roof for a few days. But even though there would be more natural light, it seemed like the most depressing place of all. There was no view worth looking at, only other buildings, and the horizon seemed so far out of reach that the town felt never-ending from up above.

She couldn't content herself just lying on her bed listening to music, so she got up, picked up the plant, and walked down to the sitting room to place it on the deep windowsill.

"Maybe this will be enough to get you going again?" she said, pushing it in so it was touching the glass. The last piece of her home was dying, or already dead, and there was nothing she could do. The town had sucked it all away from her.

She resigned herself to the fact that her plant wasn't going to come back to life and she walked back to her bedroom with her shoulders dropped. Though she had tried to pull her mind away from the crushing disappointment, it hadn't worked. It felt as if everywhere she turned there was more. She began to feel bad for Lucy, quietly letting her mother take the credit for a lovely gift, and wondered what else her mother had taken the credit for over the years.

She felt anger and sadness begin to form in her stomach, not knowing which one was stronger. She stood up and kicked the bag across the room, torn between feeling guilty for Lucy's nice gesture, and the gift of more hurt from her mother.

# Chapter Twenty-Five

THE LOUD RINGING ON her phone, high pitched and obnoxious, made Jane jump and drop her bag. Swearing under her breath, she reached over to her bed and smiled when she saw Niamh's name on the small screen.

"Is there any way to turn the sound down on this yolk?" she asked as she hit the accept call button.

"Hello to you, too!" Niamh replied. "We're down by the river. Come down and make it quick!"

"Why didn't yous wait for me? I thought you were going to ring me when yous were outside?"

"Just hurry!" Niamh said and ended the call.

Jane felt angry and left out and couldn't understand why it was happening again. She sat on the edge of her bed and tried to remember the last conversation she had with them as a group, and came to the conclusion that Connor had told them that she was a little girl who liked birds.

She felt like her time with them had come to an end. She laid back on her bed and thought that maybe they were playing a prank on her, that they weren't going to be there at all. Her mind raced and the minutes crept by so quickly as she lay there, that Niamh started calling again.

"Where are ya?"

"I haven't left yet, is everything alright?"

"Yeah, everything's great, come on! I'm dying to show you something!" Niamh replied. The excitement in her voice made Jane feel slightly better and she stood up and grabbed her bag.

"I'm leaving now, see yous in ten."

She pressed end on the call. She still wasn't using the phone efficiently and had to look properly before hitting the red button with her thumb. She carefully placed it in the middle compartment of her bag, holding it in her hand and letting it swing by her leg as she walked down the stairs. When she got outside, she realised her bunch of keys made the bag a little heavier and she smiled as she put it over her shoulder.

When she reached the clearing, an uneasy feeling grew inside her. Knowing something was about to happen but unsure what it was made her feel out of control. As she stopped to take a deep breath, she heard her friends.

"I think I hear her," Connor said.

"She's too quiet," Niamh replied. "Unlike you, you're like an elephant traipsing in and out of here. Jane is delicate."

Jane had her hands on the branches, ready to move them aside, and stopped to listen to Niamh's reply. She smiled, but that was followed by confusion; just a few weeks ago Niamh had accused her of trying to be popular and wanting other friends. She pushed the thought aside and stepped into the clearing.

"Happy birthday!" Ruby, Niamh and Connor shouted as she stepped in.

They had balloons hanging from branches and drinks and crisps neatly sitting on a large picnic blanket on the damp ground. In the middle of the blanket sat a chocolate cake and a wrapped gift. Jane put her hands up to her face and began to cry as her three friends all moved in to hug her at the same time.

"I'm smothering," Jane said through her hands after a couple of minutes. They laughed and released her.

"Are you going to be a miserable bitch all evening, or are you going to have some cake?" Niamh asked as she grabbed Jane's hand and led her towards the picnic. Jane blinked hard as she looked down at the cake in the middle, and realised it had 'Happy Birthday!' written in the middle in white icing. The writing reminded her of the handwriting on the card Stephen had given her for her First Communion; gently sloping, joined writing that flowed so beautifully. As if the writer was afraid to lift the pen from the paper in case they forgot what they wanted to say.

"Ah shit, I've no lighter!" Niamh said as she stuck three already-used birthday candles into the cake. "I wasn't even attempting to look for fifteen of them."

"Here you go," Ruby said as she pulled a pink Bic lighter out of her pocket and handed it to Niamh. Jane noticed the knowing look between Ruby and Connor, but Niamh didn't as she lit the candles. Connor and Ruby sat across from them and in unison they sang happy birthday to Jane.

A smile spread across Jane's face and, as she looked at each of her friends, tears were rolling down her cheeks for the second time since walking into the clearing.

"It's your singing, Niamh," said Connor. "It'd bring tears to a stone."

"Eh, did anyone think to bring a knife?" Ruby asked, and the three of them looked from one to the other before they all started laughing.

"I brought plastic forks," Connor said, taking them out of his backpack.

"Looks like we're eating cake as it is then, but Jane gets the first forkful!" Niamh said through laughs.

Connor handed Jane a fork and she gently stuck it into the side of the chocolate cake and lifted up a forkful. She didn't notice the chocolate icing around the edges and the cake crumbled slightly as she moved it towards her mouth.

"Oh my God," she said through the mouthful of cake. It was equally crumbly and moist, and the icing was like melted chocolate, which brought it all together on her tongue. She rolled her eyes and moved in for another forkful. The second forkful gave her the same reaction as the first, and when she moved in for a third one, she looked to see her friends grinning at her. The fork stopped moving midair, and Jane looked from one to the other and started to laugh.

"Jesus, dig in, I didn't realise yous were so polite!"

She went for her third mouthful. If she could've picked up the whole cake and ate it with her bare hands she happily would have. They all sat eating chocolate birthday cake with plastic forks on the forest floor and, as the conversation flowed between them, Jane couldn't have been happier. She ate forkful after forkful of cake, and looked up at the colourful balloons tied to the branches, trying to ingrain the memory in her mind forever. Like the writer not wanting to forget what they wanted to say, Jane never wanted to forget her first birthday with friends.

"We nearly forgot your present!" Ruby said, picking up the gift and pulling Jane from her thoughts.

"Ah lads, yous really didn't have to get me a present too, this was enough. You have no idea how happy I am right now," Jane said as Ruby handed it over.

The wrapping paper was yellow with coloured balloons similar to the ones that hung from the trees, and though she was gently trying to open the present, it ripped easily. Her mouth fell open and she looked over at Connor who was watching Jane with a quiet smile on his face.

She no longer cared about saving the wrapping paper for her memory box and tore the rest off quickly, revealing the yellow bird feeder. She held it up, smiling.

When she put it down by her side, she launched herself at Connor and threw her arms around him and whispered gratitude in his ear. He put his arms around her waist and closed his eyes as Niamh and Ruby glanced at each other.

"It was from all of us," Connor whispered in her ear and Jane immediately moved from Connor to Ruby and Niamh and put herself in the middle with an arm around each of their necks, pulling them in for a hug.

"This is the most thoughtful present I've ever got!" Jane said. A lump had formed in her throat so big that she was unsure if she'd be able to breath, let alone swallow, and she sat back down, taking a drink of Coke.

"You never told us you liked birds," Ruby said.

"Yeah that's kind of cool," Niamh followed.

"You don't think it's sad?" Jane asked, looking up.

"Why would we?" Niamh replied. "It'd be sad if you liked all the other things everyone else liked just to be cool. And anyway, you are a little sad but that's what we love about you!"

Jane playfully shouldered Niamh and laughed as they got started on the rest of their picnic. There was a cool chill in the air, and the sky started to get dark, but they didn't seem to notice as they talked, laughed and enjoyed each other's company.

# Chapter Twenty-Six

JANE WATCHED AS HER mother fixed the plastic witch's hat on her head, the elastic holding it in place sitting perfectly in one of the lines on her face. Her dark hair hung limply around her shoulders, and the black cardigan loosely from her shoulders, only bones and a protruding stomach to fill it out. Her skeletal appearance and bloated mid-section reminded Jane of the poor children on the Trócaire boxes.

Jane looked at her own plump face in the mirror and noticed her dimples and light brown hair and wondered who she looked like. She looked nothing like her mother, and only slightly like Peter. For the first time she wondered if she would recognise her father if she saw him walking down the street.

"I hope you're not wearing what you wore the other night?" her mother asked as she lit a cigarette, the smoke trailing up to the ceiling. It was becoming as yellow as her teeth.

"What? Well, I have nothing else. I know it's a bit small, but it's fine. Or do you not want me to?" Jane asked nervously.

"It's fine, just don't come into the pub and make a show of me again. You don't really have a nice enough figure for something so tight."

"Oh, I... I didn't realise. I won't wear it to the pub again."

She remembered what Darren had said to her at the end of the night, and the glow of the compliment faded away. Tears began to fill her eyes. Maybe he was only being nice after all. He was always straight up and honest with her, but her mother always told her the truth no matter how much it hurt. She thought of the whistles she had gotten as she walked in the door, and the compliments her friends gave her. She thought maybe her mother was the only person who loved her enough to tell her the truth.

Her palms ran over her belly, which now felt to be sticking out as much as her mother's, and her thumb started rubbing at the inside of her top. Feeling fat was something new. She had never felt pretty like the other girls, or felt like she stood out, but today she felt fat.

She wondered how, because she didn't exactly eat a lot. But she'd bear it in mind the next time she wanted a McDonald's. She remembered how Darren turned away quickly after paying her the compliment and she thought that maybe he was just being nice to make her feel good, but that didn't seem like his style. He was always straight up and honest with her. But her mother always told her the truth no matter how much it hurt. So who was lying?

"Can I borrow one of your cardigans to wear over it? It's too late to get anything else and I'm not going into The Hive, just meeting the gang."

"Yeah, whatever. But don't stretch any of my clothes!" Her mother was already halfway down the stairs as she shouted back up at her.

Jane picked up the empty glass and full ashtray off the kitchen table, emptying it into the bin after tapping each cigarette to make sure they were out, a trick she learned very quickly after she set the bin on fire at The Hive. She washed the glass out in the sink and turned around with her back against the worktop.

She looked at the kitchen table, next to the couch and tv, and suddenly pined for home and the separate sitting room and kitchen. There never felt like there was an escape here unless she went to her bedroom, but she preferred to do her homework at the table, finding it more comfortable. The noise from the tv never really distracted her but the tension did.

She remembered nights lying on Peter's bed, trying to distract each other from the emotional or physical tornado that was about to hit. Those nights always felt like cold winter nights. In her memory they were winter nights. The days spent playing by the stream were sunny days with blue skies.

With Peter now firmly in her mind, she knew she'd better call him. Out of habit, she grabbed a call card from her room and made her way to the lobby of the pub downstairs where four payphones hung on the wall. A checked sofa sat directly across from them, and over that hung a huge, gaudy mirror. It was spray-painted gold and flakes of paint sat on the top of the couch below.

It was a dark and depressing lobby, the dingy carpet worn with years of foot traffic and some stains in corners which would never be removed, remnants of a good night's drinking. The entrance reflected the rest of the pub: dark and uninviting. It was the opposite of The Hive, with its Beatles memorabilia and art work adorning the walls. The big windows let a lot of light and in even at nighttime it was bright and inviting.

But this pub reminded her of the customers: depressed. The older clientele, hunched over the racing section of the paper and their pints, didn't want colour or fun and especially not live music. They wanted somewhere to wallow and this was the perfect spot. The older barman looked as miserable as his customers and seemed happy to serve the pints in silence, not interrupting the noise of the racing from the screen hanging in the corner.

The smell of pipe smoke distracted her from the payphones and drew her into the darkness, hoping to find some light. The scent, which had on many a day given her comfort when she didn't know she needed it, still wrapped around her and pulled her in like a hug. She followed it now, looking for the person who smoked the same tobacco as Stephen.

She looked at the men sitting at the bar, two cracking quiet jokes with each other.

"Did ya hear Albert Reynolds broke his leg?" a man said before taking a sip of his Guiness. The glint in his eye told Jane that he still had some spark left that life, and this pub, had yet to extinguish.

"No. *Bejaysus*, what happened him?" his companion asked, flicking through the newspaper.

"The cabinet fell on him!" his friend replied before erupting into laughter and slapping his knee. His laughter stopped abruptly when his friend rolled his eyes and turned back to the horse racing.

She kept walking and found an elderly man with a walking stick sitting in a corner, smoking a pipe. The pang of sadness still came when she thought of Stephen. It was so sudden for her young brain to comprehend and her young heart to cope with. But she found herself continuing down the huge pub until she got to the skylight. The she sat at and heard quiet mutterings and clinking glasses, the one which let in no light in at all. Strangely, it was covered in bird droppings from birds she had never caught a glimpse of.

The pub was three times the size of The Hive and had less people sitting dotted around it. In the far corner another TV hung on the wall, playing the news for the deaf. A man who looked out of place at the bar shouted to the barman,

"Turn it up, I can't hear it!"

His long blonde hair and leather jacket would've fit in perfectly at The Hive, but here he looked like he didn't belong. He heard Jane laugh at his attempt at humour and he turned around. Jane looked at him, the smile fading from her face; if sadness and loneliness could be etched on someone's face, it was on his. In every line that he was too young for, and every crease he shouldn't have had, it was written, possibly by someone else's hand. Jane recognised it instantly.

"At least someone gets me. They're all miserable fucks in here. This place would drive ya to drink. Luckily for me, I've drove myself there. I'm already an alcoholic. I'm only here because I need quiet to finish me crossword. Three across is 'It moves between banks.' That's my last one. It's always the easiest ones I get stuck on."

"Stream," answered Jane.

"Fuck me, you're right. More than just a pretty face. Thanks," he said. His dirty blonde hair obscured the view of his face as he filled in the answer. "I'm going to get two double vodkas and Coke to celebrate," he said smiling over at Jane.

"Two doubles? Hardcore," Jane said, slightly impressed by his ability to drink so much and finish a crossword.

"Yeah, I'm an alcoholic. I told ya."

"And you, just know, and, admit to it?" she asked.

"I know what I am. I know why I'm an alcoholic and I know what I'm hiding. I can also spot when someone else is hiding something. What's your story?"

Jane realised he had barely looked at her for longer than a minute as he was talking to her, and she felt unnerved by his statement. She was grateful to have an excuse to leave.

"I'm hiding nothing. I thought my mother would be here, but I have to go and call my brother."

"Your mother drinks here? I already know what's eating you then. Only depressed alcoholics drink here. I'm always here. I come for the cheap booze and stay for the mighty craic. I'm Paul."

She suddenly felt uncomfortable, a stranger reading her and getting it so right felt wrong to her. She uttered a goodbye to the new stranger and walked back towards the payphones. She almost held her breath as she walked past the man with the pipe, not wanting to smell it anymore, knowing Stephen wasn't the one smoking it.

The payphones had the numbers of taxis, local chippers, and random other numbers stuck to the wall and scribbled on it. People used the phones here if the one in the phone box was out of order or in use and Jane picked up the one nearest the end, put in her call card and dialled Peters number.

"Hey, it's me," she greeted him when he answered.

"Is your phone not working, or is your credit gone?"

"Oh my God! Jesus, Peter! I'm so in the habit of coming down here that I forgot! The phone is beside my stereo!" she replied through laughs.

"No worries! Sure, ya might as well use up them cards anyway! I'd say you still have a fair few lying around? So what's the craic, Janey, do you want to come trick-0r-treating with me and Lucy? We'll take you around the estate?" When Jane giggled at his question he knew he was still thinking of her as a small child.

"No thanks Peter, me and my friends are going to watch the fireworks down by the river. But thanks."

"Right so. Be careful. Don't mess with fireworks and take your phone, please? If you need me, call or text and I'll be there. If she's bad tonight you can stay with us. Has she been bad, lately?"

"Ah she's been grand. I have to go!"

"Be safe, Janey, love you."

As Jane hung up the receiver, she thought about Peter's question. Had she been bad? She hadn't physically lashed out, but her drinking was getting worse. No longer content with Friday to Sunday it had stretched to daily. But she wasn't getting drunk daily, that was still confined to the weekends. It was the tension, the constant walking on eggshells around her that wore Jane out.

When they lived in the countryside and her mother only had access to drink at the weekends, Jane could predict what her humour would be like. She knew Monday she'd be extremely hungover and contrary and Tuesday she'd be tearful and sometimes nice, Wednesday was always a bad day because her mother called it the longest day of the week, waiting for payday and a drink on Thursday. But living here had changed that. Her moods were now unstable and there was no more nice Tuesdays, though  she didn't lash out physically so it wasn't all that bad, was it? Jane couldn't answer the question.

She walked out of the pub and started down the street. It was starting to get dark and the high-pitched screamers followed by dogs barking unnerved Jane. The streets started to get busy with groups of people in fancy dress. There was a lot of Oasis fans from what she could see, with at least five of the Gallagher brothers passing her, one with a guitar singing Wonderwall. There were Spice Girls and schoolgirls and even a couple of nuns, but Jane was unsure if they were real or dressed up.

Darkness had fallen quickly, and when she reached the park it was practically pitch black. She took each step into the park carefully as her eyes adjusted to the darkness. Just as she reached the clearing a screamer went off and frightened her, making her forget about her careful steps and she ran through the bushes, following the sound of Connor's stereo.

"Fuuuuuck! You frightened the absolute shite out of me!" Connor shouted as Jane almost ran into his arms. Her heart was racing and she was out of breath. Ruby and Niamh were laughing at Connor's outburst but he looked at Jane, frazzled and breathless, and put his hands on her shoulders and looked at her face.

"Are you okay? Did something happen?"

"No! Just one of the bangers or what ya call them went off and it sounded close and scared me!" She moved from his grip and sat down beside the girls. Though it was dark out, somehow their clearing wasn't completely enshrouded in darkness. The trees gave great shade and shelter but opened out onto the river which reflected the lights of the town. When the moon was full it made a picture-perfect image.

Connor looked at his watch and started to unload his backpack. He took out a two-litre bottle of Coke, crisps and chocolate. Niamh and Rubie followed suit. There was enough junk food lying on the ground to feed an army of guisers, but Jane felt a pang of guilt. She had come empty handed.

Niamh and Ruby pulled blankets out of their bags and suddenly Jane felt cold, her cat costume and cardigan not enough to keep the autumn night at bay. She was glad to see the blankets were enough for the four of them.

They all made their way down to the bank of the river and Niamh placed a blanket on the ground, big enough for them all if they sat close together. The three girls sat first, and Connor sat at the end, next to Jane. They all pulled in close to each other, shivering but wrapped in blankets and, as the fireworks began to light up the sky with Oasis playing quietly behind them, Jane sighed a quiet sigh and smiled. Her friends eyes glowed like small children at Christmas.

The sky exploded with colour. The still water reflected the fireworks and for a second Jane wished she had a camera. They watched the fireworks exploding, perfectly timed, in unison yet overlapping each other, creating harmony in the sky, and Jane remembered back to sitting on the wall with Peter, watching them in the distance. He'd put his arm around her then and that's why it didn't feel strange when Connor put his arm around her too.

When the display was over they made their way back up the town, helping each other navigate the now pitch-black park until they reached lit streets. Jane felt slightly nauseous from the junk food she had consumed, but she was content. Until they got closer to the street she lived on.

A familiar feeling of dread washed over her as she heard shouting; she knew instantly it was her mother. She recognised her shrill swears even from a distance and her heart raced as blind panic set in. Not wanting her friends to see her drunk mother, she hung back slightly, breathing heavily, desperately trying to think of an excuse to go in another direction. But her mind drew a blank as she started to sweat.

Connor looked back and saw Jane trailing behind the group and at first glance she looked sick. He let the others pass him and stood in front of Jane, putting his hands on her shoulders.

"What's wrong? Are you sick?"

"No. But we can't go up that street. Please, Connor. Please find another way. Get them to go a different way. Please!"

The tears were now rolling down Jane's face as she begged her friend for help. She had no way of explaining in that moment why she needed it, but her pleas didn't go unnoticed as Connor shouted after their friends.

"Lads, I'd love a caramel sundae! Can we stop off at McDonald's?" Ruby and Niamh turned around as Jane wiped away her tears quickly.

"Firstly, it's fuckin' freezing and you want an ice cream?" Niamh asked. "Secondly, are you not sick from all the shite you ate?" She was looking him up and down, but Ruby didn't question him. She was looking at Jane's face and knew something was wrong.

"Come on, it'll be quicker for me to get home this way. And an ice cream might be nice!" said Ruby.

"Sounds like there's killings on the main street, the side entrance is probably best anyway," Niamh said, following Ruby.

"Do you know the people fighting, Jane?" Connor said, holding Jane back. Jane made no reply; she looked down at her feet and wished the moment away, feeling his gaze on her. "Ah, ya know I won't push," he said. "Tell me when you're ready but Jane, I'll puke if I eat one more thing!"

She laughed and hugged him.

"I have to go, Connor. I will explain soon, I promise, but right now I really need to go. Thank you," she said, rubbing his arm before running back towards the main street.

# Chapter Twenty-Seven

WHEN SHE TURNED ONTO Main Street, Jane spotted a black handbag, its contents strewn over the road, and recognised it as her mother's. She ran onto the road and quickly picked up its contents and put them back in, while keeping an eye out for taxis and cars. She knew at this point something had happened to her mam and she started to panic.

She looked around the street but there were no signs of her mother and now the only sound she could hear was her own heartbeat, growing stronger and faster each second. Picking up the last bit of makeup which had fallen from the handbag, a spot of blood on the edge of the pavement made her stomach turn. She ran up the lane, towards the flat, and heard groaning. She stopped in the middle of the lane and closed her eyes to focus on the sound.

"Mam?" she called out. It was too dark to see anything clearly. Jane took a few more steps towards the door. "Mam?" Jane called again, this time her voice breaking.

She didn't know what had happened, but she dreaded what she was going to see as she stepped beyond the door of their flat and into the corner where the bins stood. As her eyes adjusted to the dark, she saw her mother lying on a pile of black bags between the two industrial sized bins. The left side of her face was dark and Jane realised she was bleeding.

"Jesus Christ, Jesus Christ, oh my God. What happened? Mam?" Jane rubbed her thigh, feeling for the call card that she had used earlier to call Peter, and she cursed the tight cat costume she wore. Then she remembered her phone, still sitting on the stereo in her room. "Fuck fuck fuck. Okay. Hang on, Mam."

Jane turned towards the door, unlocked both two locks, and swung it open wide. She turned back to her mother and lifted her right arm up over her shoulder. She was shocked by how light her mother's frame was as she helped her to her feet. They made their way up the stairs together and Jane lay her mother down on the couch.

"Mam, what happened? Will I call an ambulance?"

"Nooooooo," her mother moaned. "Nooo. No ambulance. M'okay."

Jane pulled a basin from the cupboard underneath the sink and a bottle of Dettol, which had a capful left in it. She filled the basin with clean water from the kettle, poured the Dettol in, and grabbed a clean cloth. She knelt down beside her mother and started to cry as she gently wiped the blood from her face, rinsing the cloth every time. Soon enough the water in the bowl had turned a muddy brown.

Jane could see a gash above her mother's left eye, just underneath her eyebrow. It was about a centimetre long and it had depth to it that looked like it needed to be stitched. Fresh blood quickly pooled on it and started to roll down her face again.

Jane sat back on her heels and thought back to the basic first aid lesson she'd been given in home economics. She ran to her room to grab a box of plasters and a pair of scissors from her dresser drawer. She kept them for when her shoes rubbed her heels and tonight she was glad her shoes were too small. She cut up a plaster into five individual strips and ran back down to her mother who was now covered in blood again.

Jane wiped it up and started peeling the backing off the strips. With one hand she pinched the wound closed and with the other stuck on the strips of plaster, hoping they would hold the wound closed enough to stop the bleeding until morning, at least. When she had all five strips on, she covered them with a bigger plaster and then held a tea towel over it to apply pressure. Her hands shook and her legs felt like jelly as she started to shiver, both from cold and shock.

She visited her bedroom briefly to change out of the cat costume and into a hoodie and tracksuit bottoms, grabbing her phone and some money and putting them in her handbag. This seemed non-sensical to her, but she felt the need to have money with her, just in case. She filled her arms with pillows and blankets from her bed and made her way back to the sitting room. The creaks and groans that each floorboard made terrified her as she quickly walked down the hall.

Her mother remained quietly on the couch, and Jane stood looking at her from the door. She was pale but at the same time full of colour, and she frowned and took closer steps to her.

"Mam?" she said while lifting the soaked tea towel off her head and replacing it with another. But there was no response.

She sat opposite the couch, wrapped in a blanket with her phone in her hand, looking at Peter's number. The smell of Dettol hung in the air and made her eyes feel as if they were burning, but she was glad of it because she didn't want to fall asleep.

As soon as the small screen on her phone would go dark, she would press a button to make it light up again and move her focus from Peter's name to the time. It had felt as if it had slowed down, that morning and daylight would never come. The quiet from the pub downstairs as the barman closed the shutters behind him made Jane feel even more alone and scared as she listened to her mother's breathing.

A loud banging on the door made Jane jump, and she froze to the armchair, wondering who could have gotten up the stairs before she realised she hadn't locked the downstairs door after carrying her mother up. The knocking was continuous, and she quickly picked her phone up from where it had fallen and shakily pressed buttons until she found Peter's number again, but she was stopped in her tracks when the knocking was joined by a loud, male voice.

"Gardai! Hello! There's been a report of an assault, and I just want to check that the occupants are okay. Hello?"

Jane stood up, the blanket dropping onto the chair behind her, and walked over to the door. Her legs were shaking and tears were rolling down her face. She had never felt more scared as she unlocked the door and opened it a crack and peered out.

The garda stood three steps from the top and she looked down on him, opening the door wider when she saw his full uniform.

"My mam's been hurt but she's okay," she said. "I cleaned her up. I don't know what happened, but she didn't want me to call an ambulance," she said, stepping back so the garda could come in. She felt the cool air rush from outside, but it wasn't much cooler than inside the flat.

The garda took off his and looked down at Jane, who stared at him with furrowed brows, her eyes red from crying. They recognised each other at the same time.

"Chris?"

"Jane?"

They both spoke in unison, and she threw her arms around his waist and began to sob.

"I don't know what happened to her," she said, "I just found her like this but I heard her shouting. If I had gone straight away, I could've stopped it. It's my fault all because I was too embarrassed for my friends to see…"

Chris put his hands on her shoulders and looked down at her. She was taller, and older, but she was still the same little girl who'd been left in a car on a hot day. Now she looked pale and worried.

"If you tried to intervene you could've got hurt too. Where is she?"

Jane took a deep breath and walked over to the couch where her mother lay. The dressing Jane put on her head was now soaked through and blood was starting to slowly roll from her temple towards her ear.

"I thought I had stopped the bleeding!" Jane said, running for another tea towel.

Chris bent down to check her pulse and picked up his radio. He spoke into it, but Jane didn't register any of the words he was saying until she heard 'ambulance' and their address.

"Your mother needs to go to hospital Jane, her head needs stitches and she's probably concussed. They'll also need to check for any other damage. Do you have anyone to stay with? Stephen?" Chris watched Jane gently hold the tea towel against her mother's head.

"Oh God," said Jane, not registering Chris' question. "I never thought of other types of damage. Oh my God she could be lying here with broken bones and I was only focused on the damage I could see. Oh my God."

"Jane, none of this is your fault, you done a great job," said Chris. "Can you stay with Stephen tonight?"

"Stephen's dead," Jane said, not looking up. "But I'm going with my mam. I'm not leaving her."

Chris' heart sunk. He had chatted with Stephen that night, into the very early hours of the morning while Jane lay in bed, and he had promised she would come to no harm when he was there to keep an eye on her. He hadn't heard of his death, which was unusual for a small county... he normally knew of every death that occurred.

Jane's defiance, her innocence and unconditional love for her mother - and Stephen's promise to look after her - was what had stopped him from calling social services, knowing full well that sometimes the devil you know really is better than the one you don't. But now he was angry with himself he hadn't made the call.

"Jane," he said. "Where does your brother live? Is he close?"

"Yeah. The estate at the top of the town. I will ring him when we get to the hospital."

"Okay. I'll follow in the squad car and I'll drive you to his house after. No arguments."

Jane felt tired. Drained, almost as if the life had been sucked out of her, and she stared into space for a moment hoping her mind would drift but it wouldn't. The sound of the sirens kept her very much in the moment she didn't want to be in.

Jane and Chris stood back against the kitchen worktop as a pair of paramedics checked her mother's vital signs. Jane's left leg began to shake uncontrollably and tears ran down her cheeks as she watched them lift her onto the trolley. Her mother didn't make a sound or open her eyes, and this worried her even more because her mother was rarely silent. Even when she was asleep she could be heard shouting through the walls at some invisible threat, or maybe a past one.

Chris could feel Jane trembling as she stood beside him, and he put his arm around her shoulders.

"Why don't you go and put on your jacket and get your phone so you can call your brother?" Jane stepped forward towards the armchair, grabbed her phone and wrapped the blanket around her shoulders.

"I have everything I need. I'm not leaving her."

"I know Jane. Nobody's asking you to."

The ambulance crew strapped her mother in tight and slowly brought her down the stairs as Jane followed. Chris took the keys out of the door and had one quick look around before he closed the door behind him and locked it. He watched Jane get into the back of the ambulance with the blanket wrapped around her and wondered what the best course of action was for this young girl. A young girl not far from adulthood who hadn't really had a childhood. His thoughts were with Stephen and his mind raced trying to remember anything of the man's death, but it kept drawing a blank.

The ambulance wasn't as noisy as Jane expected it to be. The sirens weren't as deafening as they were from the outside but the beeping of the machine hooked up to her mother is what she focused on.

"And you have no idea what happened?" the female paramedic asked.

"No. I heard shouting, but by the time I got home I found her lying next to the bins, bleeding."

"Did she walk up the stairs?"

"No. I carried her."

The paramedic looked at Jane's slight frame and wondered how she managed to carry her unconscious mother up a flight of stairs, but she knew from the weight of her on the trolley that she didn't weigh much more than her daughter and adrenaline was a powerful thing.

"What hospital are we going to?" Jane asked.

"The local one. Don't worry, she'll be in good hands."

There was something comforting about the regular beeping of the blood pressure machine that made Jane relax a little bit. It was telling her that her mother was still alive, though guilt gnawed away at her over wanting to go up the other street with her friends.

Through the one small, blacked-out window, Jane could see they were driving past Peter's estate and she looked down at her phone again, wondering when would be the right time to call him. She knew he wouldn't care for their mother's welfare, just her own. She let out a sigh as she watched the screen go dark again.

Jane watched as the paramedics wheeled her mother out the back of the ambulance and followed them down the steps and into the emergency department. Through the windows she could see the waiting room full of people, some bandaged up and some who looked as if there was nothing wrong with them at all, and she wondered why they were there.

She listened as the male paramedic quickly told the nurse and doctor what was wrong as they rushed through the sliding doors, but Jane couldn't understand what the letters and numbers were as he recited them. She pulled her blanket around her shoulders tighter, even though the heat was stifling and the smell reminded her of the Dettol she used to clean her mother's head.

The bright lights and business of the hospital overwhelmed her; she found herself standing in close to a wall as the doctor and nurses wheeled her mother into an empty bay and moved her on to a bed. She knew it wasn't good that her mother hadn't moved or woken up with all the movement, and felt tears falling down her cheeks when they closed the curtain around her.

The feelings racing through her body were mixed. She felt relieved that her mother couldn't drink and she knew where she was, but she was worried that she might never wake up again. Closing her eyes and leaning harder against the wall, a hand was placed on her shoulder. She didn't have to open her eyes to know it was Chris as he pulled her in and put his other hand on the top of her head.

"I want to go home," she sobbed.

"I can't bring you back to the flat unless someone comes and stays with you."

"No, I want to go home. To the countryside. Where I could escape all of this and be on my own for a little while."

Chris knew there were no words he could say to make her feel better. There was no way of helping her feel any less lost than what she was, but he still wanted to help.

"I'll talk to the doctor, find out what's going on, and we'll bring you to Peter's house. Do you have his number? I'll pass it onto the nurse and they can ring him and let him know what's happening.

Jane rhymed off Peter's phone number all while keeping her eyes on the still-drawn curtain her mother's broken body was behind. She wanted to see what they were doing, but couldn't bring herself to look.

When Chris stepped in behind the curtain, Jane couldn't help but notice how he seemed smaller. Her memory of Chris was a big, tall, strong man who stood head and shoulder over her mother, but here was a small, greying man, close to retirement. She felt so protected in his company that he may as well have been a giant as he stood talking to the doctor.

"They don't know anything yet. They're going to do x-rays, scans and blood tests. I'm guessing she wasn't sober when this happened?"

Jane felt anger at the accusation, at first, but her expression quickly changed when she realised that he was right, and she just nodded her head.

"Right," Chris said. "Let's get you to your brother's house. There's nothing we can do here. Let the doctors work, she's in good hands."

He put his hand on her shoulder and guided her back out the door towards his squad car, parked behind the ambulance. Jane slid into the passenger seat and felt as if she were ten years old all over again. Her stomach churned as she remembered the feeling of her mother being lost.

There seemed to be no end to the dark night as they drove through the town towards Peter's. Jane stared out the window, her breath fogging up a small portion of the glass, but she didn't have the energy to raise her hand to clear it off and waited for it to disperse before it fogged up again.

Peter's house was dark. All the lights were off, and Jane realised she hadn't phoned him to tell him what had happened. Knowing he'd panic seeing Chris standing at the door, she quickly got out of the car and stood with her back to the cold metal door. Chris kept his finger on the doorbell until a light from the upstairs bedroom came on, and Jane saw Peter pulling back the curtain slightly and peering out. It felt as if it only took him seconds to get to the front door.

"Jane! What happened?" he shouted past Chris.

"Can we come in?" Chris asked, taking his hat off.

"Yeah sure, sure, come in. Jane, are you okay?"

Chris walked in ahead to the kitchen and Jane slowly followed. Peter threw his arms around her, and she began to cry all over again.

The trio sat at the kitchen table and Lucy stuck her head in the door. Peter ushered her in as Chris began to talk.

"Your mother had an accident. It seems as if she was assaulted. She was taken to A&E by ambulance."

"Jesus Christ, Jane, why didn't you call me, that's why I got you the phone!" Peter said, looking at his sister shivering in her blanket and pyjamas.

"In fairness," Christ replied, "it was me that called the ambulance. Jane had done a mighty job in getting her up the stairs, cleaning up her head wound, and making sure she was okay. As she should have. She's a tremendous girl, Peter."

"And is she going to be okay?" Lucy asked, showing genuine concern.

"Who cares?" Peter almost shouted. "My concern is Jane. She shouldn't have to be dealing with this shite that my mother no doubt brought on herself!"

"Peter... this isn't helping your sister," said Chris.

Jane sat silently looking down at her feet. She twirled the blanket between her fingers. She had no energy to argue; she wanted to close her eyes and hope everything would be normal when she woke up. Lucy put her hands on Jane's shoulders and leaned into her.

"Come on, pet. We'll get you to bed. You've done enough for your mam tonight and you'll be no good to her if you collapse from exhaustion."

Jane borrowed Lucy's light pink fleece pyjamas. They were extremely small, even for Lucy, and fit like a second skin. They hugged her like a teddy bear and she let out a small, audible groan as she slid under the duvet and let the warmth surround her. Her eyes began to close before Lucy turned out the light and closed the door.

As Jane drifted off to sleep, she could hear Chris and Peter talking, with Lucy interjecting every so often. She tried to zone in on the conversation and pick out some words but sleep won and soon she was into a warm, comfortable sleep, dreaming that they all lived happily in that house together.

The tears rolled down Peter's face as Chris told him the story of the little girl left in the car, saying she wasn't the one lost but her mother was. He apologised for not contacting him, claiming he felt he had let them down, but relayed his conversation with Stephen. He'd been confident they'd be looked after.

"The thing is," said Peter, "he did look after both of us. We were never hungry when Stephen was alive. I always felt I had someone to rely on. He was there, in the background, watching and listening. It was like having a guardian angel . I felt so alone when he died, and I know Jane missed him shocking. She used to sit with him every day down by the stream. I wish I'd known the extent of it all, with my mother. I did know, but Jane kept it from me. Why? Why didn't she tell me?"

Before anyone could answer, Peter let out a sob. "I haven't done a very good job this far have I?" he said, wiping his tears away.

"Oh God lad, you have. You really have. You've done more than your fair share. Just try to keep your emotions in check when it comes to your mother and Jane will soon come round. I'll be here. Here's my number and there's my home number and mobile on the back of the card. I'll call back tomorrow. I'll keep in touch with the hospital and update you as to how she is. Get some sleep."

Chris stood up and put his hat back on. Peter shook his hand firmly and thanked him, knowing it wouldn't be the last time he'd see him. Lucy embraced Peter she knew, already mentally preparing herself for the never-ending cleaning he took on when he was stressed or anxious. The ripple effect of his mother's behaviour had shockwaves, like an earthquake, and Lucy was beginning to see the tremors. But she loved Peter more than she had ever loved anyone in her life and she was ready for whatever was coming.

Peter noticed the old lady in the house across from him looking out her sitting room window when he was closing the front door after Chris, and he wanted to give her the middle finger. He valued his privacy and nobody in this estate knew who his mother was or where he had come from, and he felt that a visit from the gardai would be enough to get the locals talking - especially if Mrs. Yore was the instigator of the gossip.

But his focus was on Jane and how to get her out of the situation she was in. He couldn't clear his mind as he walked back into the kitchen and knelt down at the press under the sink and began to clear it out. Lucy watched him silently, knowing there was no point in saying anything because Peter was doing what his mind needed to do and that was cleaning.

"Come up to bed when you're ready, Peter. I'll leave you to it." Lucy kissed him on the top of the head and placed her mug in the sink. When Peter looked up at her, she saw something different in his eyes this time. It was as if they were pleading for help, and Lucy knew that he was about to lose control again. She sat down on the floor beside him and grabbed his hand, pulling it away from the array of cleaning products and held it tight.

"If I get sick, who'll look after Jane?" he asked, not looking up but into the empty press as he sprayed disinfectant spray in it. "I haven't been as on top of this as I should have been." Lucy sat silently, holding his right hand and eventually he turned to look at her.

"I can't help it, Lucy."

"I know, Pete. I know. I'm going to make an appointment for the doctor tomorrow and we'll go in and talk to him about going back on your medication, okay? Let's not let this spiral. Don't push me out again. I'm by your side." Lucy replied, bringing his hand up to her mouth and kissing it gently.

"Thank you," Peter said so quietly it was barely a whisper. When Lucy stood up to go back to bed he immediately stood up himself and began washing his hands. He felt guilty washing away her kiss, but he couldn't risk getting sick.

Lucy stopped outside Jane's bedroom door and listened to the sound of heavy snoring coming from the room and felt content that she was fast asleep. With the landing light off and a glow coming from the downstairs lights the silver door handles seemed to shine, and Lucy realised that Peter had polished them earlier in the day.

Seeing the unmade bed in the bedroom was unusual because every room in the house was always immaculately clean and tidy. Peter never left any kind of mess or untidiness behind him. She found herself quickly pulling up Peter's side of the duvet before she got into bed herself, knowing he'd start pulling and tidying it up before he got in, disturbing her sleep.

"Little quirks," she called them, lovingly. These were Peter's little habits that she found endearing some days and irritating the next, but she loved him all the same. But knowing how bad he could get if his quirks weren't controlled made her anxious, and she thought about telling Jane.

It might help Jane see that Peter needed help at times as much as she felt their mother did. It might help her make the decision to move in with them.

# Chapter Twenty-Eight

KNEELING BY THE OPEN wardrobe, Jane only packed the bare essentials - the opposite of what Peter had told her to do - because she wanted an excuse to come back home and see her mother and make sure she was okay. And, after all, it was her home. It wasn't as comfortable and warm as Peter's, but it was the only place she called home and didn't want to leave her mother behind. The thoughts of doing so made her feel guilty and selfish.

With her schoolbag stuffed with her books and her uniform and an extra backpack with what she deemed essentials, she walked down the hall and dropped them at the door. The basin of bloody water still sat beside the couch and the tea towel she used to mop up her mother's blood was still where it had landed after the paramedics came in. She stayed behind to tidy up.

She replayed the whole night in her head as she boiled the kettle for hot water and put the cloths in the washing machine. The washing machine that she wasn't even sure was going to work; it was as temperamental as her mother. She folded up the throw that covered her mother that night and put it up to her nose, inhaling deeply. Her mother had a scent underneath the smell of wild garlic and cigarettes... it was a sweet smell, one which reminded her of flowers in the garden on a summer's day, but she had to inhale very deeply to find it. It lay hidden under years of bad habits and addictions and Jane knew she was the only one who could still smell it.

Tears rolled down her cheeks as she placed the throw over the back of the couch and emptied the basin into the sink. She knew things were about to change, but she wasn't sure how. She didn't want to live with Peter, but she didn't particularly want to stay living with her mother either. Both seemed to have their own challenges and she'd have to decide which was worse.

The green Heineken crate sat loyally by the outer door and Jane slid it over with her foot and stepped up on it to lock the top lock. The weight of her schoolbag nearly pulled her backwards off the crate, but she caught herself at the last minute.

"Jesus Christ, I'm destined to be a short arse forever," she said to herself as she stepped down and slid the crate back to its spot, bending down to pick up her other bag.

Out of the corner of her eye she spotted something on the ground between black sacks of rubbish and went over to get a closer look. There, amongst the filth, lay a silver miraculous medal on a piece of blue thread. She knew it belonged to her mother. She picked it up and put it in her pocket before walking up the alley.

It was a bright day with a cool bite in the air. Jane could see the changes in the clothes people were wearing: gloves, hats, scarves and heavy jackets. She wished she had a warmer jacket as she instinctively turned towards The Hive in the hope that Darren would be there setting up early.

Turning up the lane towards the older part of the town where the pub was, the perpetual breeze in this wind tunnel chilled her and Jane braced herself by pulling her jacket tighter around her. Her nose started to run, both from crying earlier and the cold. She sniffed constantly, but her heart lifted when she saw lights on behind the bar. The side door, which was well hidden and the one herself and Darren closed behind them as they finished a shift, had light pouring from behind it. It felt warm and comforting and a part of her felt as if she was home when she knocked on the door, announcing who she was.

Darren opened the door and looked out to see Jane, laden with bags and a red nose.

"Alright, Rudolph. What's the story? You off on holiday?"

Jane dropped her bags inside the door, closed it behind her, and looked at herself in the mirror behind the bar.

"Jesus Christ, my nose has frost bite. It's bitter out there," she said, grabbing a napkin from the bar and wiping her nose.

"Freeze the balls off a brass monkey," Darren replied as he lifted a full vodka bottle onto the holder on the wall.

Jane sat up on a high chair in front of the bar and watched him as he lifted the large bottle and hooked it onto the wall. The hoodie he wore didn't hide his biceps and his jeans fit nicely around his waist. She had forgotten why she called in.

"So...?"

"So what?" she said, pulled out of her daze.

Spain or Portugal?" he asked.

"What are you prattling on about now?"

"Where are you going on holidays?" he asked, nodding over to the bags.

"Oh! I wish. I'm going to stay with Peter and Lucy for a few days until Mam is home. But I think he wants me to stay long term."

"Would that be such a bad idea?" Darren asked as he reached down for four glass bottles of Coke. He poured two each into pint glasses.

"Well, who'll mind Mam?" This was the only reply Jane could give to that question.

"Give the me pros and cons. The cons of living with Peter?"

"There'll be no one to mind my mother. And... he's a bit pushy about school."

"That's it? Jane, look. I'm saying this to you as a friend, take it or leave it, but I think you'd be stone mad not to go. You could watch your mother twenty-four seven and she'd still find herself in shit. You'll end up getting dragged down with her, whether you want to or not. As for the school thing, cop on. Seriously, he's right, think about it... would you rather work in a place like this or own a place like this? Jane, you are the smartest girl I know. You have an opportunity to make something of your life. Don't throw it all away for some well-intentioned misguided loyalty to a woman who has, quite frankly, been a shitty mother."

Jane opened her mouth to argue the last point but she stopped herself. She knew he was right, she knew Peter was right, but how could she just walk away from her?

"Tell me then, how do I switch off my feelings and not let the guilt consume me if I walk away?"

"There's always alternatives, Jane. You don't have to walk away and ignore her forever. You can still call, you'll still be here, you just have to learn to take a step back. She's not your responsibility."

"I hate that you're right."

"I'm always right. The sooner you accept it, the easier it'll be for everyone. I'm never wrong. I thought I was once, but I was mistaken!"

Darren chuckled to himself but his attempt at humour was met by an eye roll from Jane as she took a mouthful of Coke.

Jane never feared Darren knowing about her mother and was more honest with him than she was with anyone. She knew it didn't matter to him and that meant the world to her. He saw her for who she was underneath the baggage of her life. He had more than once given her some food for thought, and she appreciated his advice because not only was it well intentioned and coming from a good place, but Darren also had a good way with people. He seemed to be able to read a person before they even opened their mouths to speak. He was always right, but she never admitted that to him.

"Yeah. You're right on a few of those things. Yeah. Right," she said, thinking out loud and staring down to the end of the pub.

It seemed smaller without a crowd in it, and she wondered how a full band and so many people fit into the space. But it looked duller and less colourful without the many people that crowded the pub on a busy Saturday night. Jane looked back at the tall barrel-shaped table just inside the front door and thought back to the first day she met Darren and the humiliation she felt at the hands of her mother and subconsciously rubbed her cheek. In a strange way she felt grateful it had happened because she had met her friend, gained some independence, and managed to create a life for herself all within these four walls.

She looked over at Darren and smiled a closed smile at him before she took another mouthful of Coke. Just as she was about to express her feelings to him, a knock came to the side door and they both looked at each other.

"We're not open," Darren shouted. "Five years. Five fucking years I've worked here and not one person has ever knocked on that door."

The knocking continued, followed by the sound of Peter's voice. "Is Jane here?"

"That's Peter!" Jane said as she stood up to open the side door. Peter stepped in, rubbing his hands and blowing into them. A cold wind blew in after him and Jane pulled the door shut.

"I kind of thought you'd be here. There were no lights on in the flat so this was my next guess," Peter said, looking around.

"Only a sober, observant man can find that door," Darren said, offering his hand to Peter. "Darren. Nice to meet you."

"Nice to finally meet you, too. I hear you've been looking out for my sister. I appreciate it. This is a nice place," Peter said, shaking Darren's hand and then rubbing it on his jeans, an act which didn't go unnoticed by Jane. She hoped Darren didn't notice it.

"Ah, it's grand. Gets lively at the weekends, a young crowd but good craic too. I've never seen you in, or around for that matter?"

Jane knew one of the qualities a barman possessed was an inherit sense of nosiness. They would, by the end of the night, know everything about you including your mother's mother. Jane often thought that a good barman would make a good detective, and she smiled to herself as Peter started to answer his question.

"Ah, I'm not a big drinker. I'm happier to go to the cinema or sit in with a Chinese. I go out the odd time and I do like a good band. If the mother didn't come here, I'd probably come in the odd time," Peter said.

"Well, she doesn't really as much since she met her..."

Darren stopped as Jane was looking at him wide eyed, silently pleading with him not to say anymore.

"...her new bunch of friends," he followed quickly. "More her own age who wouldn't be into the kind of music that plays here. Want a pint?"

"No thanks, I'm driving and we're going up to the hospital. Jane wants to see the mother. I might need one after, though!" Peter chuckled.

Jane rolled her eyes and drained the last of the Coke out of her glass and picked up her school bag, throwing it over one shoulder, but she felt its weight pull at her. Peter grabbed it and took it from her.

"Jesus, Jane why don't you leave some of these in your locker? You'll break your back carrying these every day!"

"Um, well, Mam never paid for the locker for me, and by the time I got in with my own money they said it was too late. It's no big deal, I never need them all every day anyway."

Darren pursed his lips together and shook his head, moving away from what he felt was about to be a private conversation, and Peter just stood and shook his head. He was about to speak when Jane put her hand out to stop him.

"Just don't. Let's just go. Darren, I'll see you next weekend."

"Alright, Jane. Listen, keep me posted, call and let me know how my best customer is."

Peter walked out the door in front of Jane, who gave Darren the middle finger as she closed the door behind her.

"Nice lad," Peter said as he pulled his collar up against the biting wind. He looked to Jane's light coat and her red nose and made a mental reminder to buy her a heavier one for the winter, which felt as if it had hit overnight. He didn't notice the change in seasons as much as she did, even with his newfound hobby in the garden.

"What's a plaza?" Jane asked as they reached the main street. Peter's mind was too preoccupied to answer as Jane stopped and pointed at a new café about to open.

"Here, what's a plaza?" she asked again. The sign had fancy cursive writing, the type that Jane's third class teacher taught them, but she didn't like it. It never felt as neat and tidy as her print writing, which had already taken what felt like a lifetime to get to an acceptable standard.

"Is that a fada over the 'e'? I don't remember learning that word in Irish," Jane said again, but she didn't say her follow up thought out loud to Peter. She didn't listen as well in Irish as she should, but he didn't need to know that.

"No, it's not a fada," Peter replied. "That's a French word for, em, well, *Jaysus*, it must mean coffee. I've no clue what plaza means though. Maybe it's French too." He rubbed his head, the cold now spreading from the tips of his fingers up towards his arm and a pair of gloves were added to the mental list along with a new coat for Jane.

"Ahh, is there French people after moving into the town? I could use some of the French I've been learning in school! *Bon-jour. Ta mere es tune grenouille!*" Jane exclaimed, but her joy turned to shock when Peter burst into laughter. She looked at him with a furrowed expression on her forehead but a smile slowly crept in when she saw him wipe away tears of laughter.

"Jane, I don't know much French, but I'm fairly certain you just called someone's mother a frog. But at least you managed hello somewhat properly!" he said after the convulsions of laughter stopped.

He put his arm around her shoulder and guided her towards the car, opening the boot to put her bags in.

Jane sat in the passenger seat, pulled her seat belt around her and clicked it into place. Her hands felt numb from the cold, biting wind, and she rubbed them together and blew into them. Though she missed her mother, she was looking forward to the warmth of Peter's house. It never felt cold and she didn't need to get overdressed just to run to the bathroom and back to the warmth of her bed if she woke in the middle of the night.

Peter sat in the driver's seat, turned the engine on, and after a few seconds he turned on the heating at full blast. Jane began to laugh.

"I remember one time when Mam was driving home and she turned the heating on in the old car, mountains of cigarette ash blew out of the vents and hit me in the face. It was like being hit in the face with an ashtray!"

"That's disgusting," Peter replied as he looked over his shoulder, ready to pull out of the parking spot.

"Yeah, I suppose it is, actually." The older she got the more she began to realise how things which seemed normal to her were in fact far from it. It was as if each one became a new revelation to her, each tinged with a sliver of sadness.

They drove through the town and Jane watched as people pulled collars of coats up around their necks. It amazed her every year how a change of season seemed to catch people by surprise, how they seemed to think that it happened overnight, and didn't even notice the gradual changes in the weather or the change in trees, plants and how birds flew. It amazed her how people had become so preoccupied living their lives that they didn't notice life going on around them.

Parking in the hospital grounds was always difficult as it was free and generally taken up by people who wanted to spend the day in town, but the car park seemed emptier than normal today and Jane figured it was because of the cold.

Nobody liked to walk into town in winter months. She liked the cold, possibly more than the heat. It was fresh and cleansing, almost like heavy summer rain. At the end of the year everyone felt the same: tired, cold and preparing for Christmas. She felt no different to anyone else at that time of year and found it easier to relate to people. She didn't have to worry about the "Where are you going on holidays this year?" question that she avoided during the summer.

Peter pulled into a parking spot, turned off the engine and let out a sigh. He held onto the steering wheel and Jane noticed his knuckles turning white.

"You don't have to go in," she said as she pulled at her jumper from the bottom. She knew it'd be too much for Peter to see their mother at all, let alone in the state she was in, but her stomach knotted at the thoughts of going in alone.

"No. I'm going with you. Come on."

He opened the door and stood out into the cold air. Jane watched him from the passenger seat as he jumped on his tiptoes lightly and rubbed his hands together, but she knew it was more from nerves than the cold.

They walked in silence towards the main door of the hospital, past patients huddled up in dressing gowns and slippers, smoking. They were like homeless people gathered around a barrel with a fire in it to keep warm. Peter looked at them in disgust and wondered how they could let doctors and nurses work so hard to make them better and then step outside and inhale badness into their lungs.

Peter asked at reception which ward their mother had been transferred to, and Jane stood reading the notices on the notice board. Some had pictures of babies being fed from their mother's breast which she had never seen before yet didn't find strange, and some had pictures of smokers' lungs on them with information on second hand smoke. Jane wondered what her lungs looked like and as her eyes scanned to the top of the board, she saw a poster for Alcoholics Anonymous. She reached up and pulled a number off the bottom of the poster and put it in her pocket before she heard Peter raising his voice.

"What do you mean signed herself out? By all accounts she was barely conscious over the last forty-eight hours and now you're telling me she's out wandering the streets?" Peter said loudly.

"Dr. Connell is still around, let me buzz him and he can talk to you. We'll find out what happened with your mam," the receptionist answered as she picked up the phone, putting it to her ear.

Jane stuck to the spot, staring at Peter who was rubbing his head and pacing before the reception desk. Her mind raced, thinking of all the places her mother could be but she kept drawing a blank. She sighed a despondent sigh and turned to look out the window.

Peter noticed her shoulders tense as she turned, and he felt angry. Angry again that Jane loved that woman so much and it wasn't reciprocated. But he was tired of getting angry, tired of being worried, and he hoped this would be the straw that broke the camel's back for Jane.

When Jane pushed open the door of the ladies' bathrooms she noticed the smell was different. The hospital itself had a clean, chemical smell but the one in the bathroom was overpowering. It was freshly cleaned and the smell of bleach took her breath away and she began to cough. Now feeling like she was running on adrenaline, as she used the toilet her mind just seemed to stop thinking.

Walking back to reception, Jane noticed the day coming to an end through the large windows. The darker evenings made the night feel longer and she watched as a murder of crows flew overhead, signalling a massive change. She heard Peter talking to the doctor but she focused on the birds, the clouds, the sky. She wondered what was going to change.

# Chapter Twenty-Nine

PETER AND JANE DROVE back to the house in silence. Jane kept her eyes on the streets, hoping to see her mother, and Peter kept his eyes firmly on the road ahead until they passed the pub where the flat was. He slowed almost to a stop and craned his neck, looking up and hoping to see some light coming from one of the windows, or any sign of life. But there was nothing. When the car behind started sounding their horn he sped up again and made his way home.

Jane was slow to get out of the car. She watched Peter fumble with the front door key and almost run inside. He didn't even take his shoes off inside the front door like he always did and she knew the few words she overheard the doctor say were bad. Fearing the worst, she didn't want to leave the cocoon of the car, but had no choice when Lucy came out and opened the passenger door.

"Jane, what happened? Peter is on the phone to Chris."

"I don't know. I think she's dying," Jane said in a tiny voice. Lucy ushered her into the house and Jane made her way to the sitting room, closing the door behind her to block out Peter's conversation on the phone. She wanted to run as far away as possible and hide. If she wasn't here, then it wasn't happening. But it was, and Jane felt that this was all her fault.

"Janey. Chris is on his way over," Peter said when he opened the door. He sat down on the opposite couch and put his head in his hands.

"What did the doctor say exactly?" Jane asked. She kept staring straight ahead and didn't look at her brother.

"That basically her liver is fucked and she'll be dead very soon."

"If she gives up drinking?"

"No. It's probably too late."

"This is all my fault. I heard her arguing with someone in the street and I was with my friends and too embarrassed to go over. If I just..." Jane trailed off. Her stomach was nauseous with guilt.

"This is caused by drinking, Jane, nothing else. It is not your fault. Jane, this is not your fault. They... they were talking about end-of-life care."

"End of life? Peter, we need to find her. She can't die alone!" Jane stood up to pace the sitting room but it just didn't feel big enough, long enough or wide enough for her to pace and she stood by the wooden mantelpiece. She didn't realise the fire had been lit until she looked down and saw the flames flicker with a tinge of blue.

She remembered sitting by a warm fire in Stephen's sitting room and asking him why sometimes there was a blue colour to the flames. He said it was the sign of a storm approaching and she knew she was about to walk into the biggest storm of her life. She wanted to curl up by Stephen's feet down by the bridge. He always knew the right things to say and sometimes the right thing was saying nothing at all. She was pulled from her memory by the doorbell ringing and her stomach knotted even more. She liked Chris but he never came because things were going well.

Peter opened the door and ushered him into the kitchen. Jane watched as they closed the door and anger washed over her.

"Why am I not being included in this all of a sudden when I've been the one minding her?" she said to Lucy and stormed into the kitchen. "I've a right to know what's going on, too," she demanded as she burst in through the door.

"Sorry, Jane," said Peter. "Yeah, you do. Chris was just asking where we think she might have gone."

"Any number of pubs. She doesn't really have friends so I don't know after that," Jane said, looking down at her hands.

She pulled a chair out and sat down at the kitchen table. She felt sad for her mother, knowing she had no special friend to call on in what was possibly her final hours. She realised that she didn't really know her mother at all. She knew what she drank, what she smoked and what her mood was from the moment she walked in the door, but she didn't really know her. She didn't know if she had a special place to go and be still, or if she even knew how. She didn't know if she had a favourite place, with the exception of a high stool in a pub. She didn't know what her favourite food was.

"I can tell you which drink she'd prefer to have on a Thursday, or that she puts vodka in her coffee in the mornings. But I don't know where she'd go now. Please find her, Chris. I don't want her to be alone," she said with tears streaming down her face.

"Jane," said Chris, "I spoke to the doctor and it's very unlikely your mother is in any pub considering the state she's in. But I'll look and if anyone serves her, I'll have their license."

Jane's first thought was to contact Darren. Contact him and fall into his arms and sob. He knew every pub in the town, and he would let her know if she appeared. Her world was melting into a blur.

"Can you give me a lift down to The Hive?" she asked. "I'll talk to Darren." She stood up, grabbing her jacket and ignoring Peter's objections.

She walked out to the squad car and sat in the passenger seat for the third time in her life. She let out a deep, slow breath and looked up at the sky, which seemed to be darkening by the minute. Black clouds the colour of smoke rolled by. They looked dirty, full of badness; even rainclouds full to bursting, didn't look as ominous as these.

Jane remembered her mother's cough, the morning smoker's cough which had started to persist throughout the day. It was hacking and sounded painful and she often spat blood into a tissue after a coughing fit. She couldn't remember the last time she had seen her eating and she looked slower on her feet. But Jane just assumed she was hungover or drunk. She let another wave of guilt crash over her as she watched the clouds from the car.

Chris started the engine and the car was silent. There was no static or talk from the radio as the car moved through the town. He drove up every side street and stopped at every alley and lane way on the way to The Hive and each time he got back into his car he shook his head solemnly before starting the engine again.

The car had barely come to a stop outside the pub when Jane jumped out and ran inside. She pushed the door open and stepped inside so quickly it was almost as if she had thrown herself in. Darren instantly stopped what he was doing and made his way over to her.

"Jane?" he said, putting his hands on her shoulders and pulling her in to his chest. Jane's tears began to flow. She smelled his deodorant through his t-shirt and in that smell found a type of comfort she had never felt before and inhaling the scent more helped control her breaths until she could speak.

"Mam signed herself out of hospital against the doctors' wishes but she's dying and she needs to get back in. Has she been here?"

She already knew the answer and pulled away from Darren when she saw some of the regulars looking in their direction.

"No, but I'll ask around. If I hear anything at all I'll ring you. I'm sorry, Jane."

She couldn't muster any more words to him as she nodded her head and turned to leave. Using her strength to tell her friend about her mother's impending death seemed to suck every other word from her. Those words, their finality, made every other word in the dictionary seem inane.

It was now her turn to shake her head as she slid into the passenger seat. She hoped after this she'd never see the inside of a squad car again.

Darkness had fallen by the time they reached Peter's house, and though Jane usually found comfort in the dark evenings, this one felt final and she couldn't understand why. Jane and Chris had barely spoken, and they both shook their heads as they walked in, exhausted, before slumping onto kitchen chairs.

The only noise to be heard was the sound of the boiling kettle and Chris breathing through his nose. These two noises drilled into every nerve in Jane's body and she couldn't focus. She looked to Peter and Lucy, wrapped in each other's arms yet lost in their own thoughts, and she wondered if they were thinking the same things. They knew each other so well and hadn't been individual people since they met at a young age. Maybe their thoughts had turned to one like their bodies were now, different yet intertwined.

Chris left the room to make some phone calls, and Jane felt suspended in time as the noise of the boiling kettle was replaced with the ticking of the clock, growing louder and louder in her mind with every second that passed.

The cold, biting wind swirled around Jane's face and neck when she stepped outside the door into the back garden, and she closed her eyes, letting it embrace her. Dark clouds had taken over the sky, and Jane could hear a seagull in the distance, letting her know that it was either very lost or so far inland it was trying to escape incoming storms. She felt envious of its ability to fly away and wondered how Mags was doing without her.

She had briefly seen some magpies since moving into the town, but nowhere near as many as she used to see on a daily basis back home. Home. The last word stuck in her mind and she turned and ran back into Peter.

"What if she went home?" she said in an almost eureka moment. "Not the flat, Peter. Home. The bungalow."

She watched as a look of realisation washed over his face and they both grabbed their coats and ran to the car.

As soon as the car left the town, a feeling of familiarity came over Jane. Although she didn't know what she was about to face, she could feel her muscles becoming less tight and her breathing slowing down. She watched as Peter chewed on his fingernails while driving, and knew he didn't feel the same way about their return.

She looked out the window at the trees she had once, as a small child, tried to count on her way home from the pub with her mother, the hedges that lined some of the fields before breaking off into fencing or stone walls. At one point she knew where every pothole on the road was, but now there were houses standing in places that lambs used to jump around in the spring. Trees had been felled to make way for big houses that looked out of place with light-up driveways which ran the length of huge, manicured lawns. They looked obscene in the once beautiful landscape, but Jane envied the view those owners had every morning when they opened their curtains. She wondered if they even appreciated what they were looking at. Did they get bored of the outside in the same way they got bored of the inside when it was time to repaint and redecorate?

She noticed some new houses they passed had felled trees but planted new ones, and imagined driving past them in twenty years, seeing tall silver birches and cherry blossoms lined up around houses and along driveways. It would be very pretty, she thought, and would like to do similar if she were ever lucky enough to own her own home.

The old school stood tall, trapped in time, with the temporary prefabs in the yard still squatting there long after Peter's time and hers. They were ice boxes in the winter and ovens on a hot day, and Jane was glad to leave them behind. She was glad to leave the whole school behind. Secondary school wasn't her favourite place but she loved her friends and with them in mind she spoke for the first time since they got into the car.

"Remind me to text or call Ruby and Niamh later. I think it's time I told them the truth."

Peter nodded and kept his eyes forward and a finger in his mouth. He didn't realise how much he had bit his nail until he tasted blood.

The lane, like the school, remained unchanged. The road still had grass sprouting up in the middle and the same potholes, filled in with loose chippings repeatedly over the years, lay unfilled again. Peter slowed his car to try and avoid them. Jane knew there was no point in rushing and getting a puncture; it would waste valuable time.

The hedges looked to be freshly cut, meaning another farmer had taken over Stephen's job of maintaining them. She still wasn't sure if she believed him when he said it was illegal to cut them during the summer, but she never had any reason to doubt him, nor had she any reason to find out for definite once she moved into the town.

As soon as Peter pulled up alongside the house, Jane knew their mother wasn't there. The house showed no sign of life. But when the car stopped, she got out and walked towards it, never taking her eyes off the little bungalow for a second, as if it were drawing her in.

The grass looked as if it had been hastily cut a few times during the summer, and remnants of the blooming garden she once tended when Stephen was alive still peeked through. Ivy was growing wild along the boundary walls, and she knew it wouldn't be long before it would reach the house and grow in the windows. The windows which rattled and groaned with wind. The windows which let the cold air in along with the sound of the birds in summer. The one Stephen had knocked on when she lay in bed, recovering from her sunstroke.

The older she got the more she became aware of why he didn't want to just arrive into a young girl's bedroom unannounced. It was sad. She knew he would never have hurt her in any way. But she also knew what people were like and how they talked.

The house looked dark, and Jane knew it would look scary and uninviting to most people, but she saw it for what it always was: home. She went to the back door and wondered why they'd called it the back door when it was at the side of the house, and nobody who visited, though visitors were seldom, used the actual front door. It had become so hard to open over time from disuse that it became ornamental.

The door opened with a creak and Jane stepped inside. *A perfect setting for Halloween*, she thought as she flicked the light switch and nothing happened. Even in the darkness she could make out the chipboard along some of the walls and the pea green colour that she swore she'd never use on any walls of her own.

Jane walked through the kitchen, running her fingers across the top of the dusty table, and towards what was once her mother's bedroom and opened the door.

"Mam are you here?" she called out, but there was nothing. Only silence.

Her old bedroom was silent, too. There were no sounds of birds. It was as if the house itself had died when they moved out and needed to be revived. She walked from room to room, calling out for her mam, until she made her way back into the kitchen.

She flicked off the useless light switch and walked out the back door and over to the wall that ran along the back of the house. Closing her eyes, she could hear the sound of the stream, and she inhaled deeply before turning toward the car.

"I checked every room, including her bedroom... her bedroom. Her fecking bedroom, Peter! Oh my God, ring Chris! I never checked her bedroom in the flat before I left! I cleaned up, but I never went into her room. Jesus Christ, she's been there all along!"

Jane rushed into the car. She watched Peter scramble for his phone in his pockets and then look for Chris' card and she breathed a sigh of relief when he found them and started dialling. She put her head in her hands as he relayed it all to Chris, then turned on the car. This time he didn't care about how many potholes he hit as he sped up the lane.

# Chapter Thirty

CHRIS RAN INTO THE room at the end of the hallway and turned on the light. He stood rooted to the spot when he saw Jane's mother lying in her bed. Her skin almost glowed yellow. When she opened her eyes, the whites looked luminous next to the bruising she had suffered days before. He knew that though her eyes were open she wasn't aware that it was him, and he walked over towards the bed.

The smell radiating from her was one of decay and death, one he had smelled off addicts before, but not as strong. A half bottle of vodka lay on the bed beside her and Chris sighed a long sigh.

"Why are you like this, Anne? You've two beautiful children, one who has given up a lot of her life to look after you and make sure you're safe. And for what?"

He began to pull at his radio to call for an ambulance, but stopped when her eyes regained focus and she came into a moment of clarity.

"I wasn't always like this, you know," she said through raspy breaths. "I was once a good mother. Ask Peter, he'll tell you. I loved him with all my heart. He was the apple of my eye."

"And Jane?"

"Beautiful. Good girl. She's a good girl." Her breath was becoming more laboured. Chris called for an ambulance.

"Peter's father was the love of my life. And he was taken from us. Then. Then when I met Jane's father... I loved him. Not like I loved John. There'd never be a man like John, but I loved him. But he loved Peter more. Then when Jane was born, Peter loved her more. Nobody had any more love left for me."

"The ambulance is on its way. We need to get you back to the hospital."

"After Jane was born, I was so horribly sad. I was sad all the time. There was cotton wool between my ears and nothing would take it away, only a drink. Then it was two drinks. Then the drink started to be... to be soaked up by the cotton wool instead of removing it, and I never felt anything. Only sad and jealous. I was jealous that they weren't sad, I was jealous that they felt things I couldn't. The funny thing is, it feels like the cotton wool's gone now. Isn't that funny?"

She closed her eyes. Chris felt her pulse at her neck and found that it was weak. Barely there. He knew now there was no rush to get her into an ambulance. He sat down beside her and held her hand.

"Where's Jane?"

"She's on her way."

Chris rubbed her hand; he was torn between hoping she would hold on to say goodbye to Peter and Jane, or getting the peace she needed now before the doctors intervened to possibly prolong her pain and misery. He knew why she'd left the hospital. She didn't want her final moments to be spent being poked and prodded by strangers. The most optimistic part of him hoped she'd also come home to be with Jane.

A breeze blew in when the door opened and Jane ran down the hall. She stopped in her tracks just inside the door.

"Mam? She's yellow."

Peter followed closely and put his arm around Jane's shoulder and tried to pull her in but she tore away and knelt beside the bed.

"We need to get her to a hospital. She's yellow! Why is she so yellow? Chris, do something! Peter, use your phone and call the ambulance and tell them to hurry up! Mam, I'm here, Mam please wake up! Mammy! Please don't go!"

Jane pleaded, though she knew. She knew there was no point but still she wanted to do something, anything, that would reverse all of this damage.

"Mam, please wake up. I'll look after you much better, I promise I will. Just open your eyes."

Anne opened her eyes and looked at her daughter who had tears streaming down her face. With the last of her energy, she lifted her arm and put it to Jane's face.

"Sorry."

Her arm fell limply away and she gasped her final breath.

Peter put his hand to his face and wiped tears away from his eyes before turning and walking down to the kitchen and sitting at the table. He put his head in his hands and sobbed, not for his mother's death but for his sister's heartache. Chris followed him down and sat across from him, patting him on the shoulder as he did.

"Anything I can get ya?" Peter, not lifting his head from his hands, shook his head. "It's early, I know," said Chris, "but there's grants to help with funeral costs and I'll help. I sure as hell wasn't much help in previous years, but I'll help now. I promise."

"I'm sad for Jane," Peter whispered, looking up at Chris. "My heart is breaking for her. But is it bad that I feel relief?"

"No lad, it's not bad. She gave yous a horrid, hard life. You had no childhood. It's not bad at all. But don't say that to your sister, so ya won't."

"God, no. I'll never admit that to anyone else ever again. But we can move on now, can't we? She's not here to always drag us back into places we don't want to go."

As Peter talked, he felt a knot of anxiety unravelling from his stomach that had sat there for as long as he remembered and he felt lighter. He felt as if a noose that had been around his neck all his life was gone.

He heard footsteps coming heavily up the stairs and he knew it was the paramedics arriving to bring his mother away for one final time and he went back into the bedroom to console Jane.

Jane sat on the side of the bed holding her mother's hand. Her fingers were stained yellow from years of smoking and her skin was rough but she rubbed it anyway. She never remembered being so close to her mother physically, and when she looked at her face she knew why she always wore such thick, heavy, make-up. She was hiding her yellowing colour. Why hadn't she noticed the yellow in her eyes?

"The paramedics are here, Jane. They're going to take Mam."

"Where? Where are they taking her? I don't want her to be on her own. I want to go with her."

Chris stepped in and knelt down on the floor on front of Jane. He noticed cigarette butts under the bed along with empty bottles and some clothing and he wondered how Anne hadn't burned the place down.

"She's going to the morgue. Because she was younger, they'll want to do a postmortem and then you'll be able to see her. The best thing you can do is go home with Peter and get some sleep. It's going to be a long few days on both of yous."

Jane nodded and stood up, bending down to kiss her mother on the forehead one last time before she watched the paramedics wheel her out.

# Chapter Thirty-One

Jane stood at the sitting room door and watched as Peter and Lucy tried to rearrange the furniture. She giggled to herself at their bickering as they stood opposite ends of the sofa, Peter wanting to move it one way and Lucy the other.

Peter had seemed different since the funeral, more at ease and he didn't seem to be quite so obsessed with cleaning. He got on her nerves about it, but he wasn't staying up until all hours bleaching the bottoms of everyone's shoes anymore. It was good to see him like this, but she still wondered why his grieving was over so quick. She wondered when she'd feel normal again, if she ever would.

Peter gave in to Lucy's suggestion and moved the sofa in the direction she wanted it to go. Jane thought maybe she never was normal and maybe she was okay with that.

It was a frosty Saturday morning, the estate shone white and a light condensation rolled down her bedroom window when she opened the curtains. She opened the window slightly and watched as her breath hit the cold air, leaving a mist. It seemed to be the day for putting up Christmas decorations; she could see the neighbours unravelling strings of fairy lights to hang outside their house as their small children watched on. Another neighbour was placing electric candles in their windows.

She tried to feel festive, but her eyes were fixed firmly on the father and his two young children. She watched on as the mother came out, still in her dressing gown and slippers, and placed woolly hats on the children's heads before returning inside. Jane felt a pang of loneliness when the father climbed down from his ladder, turned the lights on and lifted both his children up, a boy in one arm and a girl in the other. She heard their squeals of excitement when the lights flashed different colours and she tried to remember ever having a festive feeling.

She came downstairs dressed in warm clothes and placed her phone into her butterfly handbag, the one which broke her heart but she'd held onto dearly, mainly because her mother handed it to her. She didn't buy it, put thought into it, or wrap it up, but she had handed it to her and remembered her last birthday with her.

Jane found forgiveness because she knew her mam must've been in so much pain around that time. The alternative was holding onto anger and bitterness which took more energy and effort. Her heart wasn't equipped to be angry all the time.

Folding her money up and placing it in the inside pocket, beside the coins already in there, she prepared a mental list of gifts to buy. With no mam or dad to buy Christmas presents to wrap and place under the tree, Jane knew that she was lucky to have friends instead. The girls rallied around her after her mother's death and she felt loved by them more than ever. And Darren, Darren had become not only her friend, but Peter's too. They became thick as thieves, and he was now part of their dysfunctional little family.

Darren with his blue eyes would be across from her at the dinner table on Christmas day. The man who allowed her to be herself, who saw her for herself, was now welcomed in by her brother and his girlfriend. She couldn't have asked for more.

She walked into town carefully, the footpaths had a layer of ice on them and it crunched underfoot, a noise like nails on a chalkboard to her, and she tried to block it out by concentrating on her surroundings. The buses were brimming with people leaving the small town to go shopping in Dublin. Some groups of girls her age and some older women on a big adventure to the capital, a place Jane had never been.

She had heard about the Christmas lights and displays in shop windows and thought that maybe next year she'd like to have a day out with her friends, or maybe Lucy, or they could all go together. She smiled at the thoughts of all the people she loved sitting on a bus on a journey to Dublin and how the people she wanted with her wouldn't fill a bus, but knowing that their laughter and love could fill a double decker, if not more. She contented herself with that as she neared the main street.

The day of her mother's funeral was the day the Christmas lights were turned on in the town, and she felt so angry that everyone else was continuing as normal while she followed a hearse out of the town and into the graveyard. It was the only time she had felt real anger and it had seemed so irrational, to be angry over other people celebrating Christmas. She knew it was silly to feel enraged, but she felt it all the same, to her very core. It was disrespectful. But she also knew that they didn't know, nor care, that her mother had died; the world wasn't going to stop because the local alcoholic passed away.

But this day the lights cheered her. They lit up the dreary street and with the rooftops white from the frost and carol music coming from the busy shops it did indeed look magical. Jane stopped to take it all in.

She didn't feel the sense of panic that every other shopper seemed to sweat from their pores as they picked up gift sets and moved to the next aisle. Taking her time, she wandered from store to store picking out what she thought would be the most perfect gifts for her friends and family, little tokens to show she listened to them and cared deeply for them. She even picked up a box of chocolates for Ruby's parents who sent so much food over after her mother died that they didn't have to cook for a fortnight.

She was grateful to those who came to her and Peter in their hour of need and she regretted not speaking up sooner. Perhaps they would have helped her mother recover and get better, and she could be celebrating Christmas with them now. But she knew that wouldn't have happened. Her mother wanted to live her life in the way that she did. She had her reasons.

Laden with bags, she made one last stop to pick up a notepad and pen. She liked stationery and pens and loved more than anything writing little notes to her friends in school. She was glad she didn't have to repeat a year after all she'd missed; school seemed different now she was putting some effort in. She tucked her new stationery into her handbag and made her way up to her new home, her new home that still didn't feel like home in some ways, but was filled with warmth and love, and food.

As she passed the flat, she looked up towards the window she used to sit by, watching for her mother stumbling home or just watching people, and she didn't miss it. She didn't miss anywhere like she missed the bungalow and vowed to one day return and reclaim her place down by the stream. But for now, she found happiness in Peter's garden. The small birds returned to the bird feeder she placed at the end of the garden and robins nested in the bushes. She had even seen some magpies. It was as close to home as she would get for now.

There were smiles and laugher when she helped Peter and Lucy decorate the tree, an artificial one that smelled musty from being in the attic. They hung baubles on the branches and the lights glowed different colours, and Jane felt a warm glow and a longing when Peter and Lucy hugged each other.

Looking out the sitting room window, the houses in the estate were lit up with lights hanging from gutters and Christmas trees and candles glowing from windows. The dark sky was clear and the stars shone brighter than Jane had ever seen them shine since moving into the town. She wondered which one was the north star and, if she followed it, where would it take her.

"Do you think she's in heaven, Peter?" Jane asked, her eyes fixed on the Christmas tree.

"I don't believe in any of that," he replied, "but she did. Let's hope she has found the peace that she didn't have in life. So yeah, I do think that would be heaven for her."

Jane went out into the hall and pulled at her light grey jacket, the one that wasn't fit for the cold months - until recently, the only one she owned - and pulled the miraculous medal from her pocket. She held it up by the blue thread and asked Peter if she could hang it on the tree.

"Of course, Janey, it's your tree too," he answered, putting his arm around her shoulder. A single tear rolled down her face as she hung her mother's religious medal from one of the top branches.

That night, all the gifts she had bought for her friends and family were wrapped neatly and sitting on her dressing table next to the aloe vera plant, thriving in its new home. Jane lay in bed thinking about the family across the road and she pulled out the notepad and pen from her handbag and started to write a letter.

*Dear Dad, My name is Jane and I'm fifteen years old. My mam passed away a few weeks ago and I'd really like to meet you.*

The scrawl of a girl not yet quite an adult but no longer a child told a story of loneliness, loss and regret with touches of happiness here and there. She'd wait until the new year to send the letter. For now, she'd try and enjoy her first Christmas without her mother, the first in her new home.

# acknowledgements

I DON'T WANT TO do the cliché of calling this a journey, but that's what it has been. A journey on a rollercoaster that was set on fire. In that, there were glimmers of light that shone through a very dark tunnel; at the top I almost felt as if I could reach the stars and even at the bottom, the part where my stomach lurched and spun, I was pulled right back up to the top by friends and family.

I have an army of people to thank, from the Bull's Arse and Wordly Worders writing groups who helped me get started, to the very special friends I have made through my own ad writers' group. Fiona Sherlock, for seeing something in me at the very beginning and offering me a mentorship. To the class of '24 in John Mackenna's creative writing class in Maynooth. Thank you for allowing me to share, for the feedback and for your encouragement.

There's an army of silent warriors behind me; you have stood in the shadows and appeared at my darkest times and I cannot thank you enough for what you have done for me. You know who you are and know that I love you with all my heart.

I have a great family: my Mam, my Nanna, the whole Gilsenan clan who I just don't see enough of, thank you for being behind this. Obviously my kids, my biggest supporters...thank you.

There's one person I have left to thank. Without him this wouldn't have happened. My publisher from Chicory Press has been more than a publisher, he has now become a true friend. Steve, thank you for all your hard work and dedication to this novel, I would've given up long before you!

—Amanda Gilsenan

# about the author

Amanda Gilsenan is from Kells, County Meath, and has rarely left it. She founded the aSpired Writers group and co-hosts a podcast by the same name. She has completed a short course in Maynooth University and it hasn't at all helped her grammar but definitely helped her enthusiasm for sitting and looking at a blank screen. Some people are either night owls or early birds...she's a permanently exhausted pigeon who gets great ideas at three in the morning. Her next great idea is to gain a degree in this and learn some punctuation

# a note from the publisher

Chicory Press Independent Publishers thank you for reading One For Sorrow by Amanda Gilsenan. We hope you've enjoyed this book, and invite you to check out more great stories at ChicoryPress.com. Be sure to follow both us and Amanda on social media, and review this novel on Goodreads and other sites. Your ratings and reviews help authors get their work seen by other readers.

*Go raibh maith agat*

Scan below to listen to the official *One For Sorrow* playlist on Spotify: